PORTRAIT OF THE DUKE

Suddenly a Duke Series
Book One

Alexa Aston

Dragonblade Publishing, Inc. is an imprint of Kathryn Le Veque Novels, Inc.
P.O. Box 23
Moreno Valley, CA 92556
ceo@dragonbladepublishing.com

Produced in the United States of America

First Edition January 2023
Trade Paperback Edition

ARE YOU SIGNED UP FOR DRAGONBLADE'S BLOG?

You'll get the latest news and information on exclusive giveaways, exclusive excerpts, coming releases, sales, free books, cover reveals and more.

Check out our complete list of authors, too!

No spam, no junk. That's a promise!

Sign Up Here

www.dragonbladepublishing.com

Dearest Reader;

Thank you for your support of a small press. At Dragonblade Publishing, we strive to bring you the highest quality Historical Romance from some of the best authors in the business. Without your support, there is no 'us', so we sincerely hope you adore these stories and find some new favorite authors along the way.

Happy Reading!

CEO, Dragonblade Publishing

Embracing the Earl
Defending the Duke
Suddenly a St. Clair
Starlight Night (Novella)
The Twelve Days of Love (Novella)

Soldiers & Soulmates Series
To Heal an Earl
To Tame a Rogue
To Trust a Duke
To Save a Love
To Win a Widow
Yuletide at Gillingham (Novella)

The Lyon's Den Series
The Lyon's Lady Love

King's Cousins Series
The Pawn
The Heir
The Bastard

Medieval Runaway Wives
Song of the Heart
A Promise of Tomorrow
Destined for Love

Knights of Honor Series
Word of Honor
Marked by Honor
Code of Honor
Journey to Honor
Heart of Honor
Bold in Honor
Love and Honor
Gift of Honor
Path to Honor
Return to Honor

PROLOGUE

London—1801

L ADY MARGARET TOWNSEND watched her older sister flirt with one of the gentlemen who had called upon them this afternoon. It was Dolley's first Season, and from everything Margaret could tell, Dolley's come-out was a spectacular one. At least according to the gossip columns, which Margaret read voraciously when no one was looking. They referred to Lady Dolley Townsend as a diamond of the first water and the most impressive debutante of this Season.

Margaret couldn't stand Dolley.

She found her sister petty and annoying—and that was on a good day. Actually, her mother was petty and annoying. Dolley was merely cut from the same cloth. Both women prized money and titles above all else. Thank goodness, she took after Papa and understood what was truly important in life. Learning. Friendships. Family. At least family who acted like family toward one another.

Mama had never taken to Margaret and because of Mama's attitude toward her younger daughter, neither had Dolley. Both her mother and sister were petite blonds with round, blue eyes like a doll's. Margaret, on the other hand, was already two inches under six feet at age fourteen, all gangly arms and legs. But it was her red hair which sealed the deal and what she believed made Mama dislike her so much.

Grandmama had had the same fiery red hair as Margaret. At least it had been a vivid red when Grandmama was young. By the time Margaret came along, Grandmama's hair had begun to turn white and was completely so by Margaret's fifth birthday. Since Mama had never liked anyone on Papa's side of the family—Papa included—Margaret's red hair marked her for derision from her mother and sister.

She didn't care what Mama or Dolley thought of her. She especially didn't care for fancy clothes and making her come-out. It all seemed a waste of time to her. She would rather be painting. Or riding. Or doing anything outdoors instead of sitting in this stuffy drawing room and watching preening suitors fawn over Dolley. Every afternoon, their drawing room drew at least a dozen men and was filled with bouquets which tried to show Lady Dolley Townsend just how much these suitors thought of her. Mama dragged Margaret to the drawing room each day and told her to pick up her embroidery and sew. Mama did the same, keeping an eagle eye on each of the men present, noting which ones spent the most on obscenely huge bouquets and how often they called.

Since her mother was engrossed in listening to the conversation Dolley was having with two earls and a marquess, Margaret decided now was as good a time as any in which to make her escape. The clock had just chimed, and she knew Dolley was to go driving in Hyde Park with some suitor in a quarter hour. Mama wouldn't miss Margaret.

Slipping from her seat, Margaret left the drawing room and proceeded downstairs. She had left a book in her father's study, the one place where Mama never thought to look for her. She would retrieve it and read for a few hours until supper. Another of the endless balls was being held tonight and her family would have a light meal before Mama and Dolley dressed and they left for the ball, Papa as their escort.

As she descended the stairs, she saw a handsome gentleman being admitted by Benson, their butler.

"I will tell Lady Dolley you are here, my lord. Would you care to wait in the parlor?"

"No, here is fine," the caller replied.

Benson passed her on the stairs and winked. Margaret smiled. The butler had always had a soft spot for her and often sneaked the newspapers to Margaret.

Reaching the foot of the stairs, the stranger looked up, his eyes flickering over her and moving on. Margaret was used to it. Dolley was the true beauty in the family. But it didn't mean she liked being dismissed. She decided to force this gentleman to be at least slightly polite to her.

Even if she had no intention in being the same in return.

"Good afternoon, my lord," she said breezily.

He had turned from her and had to look back. "Good afternoon," he said brusquely.

"You really should be nicer to me," she pointed out. "After all, I am Lady Dolley's sister, though not a beloved one. You would think a gentleman—and a potential suitor—would have better manners than you are displaying."

He looked taken aback by her frankness. And speechless.

Taking the bull by the horns, she said, "Since no one is here to introduce us, I will take it upon myself to do the honors. I am Lady Margaret Townsend. And you would be?"

"I am Lord Browning," he said stiffly, obviously bothered by her deigning to speak to him.

"What kind of lord?" she inquired. "I hope you are a marquess."

"Why?" he asked, wariness in his gray eyes.

"My sister is considered the beauty of her come-out class, my lord. Mama thinks she should settle for no less than a marquess and would prefer Dolley be wed to a duke."

"I am a viscount," he told her.

"Pity," she murmured, just loud enough for him to hear. "Of

course, you are quite handsome with that coal black hair and wonderfully broad shoulders. You could stand a bit straighter, though. Posture is important. Your clothes are beautifully cut, however. That will impress Dolley. She insists on a man who dresses in the latest fashions."

"You are quite impudent, you know," he told her. "How old are you?"

"I am fourteen. Fifteen tomorrow."

His brows arched. "June first is also my birthday. I will be two and twenty tomorrow."

Margaret looked him up and down. "You are young to be courting my sister. Most of her suitors have at least five to ten years on you. Why are you participating in the Season? Are you especially interested in claiming a bride?"

"Not really," he admitted. "I recently finished up at university, and my parents wished me to attend a few events."

She sighed in an exaggerated manner. "Then Dolley won't be interested in you at all, no matter how good looking you are. She wants an impressive title and a wedding after this Season ends. She would not be willing to wait around for you, my lord."

He frowned. "You don't believe in holding your tongue, do you, Lady Margaret?"

"I think telling the truth is refreshing, my lord. So few in Polite Society do so."

"You had better change your tune come your own debut," he warned.

"I don't even know if I want to make my come-out," she admitted. "I think I would find all the events boring. It would be as if I am a horse and all the men present at the various balls have come as they do to Tattersall's—to look over the eligible ladies and discover the pedigree. Focus on their lines. See which young filly would be a good brood mare for them so that they might get their required heir and spare."

"You are dashed cheeky," he proclaimed, shock upon his handsome face.

"I will admit I am not one for the womanly arts. If you saw my embroidery, you would know what a horror I am with a needle in hand. Why, I stab myself as often as I do the cloth itself, and all of my stitches are sloppy and crooked." She grinned. "But I can ride like the wind and believe one day I can become an accomplished portrait painter."

For the first time, he appeared interested in their conversation. "You paint? Portraits?"

"Yes," she said, enthusiasm bubbling over. "I practice on all our servants. Sometimes, I even pay children on the street to sit for me. That is what I truly believe my calling to be, not being a wife to some stuffy lord and playing hostess for him and having babies he won't even bother noticing."

A look of disdain crossed his face. "Men do not play with babies."

"Well, they should!" she declared. "Not only babies, but fathers should play with their children as they grow older. Spend time with them. Get to know them and love them. My papa lets me accompany him everywhere. We are inseparable and I know he loves me very much."

The viscount shook his head. "You are a handful, my lady. I am not certain any man would want to wed you. You are far too brash and opinionated."

"See?" she asked, a triumphant smile lighting her face. "I don't really want a husband after all. Therefore, I shouldn't waste my time with a Season."

Voices drifted down to them, and Margaret saw a large group of men heading their way, the last of the suitors leaving after paying their respects to Dolley and Mama.

As they passed, several called out greetings to Lord Browning, while two stopped in front of her.

"Good afternoon, Lady Margaret," Lord Lunsford said. "It was good seeing you this afternoon."

"Have a pleasant day, Lady Margaret," Lord Wilson added.

"A pleasure seeing you again, my lords," Margaret said sweetly, curtseying as they passed.

When they were gone, Lord Browning asked, "How do you know Wilson and Lunsford? You are not out yet."

"They are two of Dolley's more clever suitors," she explained. "When she is flirting with others and not paying them much attention, they come and speak to Mama and even me. They know fawning over Mama might earn them her favor, and she could sway Dolley's opinion. Alas, Lord Lunsford is merely a viscount, and so he is not in the running, despite his impeccable attire and handsome features. Lord Wilson might have a chance, however, even though he is only an earl. He is worth quite a bit more than the average peer. He is too intelligent for Dolley, though. At least that is what I believe."

"Why do you say that?" Lord Browning asked.

"I have read his speeches in the newspapers," she shared.

"You . . . follow . . . politics?" he asked, doubt in his voice.

"Of course, I do. I am very interested in what happens in England and the war with Bonaparte."

"You are not quite what you seem, my lady," the viscount told her.

She shrugged. "Most people pay me no attention at all. It allows me to be who I want to be."

"There you are, Lord Browning!" a voice called out.

Margaret turned and saw Dolley descending the stairs, the picture of feminine beauty and grace. For a moment, a frisson of jealousy ran through Margaret. She wished she could be graceful and hold the attention of the handsome lord standing next to her.

"Benson told me you were here, my lord," Dolley continued. "I am happy you asked for me to drive with you through the park this afternoon." Her eyelashes dipped, and she looked up through them, looking utterly appealing.

"I am grateful you wanted to drive with me," Lord Browning said. "And since Lady Margaret is here, perhaps she would wish to accompany us." He looked at Margaret intently.

For a moment, her heart raced. Then she realized how angry Dolley would be if she agreed to accompany them.

"No, I cannot intrude," she said demurely.

"Oh, it wouldn't be an intrusion," the viscount insisted. "We would be happy to include you. Wouldn't we, Lady Dolley?"

Her sister's eyes narrowed, and then she pasted on a bright smile. "Of course, my lord. I have always said that family is so important. Margaret is certainly welcome to come along with us."

"Then it is settled," Lord Browning said, turning.

As he did, Dolley pinched Margaret's arm. Hard. She knew enough not to utter a squeak and merely shrugged helplessly as she walked to the door and ventured outside to where Lord Browning's vehicle stood.

He offered his hand to Dolley and helped her up before turning and doing the same to Margaret. When she placed her hand in his, a burst of electricity seemed to run through her, making her scalp tingle. He frowned at her, as if somehow displeased, and she stepped up into the barouche.

Dolley wore a sour face, and Margaret knew her sister was furious. The game had gone on long enough. She had warned Lord Browning that Dolley wouldn't be interested in him. Her fun was now done.

"Oh!" she said, exaggerating a bit. "I just forgot. I was to finish writing my report on the book my governess gave me to read. She wanted it by day's end." Turning to face the viscount, she added, "I cannot disappoint her. I will stay here, and you and Dolley can enjoy your drive through Hyde Park."

The viscount's gray eyes took her in, making the tingles spread through her. "Then I shall escort you back inside, Lady Margaret." He glanced at Dolley. "A moment, my lady?"

"Of course, my lord," Dolley said, her tone sweet. "I am sorry you won't be able to accompany us, Margaret."

"Perhaps another time," she said cheerfully, knowing that would never happen.

Lord Browning extended his hand, and she took it again, feeling a rush of warmth run through her as he helped her down. He led her to the front door.

"There is no book or report, is there, Lady Margaret?" he asked softly.

Grinning cheekily, she said, "There is no governess, my lord. Most of them found me to be incorrigible."

"Then why the excuse?"

"Because Dolley would take it out on me long after today's drive," she admitted. "She already dislikes me as it is. I do not wish to alienate her further."

"Why the animosity between you?"

"Mama doesn't like me either. It's the red hair. They both say it is vulgar. It's not as if I can change that." She sighed. "Go enjoy your ride, Lord Browning, but remember you have been warned."

"Yes, I remember. I am not a marquess or duke and haven't a chance with your sister—even if I am handsome."

"And arrogant," Margaret added playfully. "As long as we're being honest with one another."

"I hope we always will be, my lady. I look forward to seeing you in a few years at your come-out."

"Don't count on it," she said saucily and opened the door, stepping inside the foyer and then closing it behind her.

She left the startled footman looking at her as she raced into the parlor and peered out the window, watching Lord Browning climb into his barouche and take up the reins. He was a handsome devil, handsome as sin, some might say. Margaret watched them drive away and then retreated to her bedchamber, where she removed drawing paper and her charcoals. She had an overwhelming urge to draw Lord Browning.

And paint him.

She had finished a portrait of her beloved grandmother yesterday. Seeing how well it had turned out gave her the confidence that she could do justice to one featuring Lord Browning.

He would never see the portrait, but she felt compelled to produce it, nonetheless. Though he wasn't a paying customer, he would be her first effort at painting a member of the nobility.

Margaret prayed he would not be the last.

CHAPTER ONE

London—Ten years later . . .

MARGARET ROSE FROM the rocker, her niece in her arms, the baby's eyes now closed. She crossed the nursery and placed the sleeping child into the crib staring down at her for a long time.

She wanted a baby. She wanted a life of her own. Hopefully, her wishes would become a reality soon. At least the part about creating and managing her own life. A baby would have to wait because Margaret wasn't interested in marriage—and it took a husband to have a baby.

Actually, it didn't. She had known one of their maids who had found herself with child, and the servant certainly wasn't wed. It became a scandal, though, one which Margaret's mother had swept under the rug. The parlor maid had been dismissed, along with a groom from the stables. He was the man the girl had named as the father. Margaret wondered where the couple had gone once they left the country estate without references. It was just like her mother to send the pair off so cruelly, even though both had served the Townsend family well for several years.

Perhaps she could help some young woman in need and take on her baby and raise it as her own. It would certainly be shocking. Then again, Margaret's plans to have a career would prove scandalous. More than anything, she wanted to become a portrait artist. She had practiced for years. Her favorite paintings she had completed were of her grandmother and a man she had met only once. Grandmama had died when Margaret was ten and so had not lived to see the portrait her granddaughter had created. It was still a wonderful reminder of the woman who had loved and supported Margaret during her childhood.

As for the stranger? She had never seen him again. He had come to court Dolley, and she had warned him that a viscount wouldn't be considered. Dolley and Mama had been far too ambitious. The pair had settled upon Lord Baxter, a wealthy marquess. Dolley had wed, and the autumn after her come-out had given birth to a boy who was now nine. She also had a girl who had just turned two. In typical fashion, her sister rarely saw either child, claiming they dirtied her gowns and were too loud and demanding. It was the nursery governess who was raising the pair. Since Margaret had come to live with Dolley and Baxter, she had done her best to spend as much time in the nursery with her nephew and niece as she could. She enjoyed their company and had a marvelous time playing with the children and teaching them small things, seeing the wonder in their eyes, and accepting their sweet kisses.

Turning from the crib, she nodded a thanks to the nursery governess and left the nursery. Knowing teatime would be in half an hour, she ventured down the stairs and decided to take a brief stroll in the gardens before heading to the drawing room. She opened the French doors and stepped outside. The day was cool but sunny, and she entered the gardens, glad to have a bit of time to herself.

The Season approached, something she dreaded. She had no interest in finding a husband because he would tell her what to do. If anything, Margaret was highly independent and didn't think a husband would suit her. Mama had claimed Margaret was spoiled because Papa let her accompany him about the estate. Her father had taught her many things, from how to keep ledgers to the way tenants should be treated. Since neither her mother nor Dolley ever visited their tenants, that task had fallen to Margaret, and she thoroughly enjoyed it. She had celebrated births and marriages alongside them, as well as mourned the passing of their family members.

The only reason she had agreed to attend the Season was so she could try and make social connections. If she could convince a few influential members of the *ton* to allow her to paint them, she hoped her reputation would spread. Then she could begin her artistic career, something a husband would forbid. Margaret believed God gave her the talent to paint, and it would be wasteful not to use it. If that meant no children, so be it. She would rather paint than do anything else.

Bending, she sniffed an early blooming rose, enjoying its sweet scent. Then she heard voices and realized her sister and brother-in-law were sitting in the gazebo just on the other side of the rose bushes. She started to turn and leave them in peace until she heard her name. Knowing eavesdroppers never heard good things about themselves, she still chose to remain.

"It is not that Margaret is exactly a bother. It is merely my opinion that your cousin should be the one responsible for her," Lord Baxter complained. "After all, he *is* the new earl and head of your family. With your father's death, Margaret became his responsibility. Not mine."

"I agree," Dolley said. "But he is already wed and has five children. He said there was no room for Margaret. Besides, he and his wife never attend the Season. If Margaret has any chance of landing a husband, then she simply must do a Season. How the chit will ever find a husband, though, is beyond me."

Baxter harumphed. "At least your father provided a wardrobe allowance for her, along with her dowry. If I had to clothe the woman, it would have been asking too much. As it is, you almost bankrupt me each year with the new wardrobe you demand for each Season."

"Am I not worth it, Baxter? I still possess my looks and figure, despite the fact you have already gotten two children off me. People still comment on my beauty and how fortunate you are to have claimed the most beautiful debutante of my year."

"I could still stand to have a spare to my heir," the marquess complained. "Especially since I am having to put up with housing your sister and escorting her to events."

Margaret winced at his tone. She did her best to avoid both Baxter and Dolley and rarely saw either of them so she knew she was not an inconvenience. They were both selfish and self-centered, however, and she would never be able to change that.

"Thank goodness Margaret's dowry is large. It will help her to land a husband," Dolley said. "Her dowry will be the only way she will attract one. You and I both know there are gentlemen of the *ton* who will overlook Margaret's many faults simply because they are in need of the money she would bring into a marriage."

A long sigh sounded. "It may take time, though, Baxter. After all, look at her. She's absolutely hideous, with all that horrible red hair. And her height! Why, I have never seen a woman so tall in my life. It's simply unnatural. The fact she is my sister is hard enough to bear. She will stick out like a sore thumb in ballrooms and be an embarrassment to the both of us. Still, we must do our duty to her. We will garner sympathy from Polite Society for having to put up with her."

"I still say despite her dowry, attracting a husband will be nearly impossible. Why, she's on the shelf," Baxter insisted. "Four and twenty and making her come-out? Besides, I don't like her. I never have. She is far too opinionated for a woman. The gentlemen of the *ton* won't like her either. You know I am right."

"That may be true," her sister admitted.

"It is," Baxter insisted. "She reads the newspapers, for goodness' sake. She spouts opinions about politics and economics and laws which have been passed or ones she thinks Parliament should pass. No man of Polite Society enjoys a bluestocking. Especially one so old and still unwed. I say despite the size of her dowry, Lady Margaret will have a difficult time finding a husband. Then we'll be stuck with her."

"No, we won't," Dolley shared. "She turns five and twenty at the beginning of June."

"What difference does that make?"

"It means legally, she will have access to her dowry," Dolley said, her tone soothing her rankled husband. "If my sister cannot find a husband, she would be of a mind to take her dowry and live off it."

"Does she know this?" Baxter asked.

Of course, Margaret knew it. She had insisted upon it when she pumped Papa for information about her dowry. That had been after Mama had grown ill and Margaret's come-out was delayed in order for her to care for her ailing mother. For three, long years, Margaret had spent a majority of her days in Mama's sickroom, tending to her ungrateful parent, who constantly bemoaned the fact that it wasn't Dolley taking care of her. Margaret reminded Mama daily that Dolley had wed and had a husband and a child to care for.

When her mother had finally passed, Margaret began her year of official mourning, only to have Papa struck with apoplexy. It had left him paralyzed on one side and unable to speak. He fully understood all that went on about him but could only grunt to communicate. Finally, they arrived at a tapping system since he could move his left hand. Through careful questioning, Margaret pieced together what Papa wanted done on the estate and saw to it herself, with the help of their steward. She had become the de facto earl and ran the property, seeing to their tenants and managing the crops and ledgers on her own.

Her painting had been sorely neglected during those two years. She had finally gotten back to it during this past year of mourning after Papa's death. That was another reason she rarely saw her sister or brother-in-law. Between playing with the children and concentrating on her art, Margaret remained busy and out of the way.

"You are saying she would access her dowry and live off it?"

Baxter asked, his tone perplexed.

"That is exactly what I am saying," Dolley told her husband. "You know how independent she is. The dowry would give her a way to live on her own. Simply, of course. And obviously, she would not take part in Polite Society. Then again, I find it hard to picture my sister at any event, be it a ball or rout or going to the theatre. After all, she will be following in my footsteps. No one could do so after the spectacular impression I made upon the *ton*."

Margaret almost gasped aloud at her sister's audacity but remained silent.

"Then I suppose I can tolerate her for a few more months," grumbled Baxter. "I still think this idea of her painting portraits is mad."

One evening at dinner, Margaret had shared what she wished to do with her life. Baxter hadn't said anything at the time, but she now knew his opinion.

"No one will commission her to do so," Dolley agreed. "Margaret is foolish to believe so. In a way, it is a bit sad. She is quite talented, you know. I have seen a few of her pieces. Why, I have an idea, Baxter!"

"Will it cost me money? Your ideas always seem to."

"It won't cost you a farthing," Dolley guaranteed. "I will ask Margaret to paint our portraits. We have yet to have it done, and she would be delighted to do so. I will tell her it will be good practice for her." Dolley chuckled. "Besides, if for some odd reason she ever did become famous, we would have an original work by her."

"It would be a decent way for her to repay our kindness. For housing her for these past few months. Having her accompany us to upcoming *ton* events this spring and summer."

"Exactly. I will bring it up at tea. Support my idea," Dolley commanded. "I have a way to make her think it would be her idea, after all. She won't suspect a thing and will be happy to do this for us. Perhaps I can even talk her into doing one of the children together since she seems to spend an inordinate amount of time with them. Why, I cannot fathom. But it will be good to finally be rid of her. She will only be an embarrassment to us for a bit longer, then we can wash our hands of her."

Margaret had heard enough. She hurried from the gardens back to her room to freshen up. Once in her room, she tidied her hair, staring into the mirror to see if she found any wrinkles on her face. She did not think four and twenty was so very old. Then again, she should have made her come-out years ago, at eighteen, when she was young and fresh faced. She studied her image.

Her red hair was abundant and pulled away from her face. Her green eyes stood out against her porcelain skin. She was no beauty like Dolley, but she still was more than passable in looks. Her breasts were full and her waist small. The only drawback would be her height. She was like her grandmother—extremely tall. Grandmama had been almost six feet, highly unusual for a woman, and Margaret was but two inches under six feet. That alone would probably keep away any potential suitors. Gentlemen would be drawn to delicate creatures such as Dolley, who was two inches over five feet, small boned with delicate features, along with blond hair and blue eyes. Margaret had always felt like a giant when standing next to her petite sister. It would most likely be the same with the other girls making their come-outs. And girls they would be, most seventeen or eighteen years old.

She laughed aloud. She would be the opposite of her sister, as she always had been. While Dolley had been the noted beauty and diamond of the first water, Margaret would be the ancient giantess and most likely the leading wallflower of this Season. It was a good thing she was not interested in a husband and would gain access to her dowry in a few months' time. Dolley was right in assuming Margaret would want to be on her own once she reached the ripe old age of five and twenty. While she would remain in this household until the end of the Season, she had plans to find a place of her own. Her funds would not allow her to let both a place in town and one in the country, though. That would be the only drawback. She would miss the country.

Walking. Riding. Visiting with the tenants and their families.

But farmers did not have the money—much less the inclination—to have their portraits made. That would be for the aristocrats who came to London each year for the Season. Actually, a small portion of Polite Society did remain in town year-round. She hoped to tap into that market after this Season ended and establish her reputation over the next year so that by the time next Season rolled around, she would be able to find patrons who commissioned her.

That meant she would tolerate attending the events during the next few months. She would paste on a bright smile and try to meet as many potential clients as possible and arrange to paint portraits of those who would stay in London. She would also need to meet with Papa's solicitor, whose name she had, as well as find a place to let. They hadn't been in town long enough for her to explore it, but she would also do that soon. She needed to find a place to live in a decent part of town where her funds would stretch further than they might in fashionable Mayfair, where Baxter and Dolley lived. Perhaps somewhere nearby so that she could easily reach it by a short hackney cab ride.

She also wanted to find an art supply shop and restock her meager supplies. She hadn't brought any blank canvases with her, only her favorite brushes. She couldn't wait to explore the selection of paints available. In the country, she had made her own, only using prepared ones Papa brought from London for her after he and Mama returned from the Season each year.

As for finished canvases, she had only retained possession of two—that of Grandmama and Viscount Browning, Dolley's long-ago erstwhile suitor. While she had a servant hang her grandmother's portrait in her bedchamber at the Baxter townhouse, she had not removed the cloth protecting Lord Browning's painting in many years. She had merely brought it along with her to London when she left the country. A footman had taken it to an empty room on the top floor of the Baxter townhouse.

She wondered what the viscount now looked like. He had

been seven years her senior and not interested in settling down, a fact she was grateful for since Margaret had warned him off pursuing her sister. Did Lord Browning now have a wife? He hadn't been in the market for one all those years ago. Surely by now, he would have settled down, though. Would he have children? She wondered if he would be a good father and decided he wouldn't. He had been a tad too arrogant for her and would probably pursue custom and not have much to do with his children, as Baxter and Dolley.

Margaret shook her head, thinking on all her sister was missing out on. Each day she had been here, she had seen her nephew and niece grow and change. Their vocabulary expanded. Their curiosity abounded. Yet Dolley—and her husband—constantly ignored their offspring. If Margaret wed—and she sincerely doubted she ever would—she would spend several hours a day in her children's company, enjoying how the babies became small people in their own right, with their likes and dislikes and habits and peculiarities.

Sighing, she decided it was time to go down for tea with her sister and brother-in-law—and have a bit of fun with Dolley as she tried to subtly persuade Margaret to paint the portraits of Lord and Lady Baxter.

With one last glance in the mirror, Margaret smoothed her hair and then returned to the drawing room. She would agree to paint Dolley and Baxter simply because she needed the practice. Their clothing would also be far more elaborate than the servants she usually painted. If pleased, her sister might actually recommend Margaret to her friends, especially if Dolley thought it would take Margaret off her hands.

Resolve filled her as she entered the drawing room. She would make certain these portraits would closely resemble her sister and brother-in-law, while flattering them at the same time. She had to.

They would be her stepping stone to the future.

CHAPTER TWO

D ANIEL JUDSON, DUKE of Westfield, sat behind his desk, his thoughts scattered. The Season was fast approaching.

It was time to find a wife.

He had put it off long enough. His first Season he had recently graduated from university and went as a lark, mostly to please his mother, who wished for him to attend. He had found the young ladies making their come-outs to be vapid and dull. Only a handful were pretty, and one truly stood out as the beauty of the group of newcomers. That had been Lady Dolley Townsend, now Lady Baxter. She had wed a marquess, just as her sister had predicted.

He wondered what had become of Lady Margaret, she of the flaming hair and moss green eyes. Daniel had teased that he would see her at her come-out, and yet she had not made an appearance three years later when his sister, Lilly, did so. He almost thought to ask Lady Baxter where her sister might be but after approaching the marchioness, he thought better of it and turned away. Still, he had kept an eye out for the remarkably frank Lady Margaret and had been disappointed when he never saw her that entire spring or summer.

She hadn't occupied his thoughts for long, though. Daniel had had his hands full. His father had passed away suddenly and his mother followed soon after. It was up to Daniel to see his two younger sisters launched into Polite Society. He did so with the help of the Dowager Duchess of Westfield, his grandmother, who helped prepare Deborah and Lilly for their come-outs. Deborah had made her debut first. She was five years younger than Daniel and a bit of a featherhead, though no one was sweeter than Deborah. She had wed a Scottish laird at nineteen and in six years of marriage had produced two sons. Deborah hadn't liked the trappings of the Season, and she and her laird now remained in Scotland year-round.

Lilly, two years Deborah's junior, had married a jovial baron the year after her come-out and had one daughter and another babe on the way. Because of her delicate condition, Lilly and her husband had decided to stay in the country to await their babe's September birth. Daniel would miss seeing his sister and planned to visit with her once the child arrived.

In the meantime, it was time to get serious about finding a bride for himself. After all, he was a duke and needed to produce the requisite heir. He had skipped last Season simply because his grandfather had died in February, thrusting the dukedom on his grandson's shoulders. Daniel had sowed quite a few wild oats and knew it was time to settle into his role and responsibilities. He had spent the entire past year at Westwood, learning about the land and its people. He now could speak with ease about crops and cattle and sheep.

He had also taken a portion of his wealth, which had been much smaller than he would have thought a duke might possess, and begun investing it, seeing large returns in the past year. It seemed he had the Midas touch and now Westwood would be safe for several generations to come. That meant he did not have to seek out a bride with an enormous dowry. He could wed a woman of grace and good breeding and work on getting a few sons off her. Aware he was now past thirty, Daniel knew it was time to secure a wife and then the subsequent heir.

A soft knock sounded on his study's door. "Come," he called.

His butler entered. "Her Grace requests that you take tea

with her this afternoon, Your Grace."

"All right, Hampton. I shall be there shortly."

The butler left, and Daniel sighed aloud. He loved his grandmother dearly, much more than he had his parents. No love had existed between Daniel and them. The two had been totally self-centered, ignoring their three children and living lives of indulgence. The three Judson children had rarely seen their parents. Once, he and his sisters had a discussion, wondering what color their mother's eyes were. None of them could recall their color—and it had taken eight months before they had actually been in her company to see for themselves what shade they actually were.

Daniel thought family was important. That was why he had taken special care that his sisters wed decent, honorable men. Both seemed quite happy from the letters they had written to him. He wondered if he might find happiness in his own marriage.

He certainly wasn't interested in finding love.

Duty meant everything to him, though, and so he would wed as was expected and have children. He would treat his wife with utmost respect and dote on his children without spoiling them. Now, he had to find said wife. One who wouldn't bore him to tears, prattling on about her latest gown and sharing gossip about the *ton*. Was it asking too much for decent conversation?

Most likely, the answer to that question was a resounding *yes*.

He had yet to meet any woman he would wish to wed. Perhaps since he had been away from Polite Society for a while, some remarkable creature had now entered the social scene and would catch his attention.

Daniel chuckled at that, deeming it highly unlikely.

He rose, knowing he shouldn't keep his grandmother waiting. A slight dread filled him, however, as he made his way up the stairs and to the drawing room. She had been harping lately about him taking a wife.

And having fun.

Fun was not a word in a duke's vocabulary.

Entering the drawing room, he saw her seated next to the teacart and greeted her. "Good afternoon, Gran. I hope you have had a lovely day."

He took a seat, and she poured out for them, handing him a cup and saucer.

"What have you been doing today, Daniel?"

He liked that she still called him by his Christian name. No one else did, not even his sisters when they addressed him in person or through letters. It was as if when he became a duke, the Daniel part of him had ceased to exist.

"Scouring my investments, Gran," he told her.

She shook her head. "You work too hard, Grandson."

"I have a multitude of responsibilities and many properties to see to, Gran. You should know after having been married to Grandfather for so many years."

She snorted. "Even Westfield did not bury himself in his ledgers as long or as often as you do, Daniel. You used to have friends coming and going at all hours of the day and night. When are you going to have a little fun?"

"Dukes don't get to have fun. They are to be serious men who lead Polite Society," he replied, sampling a bit of a lemon cake.

"You are too serious, my boy," she cautioned. "You used to sparkle in conversation. You enjoyed life. You always had friends surrounding you."

"I have far too much to do to waste time the way I did for most of my twenties, Gran. I led the life of a carefree, happy bachelor. No London gentleman enjoyed his life more than I did. At the same time, I made certain my sisters found good husbands before I abandoned *ton* events altogether."

She sniffed. "The Season is not all it is made out to be. It can become rather boring unless you have good friends to share it with."

"I shared many good times with friends from school and

university for years at my clubs. I was never one to pass up a drink or a visit to a gaming hell." He paused. "Nor did I hide the fact from you that I have had several mistresses. But you will be happy to know I plan to wed this Season. Or after the Season. I suppose that is when weddings occur. Betrothal during the Season and marriage to follow. At least that how it was for Deborah and Lilly."

Gran frowned. "You make it sound as if it is one of your business transactions, Daniel."

He took a sip of tea and set down his saucer. "Well, it is a bit of that, I suppose. I will search the Marriage Mart. Find an appropriate woman who will make for an excellent duchess. Then I can be done making nice with Polite Society. If I never attend the Season again, I would be happier for it."

"And what of this wife you are wishing to claim, Daniel? Does she have any say in this? She might enjoy the Season. The dancing. The parties. Wearing new, pretty gowns. Visiting with her friends."

He hadn't thought of that.

"I suppose it truly won't matter. Once I am wed, I can do as I want and so can my wife. As long as she provides the heir I need, she may come and go as she pleases. If that involves enjoying the Season with her friends, so be it."

Gran's frown deepened. "I suppose you will be kind enough to provide her with a new wardrobe and the appropriate pin money."

He picked up the sarcasm dripping from her. "Gran, do not chide a duke. We are supposed to make our own rules, and Polite Society then forgives us anything."

"What of love, Daniel?" she challenged.

"What of it? You and Grandfather did not love one another. My parents shared no love or intimacy. Truly, it is not a consideration of mine. Love is for others. Not me."

Her eyes narrowed. "I beg to differ, Grandson. I think love is for everyone. It will enrich your life. It will make you a better person. It will give you hope and the very reason to live." She paused. "I speak from experience, Daniel."

"What? I don't understand." He looked at her with new eyes, for the first time not thinking of her as his grandmother, but a woman who was once young.

"I was madly in love once upon a time," she said, a wistfulness in both her tone and her eyes. "He was everything to me. *Everything*. And then I lost him."

"Did he . . . die?"

"No. I did," she revealed. "My parents longed for a strong social connection in order to further their own. I was only a viscount's daughter—but I had beauty and charm. I caught the eye of the Duke of Westfield. The rest didn't matter."

She hesitated and then continued. "I told Westfield I did not love him. That I never could. That I loved another. He *laughed*. I can still hear him now." Her face transformed into a gruff exterior, and she lowered her voice, imitating her husband. "Love doesn't matter, my lady. You are beautiful, and you are who I want. I am a duke. Your father will never tell me no. Neither will you."

Gran's hand shook as she raised her teacup and sipped from it. "Westfield was right, you know. No one ever told him no. I learned dukes do not know the meaning of that word. I had to break the news to my sweetheart that I was to wed another."

She paused, her eyes growing hard. "He killed himself on my wedding day. I have mourned him every day since."

Her words took Daniel aback. He reached for her hand and squeezed it. "I am so sorry, Gran."

She smiled wryly, patting his hand. "Oh, it is all right, my boy. I have led a good life. A comfortable one. I used my power and position as a duchess for good."

He thought of the charities she supported, more so now than when his grandfather was alive.

"I never did come to love Westfield. I couldn't bring myself to love a man with such a cold heart." She gazed deeply into

Daniel's eyes. "But there is still hope for you. Your father didn't make a love match, though I urged him to do so. He thought the notion foolish." Her brows arched. "Much as you seem to think so yourself. Still, I have hope for you. That you will learn to love. To laugh. To celebrate life with a wonderful woman by your side. I want you to enjoy your relationship with her and spend time with her because you want to. Not because you have to. I want you to fill this house with children and love them as much as I do you, dear boy."

She set down her teacup. "Do not disappoint me in this, Daniel. Do not look for a woman who would make for an appropriate duchess. In fact, do the opposite. Look for one who is someone you can love. A woman who will challenge you. Adore you. Make you a better man."

"I think you ask the impossible, Gran. I don't believe such a woman exists. Especially not among the young women making their come-outs this year."

"Oh, you do not want a girl fresh from the schoolroom, Daniel. You need a more mature woman. Even a widow might do. I want you to promise me that you will be open to the idea of love. It may—or may not—find you. I simply encourage you not to shut the door on it before your search even begins."

Daniel nodded. "I will do as you ask and remain open to the idea."

He doubted love would come. It was rare in the *ton* to make a love match. Still, knowing his grandmother had once loved passionately and been denied by her family left him with a heavy heart. It also reminded him again of Lady Margaret Townsend and how her mother had pushed for her older daughter to make a match based upon a title alone.

Where was Lady Margaret?

Daniel decided he would find out.

CHAPTER THREE

M ARGARET'S BELLY ROILED as a maid helped her into her ball gown. Tonight, she would finally make her come-out into Polite Society. Nerves flitted through her as the maid brushed her hair. She didn't have a lady's maid. She'd made do without one in the country all the years she'd cared for her ailing parents. She hadn't gone anywhere and had dressed with the help of their housekeeper, and cared for her own hair.

When she had gone to live with Dolley, her sister refused to share her own lady's maid with Margaret. That left a different parlor maid pressed into service each morning and evening. While the servants were very kind, none of them had experience with a lady's wardrobe and hadn't a clue what to do with Margaret's hair. Because of that, she waited until the girl finished and then wound her hair into a simple chignon herself, securing it with pins.

Turning her head one way and then the other, she checked for any stray strands of hair and found none.

"Would you fasten my necklace?" she asked, reaching for the box that contained the only jewelry she owned.

"Of course, my lady."

The servant removed the strand of pearls and placed them about Margaret's neck. Papa had given her the necklace the Christmas before she was to make her come-out, saying every young woman needed a fine set of pearls. He had teased her, telling her it would always be her favorite necklace; even though he was certain her husband-to-be would shower her with jewels.

She blinked away the tears that rushed to her at that sweet memory. She had always been so close to him, accompanying him everywhere in those years before her mother's illness struck. Then she had watched Papa waste away after he, too, fell ill. She stood, smoothing her gown, glancing in the mirror, and thinking he would be proud of her. She would do him justice and attend this ball with her head held high and his gift around her neck.

"My, don't you look pretty, my lady," the maid said. "You'll have gentlemen falling all over themselves, wanting to dance with you."

Margaret wasn't certain that would occur. She believed she would be relegated to the sidelines with the other wallflowers, young women who were plain or shy or lacked a decent dowry. Her age alone would most likely place her there. She wouldn't allow that to interfere with her plans, however. She didn't need young swains fawning over her. They weren't the ones who would be interested in having their appearance captured on canvas. It would be older couples who wanted to preserve their likenesses, ones who had already wed. She hoped to arrange to paint some who had recently wed, playing on their likelihood of wanting to be captured while they were at the height of their looks. Then again, she would press others to have their children painted. She also would suggest older couples have their portraits done, having settled into their years, perhaps even mentioning they might want portraits of themselves as a couple or as an entire family.

"Thank you," she said politely to the maid. "I appreciate your help in getting ready this evening."

The girl looked at her, starry-eyed. "Will you tell me a bit about the ball tomorrow, my lady? I would ever so much like to hear what one is like."

She smiled. "I can certainly do that."

"I want to hear what the other ladies wore. What they serve at the midnight buffet. I have helped in setting up our ballroom here, but I've never been allowed near it once the guests arrive. I'm usually sent to the kitchens to help the scullery maids. Cook is always running about like a chicken with her head cut off, worrying about all the dishes."

"I will share everything I can remember," she promised, dismissing the maid.

Margaret swallowed and took a deep breath. She found taking several breaths to always be calming and did so now before she left her bedchamber and went to the foyer downstairs. Baxter was already there in his evening clothes, a cross expression upon his face.

"Good evening, my lord," she said.

"Good evening," he replied curtly, drumming his fingers on the banister. "You didn't happen to see Lady Baxter?"

"No, I did not. You have been married to Dolley for several years now, my lord. You must realize she takes a good while to dress for a formal occasion."

"I don't wish to be late," he grumbled. "The opening night of the Season is already crowded enough as it is. If we don't leave soon, we will be in a mass of traffic. Why, last year, our driver couldn't get us within three blocks of our destination—and we were made to walk all that way."

She stifled the laughter that threatened to bubble up. Walking a few blocks seemed a small price to pay for being able to attend a grand ball. Then again, Baxter and Dolley were the type of people who would ring for a servant to bring them something that sat only a few feet away so that they didn't have to reach for it themselves.

"Finally," the marquess muttered as Dolley glided down the staircase.

"Have you been waiting long?" she asked, knowing her husband was champing at the bit by her tone.

"You're here now. Shall we?"

He escorted them to the carriage waiting outside the front door, and within two blocks their carriage came to a standstill, faced with the traffic Lord Baxter had predicted. They crawled another block before a knock sounded at the coach's door, and the coachman opened it.

"My lord, this is as far as I can get you unless you want to wait another hour or two," the driver said.

Dolley sniffed. "I suppose we shall have to walk. This seems to happen each year when the Season begins."

"If you would deign to come downstairs earlier, this situation could be avoided," her husband said, glaring at his wife.

The marquess proceeded to exit the vehicle. Dolley followed and then Margaret joined them as they gingerly picked their way between carriages and joined the throng heading to Lord and Lady Villafield's townhouse.

"I do wish someone other than the Villafields were hosting this opening ball," Dolley said. "Lady Villafield is so common."

"Isn't she a countess?" Margaret asked, having seen the invitation and knowing it was an earl and countess who were their hosts for this evening.

"She is but a baron's daughter," her sister said. "Plain as a day is long—but her dowry was large enough to entice Villafield to offer for her."

"What do you think gentlemen will think of my dowry?" she demanded. "And exactly how do others find out the size of a lady's dowry?"

"It is common enough knowledge," Baxter said. "The topic comes up frequently at my club during the Season, along with the looks and connections an eligible lady possesses."

It horrified her to think of how little men thought of women. She could imagine them sitting in White's, brandy sniffers in hand, as they discussed the assets of women who were being paraded about the Marriage Mart. Thankfully, she did not need a husband and thanked her stars that Papa had made certain of that by guaranteeing that Margaret would have full control of her dowry once she turned five and twenty.

In a way, she should be happy her come-out had been delayed. If it had not been, then most likely she would have wed quickly and her husband would have maintained control of her dowry. He would also have controlled her. She doubted he would have given her leave to be a portrait artist. By waiting until now to debut into Polite Society, Margaret was at a point where she was almost self-sufficient and had no need of a man ordering her about, telling her what to do. That put her at an advantage. She didn't have to worry about what bachelors of the *ton* thought of her, as long as their parents and other married couples decided to engage her services.

She did know that she looked her best, though. Papa had made provisions for her come-out wardrobe, and Margaret had been taken to Dolley's modiste, one who accepted a handful of new clients each Season and only those by referral. Being the sister of a marchioness did have a few advantages.

Margaret had been astounded at the number of gowns that were required for a Season. Since she had been buried in the country for years, Dolley had been appalled at her sister's wardrobe. Besides dozens of ball gowns being made up, the modiste also provided dresses for every occasion. Routs. Garden parties. The opera and theatre. Receiving guests at home and ones for calling upon others. Even the number of new undergarments she possessed shook her to her core. The fact that Dolley replenished her wardrobe each year for the Season gave Margaret an inkling of just how much Lord Baxter spent on seeing that his wife was properly outfitted.

At least now that she had such fine clothes, she would not need more for years to come. Yes, fashions changed, but she would likely not partake in another Season in the future. If she established her clientele, she would no longer need to go to *ton* events. She had plenty of day gowns to wear and even then, she would wear smocks to cover them while she painted. She didn't have to be fashionable.

Only talented.

Once again, Margaret prayed that she would find a few members of Polite Society who would take a chance on her and give her a commission. She need not charge much. In fact, she had figured out that most people in Polite Society actually enjoyed getting a bargain. If she charged a reasonable amount for her first few portraits, then she could raise her prices accordingly as commissions came in. Those who ventured early to claim her services would then truly have gotten a bargain. It would all be in the timing—and if she could secure a few engagements to paint.

They reached Lord and Lady Villafield's townhouse and entered it, joining a lengthy receiving line. While others might have been bored, she relished the time she could spend in it, focusing on what guests wore and thinking how she would paint those who stood around her. Dolley chatted with a few people and was aware enough of her duties to introduce her sister each time she did so. Even Lord Baxter managed to do the same.

By the time they reached their hosts, Margaret had already made the acquaintance of well over a dozen people and their spouses. She was clever enough not to mention anything about painting, though. It was important to secure the social connection first—then draw upon it and convince a potential client that they needed her services—and that she was the one to provide it to them.

Entering the ballroom with Dolley and Baxter, her brother-in-law gave a quick glance and said, "I will be in the card room." He turned and abruptly left.

"Does he always abandon you with such haste?" she asked, surprised at the marquess's quick exit.

Dolley waved a hand in the air. "It is what men of the *ton* do, Margaret. They wed for money, usually choosing a spouse to help them rise to a loftier position, and then go about their own business. Baxter has his friends. I have mine. We have our own interests and share little—if anything—in common."

Her sister's words were puzzling. "Then why did you bother

to wed him? I notice he is rarely at home, and you are not often in one another's presence. Here, tonight at the opening of the Season, he has already fled your side."

Dolley stared at her as if Margaret had sprouted another head. "Why, he is a marquess. The fact that he cut a fine figure and was quite wealthy only supported my decision." She patted her hair. "After all, I was the great beauty of my Season. Baxter was fortunate to win my hand."

"Do you ever talk to him?" she asked.

"About what? I told you. He has his life, and I have mine. Yes, we come together upon occasion and I do my wifely duty, unpleasant as it is. He has already gotten two children off me." Her nose wrinkled. "And possibly a third."

"You are with child?"

"Perhaps. I will know in the next few days but already my breasts are tender and my appetite is dull in the mornings." Her sister's stern face warned Margaret not to mention anything to anyone.

Immediately, Dolley's features softened. "Ah, I see others moving this way. I will now introduce you to as many people as I can, Margaret. Promise me you will be demure and keep your opinions to yourself, else you will never land a husband."

Her sister placed a warm smile upon her face. "Ah, Lord Neville. How good to see you."

After that came a parade of others, both men and women. Margaret quickly realized people came to them and not the other way around. Dolley, as a marchioness, must hold an exalted place within the *ton*. She witnessed her sister transform into a woman of sincerity, full of kind smiles and doling out bits of gossip. Dolley did her duty and made certain Margaret met everyone who came their way.

It surprised her when some of the men asked to sign her programme, which she had received from a footman as they entered the ballroom. She handed it over, and soon saw it half-filled. She hoped she remembered how to dance. She had learned to do so years ago but hadn't had an opportunity to practice—and hadn't thought it necessary to do so.

Then she sensed eyes upon her and turned, glancing toward the entrance to the ballroom. Two people had entered and gazed in her direction. The woman was elderly, with abundant white hair and a regal air about her.

But it was the man who drew her attention.

He was very tall and broad-shouldered, with a commanding presence that would draw the eye of man and woman alike. His black evening clothes were immaculately tailored. His hair, black as a raven, was a bit longer than fashion dictated.

Then she realized exactly who he was.

Viscount Browning . . .

She had painted him once upon a time and should have recognized him. Time had passed, though. He had been a brash young man that day they had met, fresh from university and about to turn two and twenty as she turned fifteen. That meant almost nine years had passed. In that time, Lord Browning had certainly grown into his looks. Before, he had been boyishly appealing.

Now, he was a man.

One who now headed in her direction.

CHAPTER FOUR

DANIEL WAITED AT the foot of the stairs, admiring his grandmother as she descended the stairs. Though she had recently turned eighty, she still walked erect and with confidence, unlike many of the stooped matrons much younger than she was. Her snow-white hair, still abundant, was piled high upon her head, and diamond earrings dangled from her earlobes. Her gown, a dusty rose, was the height of fashion.

As she reached the bottom step, he took her hand and kissed it. "You look incredible, Gran. How can I find a woman to wed when you have set such a high standard? You are every inch a duchess."

Her smile told him how pleased she was with his compliments. "You are a dear boy. Actually, a dear man. You will find the right woman to be your duchess, Westfield."

"So, we are back to formalities?" he asked, already dreading being the Duke of Westfield again with all of Polite Society.

"We are. Terms of endearment have no place at *ton* events." Gran's eyes lit with mischief. "Unless you are smitten with a lady and wish to call her some pet name."

He snorted in disgust. "I may be perusing the Marriage Mart this year, Gran, but I am looking for a wife. Not love. Pet names will play no role in my marriage. Come along. The carriage awaits us."

Once inside, she took his hand. "Daniel, I want you to listen to me."

"Oh, so *now* I am Daniel. When you want something from me."

"Pish-posh," Gran declared, pushing away his hand. "I merely wanted to remind you that you promised me you would be open to the idea of love."

"Whatever that is," he mumbled.

"I caught that. My hearing is still quite good, young man. Even better than my eyesight." She sighed. "Oh, Daniel. I have such high hopes for you making a love match."

"And I would tell you to lower your expectations, Gran."

"Why don't you let me find you your duchess?" she asked.

He had never considered that possibility. Of everyone in the world, he trusted no one as much as he did his grandmother. She had been a duchess for over sixty years. She would know what qualities would be necessary.

"I think that is an excellent idea," he declared, thinking it would take the pressure off him. Already, he knew doting mamas would be pushing their daughters to spend time with him once he continued to show up at *ton* events. It would be obvious to Polite Society that the Duke of Westfield was finally looking for his duchess. He dreaded the number of ladies he would have to ask to dance. Knowing he would actually have to converse with them caused him to shudder. Then there was the actually calling upon various ladies he thought to be suitable. All those wasted hours in drawing rooms with chaperoning parents hovering nearby and a room filled with other men paying suit made his belly turn. The thought of a lengthy Season and a hunt for a bride bored him. If Gran could find an appropriate woman to serve as his duchess, he should allow her to do so.

"You agree that easily?" she asked, her surprise clearly written on her face.

"I do. You may inspect and scrutinize the available ladies. Study their behaviors. Inquire about their reputations. Consider which ones possess the character to make for a perfect Duchess of Westfield. You are a truly a wonderful judge of character, Gran. I should have thought sooner to place you in charge of this mission."

"You are not getting off Scot-free, my boy," she warned. "Once I begin compiling a list of appropriate candidates, I will require you to spend time with them. Dance with them at functions. Take them to the theatre or for drives in Hyde Park. Most of all, you will need to call upon them several times to see if you believe you suit with one another."

He frowned. "I wish you would do all that for me. Just pick someone, Gran. Anyone will do."

She clucked her tongue. "I am not the one who will marry the girl. You are, Daniel. While I may cull through the pack, you will still have to put in the time to make your selection." She paused. "Do you agree?"

Sighing, he said, "If you will do your part, then I will do mine."

Daniel settled back into the cushions, pleased with the bargain he had struck with his grandmother. He would allow her to do all the work, knowing she would select a woman who would be ideal as a duchess.

"Wipe that smug look from your face," she ordered.

He glanced in her direction. "What?"

"You heard what I said. Just because I am going to be doing most of the legwork in finding you a bride does not mean you are off the hook this evening, my boy. You are not to disappear into the card room until the end of the ball. You will remain in the ballroom the entire evening. You will make certain you fill the dance cards of the women I indicate to you."

"But Gran," Daniel protested, "you haven't even spoken to any of these young ladies yet."

"I have a discerning eye. At least that is what you seem to be telling me. It is true that I may not know the young girls making their come-outs this Season. Then again, I don't foresee you being happy with a chit straight from the schoolroom, one prone to giggles or hysterics—or both."

He shuddered. "Very well then. If you know of a few eligible young women this evening, I will be perfectly content to dance with them."

"*And* make conversation with them, Daniel. It won't be enough for you to smile lazily and take a woman's breath away with your fine looks. Finding a marriage partner—a good marriage partner—takes work. On your part, as well as mine."

"Do you have any appropriate topics of conversation for me?" he asked sarcastically.

She glared at him, making him feel he was once more the small boy who had fallen from her good graces. "I will trust that with your outstanding education and sparkling personality, you will be able to converse without my suggesting topics to you," she said tersely.

They continued the remainder of the way in silence, the carriage pulling up in front of the Villafields' townhouse. Daniel assisted Gran from the vehicle and realized due to the dearth of carriages around them, they must be some of the last guests to arrive at the inaugural event kicking off this Season.

Going inside, they joined the receiving line and soon found themselves face to face with their host and hostess. Lady Villafield smiled at him, stars in her eyes, while Lord Villafield fawned over Daniel as everyone seemed to do since he had become a duke. He hated the fact that merely being a duke had people act in such a silly fashion.

"I cannot thank you enough, Your Grace, for choosing to attend our humble ball," the earl said. "Why, it will be a success merely because you and Her Grace are in attendance."

"Yes, well, thank you very much for your gracious invitation," he said. "I would like to have my grandmother go inside now so she may greet her old friends."

Finding her voice, Lady Villafield said, "And perhaps you, too, may see friends of your own, Your Grace?" Her eyes gleamed and she added, "There are a good number of beautiful young ladies making their come-outs tonight. I hope you will be generous with your time and dance with several of them."

Daniel grimaced inwardly but smiled politely. "Of course, my lady. After all, a ball is for dancing, is it not?"

The countess tittered at his remark, and he took the opportunity to take Gran's elbow and guide her beyond their hosts and into the ballroom itself. He had not attended a ball in a good many years, not since Lilly's come-out Season. Once his sisters had secured husbands, Daniel felt his duty complete and spent most of his evenings while in town at his club, drinking with friends, or in gaming hells.

Or with one of his mistresses.

He found being with a mistress far easier than waiting on young debutantes. With a mistress, he knew where he stood. He knew what the rules were and treated the women accordingly. He never kept the same one for long, however, buying them off with some pretty bauble and moving on to the next one. At least he had during his carefree days when he had been Viscount Browning. Ever since he had been the Duke of Westfield, he had no time for a mistress.

He wondered if he would do the same after his marriage and supposed he would. Gran and her notion of love simply did not interest him. Yes, she had found it as a young lady, yet look what had happened to her. She had wed the Duke of Westfield instead at her parents' insistence, making her miserable. The fact Gran's lover killed himself was a bit shocking and made Daniel all the more determined to keep his heart encased in ice instead of giving it away, where he would have no control over it.

As they stepped through the entrance of the ballroom, he glanced about quickly to see if he could spy anyone he knew. He did see a few acquaintances, but most of his friends were the same as he and had no interest in *ton* events.

Then he saw her.

Lady Margaret Townsend.

He had looked for the impudent young woman when his sister, Lilly, had made her come-out since they were the same age. Lady Margaret had warned Daniel she was not interested in making her debut into Polite Society, and he had not seen her at a single event that year. Since he had been a ghost at Season events since then, he wondered when she had started attending them.

His gaze locked with hers, and Daniel tried to recall just how long it had been since their long-ago meeting, determining it had been almost ten years ago, after he had graduated from university. In that time, Lady Margaret had grown from being average to quite spectacular. She stood next to her petite sister, Lady Baxter, a large circle around them.

"Oh, my goodness!" exclaimed Gran. "She is finally here."

Daniel looked to her. "Who?" he demanded.

"Why, Lady Margaret Townsend, that is who."

Gran knew Lady Margaret?

Gran smiled and said, "She is the very image of my closest friend, Dorothy, from years ago. Dorothy and I were closer than sisters when we made our own come-outs. Once we both wed, however, we grew apart, rarely seeing one another. We did come across each other once, however, when Lady Margaret was but five years of age. Already, she had the fiery red hair of her grandmother, as well as Dorothy's spirit. I have looked for her at *ton* events for many years now. This is the first one she has ever attended."

For some reason, that pleased Daniel very much.

Gallantly, he said, "Then I suppose we should go and have a word with your dear friend's granddaughter."

Gran's eyes lit up. "I think we will need more than a word, Westfield. I believe I shall ask Margaret to tea. As for you, you will sign her programme. Is that understood?"

For once, he and his grandmother were in complete agreement.

"Naturally, I would honor your wish, especially if this is the first ball Lady Margaret has ever attended. She may not know many others, and it would be the polite thing to do."

Gran chuckled low. "You do not fool me, Grandson. I can tell you are already intrigued by her. Let me say this. If she lived up to the potential she showed me when she was only five, she would make for an outstanding duchess."

Daniel thought so, too.

He escorted Gran across the room, but it took several minutes before they arrived because so many wished to speak to the Dowager Duchess and Duke of Westfield.

Finally, they arrived at their destination, and Lady Baxter smiled at them both.

"Your Graces, how lovely to see you this evening."

Daniel wondered if Lady Baxter regretted not giving him more of a chance when she was seeking a husband. He might not have had the ducal title at the time and had truly not expected it. He did possess it now, though, along with all the power and influence that went with it.

"The same, Lady Baxter," Gran said smoothly. She turned to the towering beauty that stood next to the small blond. "We need no introduction, my lady."

"We don't?" asked the redhead, her head cocked, a quizzical expression on her face as she concentrated upon his grandmother.

He thought it amusing that while Lady Margaret had studied him at length as he and Gran made their way across the ballroom, now that he stood in front of her, she ignored him.

Gran clasped Lady Margaret's hands and said, "I last saw you when you were but five years old. You were with Dorothy."

Daniel's breath was snatched from him at the dazzling smile Lady Margaret shone upon Gran.

"Oh, my goodness. You are Grandmama's friend. I recall meeting you in the bookstore." She paused, her eyes growing misty. "You even recommended a book which Grandmama bought for me after we parted company. It became a favorite of mine. How lovely to see you again after so long a time, Your Grace."

"It is good to see you finally making your come-out in Polite Society, my dear," Gran said. "It was easy to spot you even though the ballroom is crowded."

Lady Margaret blushed. "Yes, my height and hair do give me away."

"Might I introduce my grandson to you?" Gran asked, releasing the young woman's hands and indicating Daniel. "This is Westfield."

Finally, her gaze met his. "We met years ago, Your Grace. You were Lord Browning then, I believe."

Daniel took her gloved hand and bent over it, pressing a kiss to it. That same spark of electricity which had run through him years ago occurred again. He had forgotten it.

Until now.

He rose, still keeping her hand in his. "I do recall that meeting, Lady Margaret. I believe you had a book report to finish for your governess."

Color filled her cheeks. "I did indeed, Your Grace. You have quite a good memory."

"How could you ever recall such an inconsequential detail?" Lady Baxter demanded, clearly unhappy she had been left out of their conversation.

Daniel looked at the matron. Once, he had thought her to be the most beautiful female he had ever seen.

Now, he knew her sister was far more beautiful than any woman of his acquaintance.

"I have an excellent memory, Lady Baxter." He turned back to Lady Margaret and squeezed her fingers gently. "Might you still have a vacancy upon your dance card, my lady?"

"I do, Your Grace," she replied, passing her programme to him.

He studied it and saw about half the dances had been taken. Since it was her first *ton* event and she was a fresh face, this surprised him. Then again, she would tower over many gentlemen of the *ton*, who might be reluctant to partner with her.

Quickly, he scribbled his name beside two places and returned it to her. Glancing toward Gran, he saw her smile of approval.

Lady Margaret stared down at the card and then looked to him. "You have made a mistake, Your Grace. You—"

Gazing directly into her eyes, he said, "I never make a mistake, my lady." Then with a smile, he added, "After all, I am a duke."

Her quick intake of breath and wide eyes had him bite back the laughter that threatened to erupt. Turning to his grandmother, he said, "We should get you settled, Gran."

"Yes, of course," she said. "First, I would like to ask Lady Margaret if she might wish to come to tea tomorrow." Gran offered the young woman one of her rare smiles. "Would you be available to do so, my dear? I know you most likely will have several callers tomorrow afternoon. If it would be convenient, my grandson could be one of them and then return you to me so that we might have a good, long chat about the old days and all the fun I used to have with your grandmother."

"I should come along, too, Your Grace," offered Lady Baxter, clearly not wanting to be left out of an invitation from a dowager duchess.

"Oh, we can do so another time, Lady Baxter," Gran said loftily. "Tomorrow, I shall catch up with your sister. That is, if you are available, Lady Margaret."

Her cheeks burning, Lady Margaret said, "I would be happy to come to tea, Your Grace. However, His Grace need not call upon me nor convey me to your townhouse. I will see to getting there myself." Her smile was polite, but her tone sounded defiant.

"I would be happy to call upon you and convey you to my grandmother's for tea," he offered. "It is no imposition."

Her eyes sparked with something that almost looked like anger. "Thank you for your kind offer, Your Grace, but there is no need for you to call upon me. I am certain you must have made other plans."

Daniel refused to be put off. "I have no other plans, my lady," he said breezily. "I look forward to visiting with you tomorrow and then accompanying you afterward. Shall we, Gran?" he asked and quickly led her away.

"She certainly did not want you to make an effort on her behalf," Gran mused as he led her to the section of chairs designated for matrons to watch the dancing. "And you actually met before?"

"We did. I had come to call upon her sister. Lady Margaret warned me I had no chance with Lady Dolley, who was looking for a better title than I possessed."

Gran snorted. "She actually said that to you?"

"She did. She was quite impertinent and brazen. I believed I called her cheeky."

"To her face?"

He nodded. "She deserved it. There I was, fresh from university and thinking I was quite handsome and charming. Lady Margaret told me I was arrogant and managed to knock me down a few pegs that day."

"You do seem to recall a meeting so long ago with clarity," Gran mused as they reached the seats. "Should I read anything into that, Westfield?"

"Not at the moment," he told her. Then he grinned. "Ask me after I have danced with her."

"I noticed you signed her programme twice. You do know that will draw unwanted attention upon the both of you, Westfield."

"I do. And I won't do it again with any other partner this evening. If you will excuse me, Gran, I need to sign a few more dance cards if you will make some recommendations to me."

Quickly, she named a few names and located the individuals in the ballroom. Daniel then seated her and made his way through the room, signing here and there. His thoughts remained with the tall, beautiful, saucy redhead, however.

He looked forward to their next conversation.

CHAPTER FIVE

As THE DUKE of Westfield turned and led his grandmother away, Margaret felt her knees wobble and willed herself not to collapse.

She was stunned that he had remembered her after almost a decade. He had even recalled the falsehood she had told regarding an imaginary governess who required her to complete a book report, which she had used as an excuse to get out of accompanying the viscount and Dolley on their carriage drive through Hyde Park. She glanced down at her sister and saw the eerie calm in Dolley's eyes. No one would know it—but Dolley was about to explode.

And it would be directed at Margaret, possibly ruining this night for her, as well as others.

She couldn't allow that to happen. Any tinge of gossip would harm her chances of arranging commissions to paint influential members of the *ton*.

Smiling shakily at her sister, she said, "I believe I need to visit the retiring room. Do you wish to accompany me?"

Dolley murmured her assent and made their goodbyes to those gathered around them. Margaret saw she wasn't the only one stunned by Westfield's attentions to her, as she noted envy in the eyes of every woman wishing them well as they departed the circle.

Dolley actually linked arms with Margaret, and they skirted the edge of the ballroom. She did not know how soon the first dance would occur, but no one had asked for it. If they missed it, it would not reflect poorly on either of them, as she knew Baxter never danced with Dolley since their marriage.

They only stopped twice and murmured a few greetings before escaping the ballroom and moving along the deserted corridor to the retiring room. Entering it, Margaret saw it was empty, which did not surprise her. She knew throughout the evening various ladies would be here primping. For now, since it was the beginning of the ball, everyone already looked their best. This was why she had suggested to come here in order for them to have a private conversation. The only others present were two maids who served as attendants for the evening. Dolley would not consider them people.

As expected, Dolley pushed her away and hissed, "What on earth was *that* about?"

For once, Margaret played dumb. "I am not certain what you mean."

Dolley's eyes narrowed. "You know exactly what I mean, Margaret Townsend. Westfield. The attention he paid you. How could the man recall a single conversation he held with you a decade ago? Of course, you were an insolent girl and probably said something horrific to him, whereby he would remember you all these years later."

Since they were alone, she decided to stand up for herself. "If I was so rude to His Grace, who was only a viscount then, if you recall, then why would he have asked me to accompany you on your drive through the park?"

Dolley stiffened. "Because he was a gentleman," she said after a moment's thought.

"And you still think he is being a gentleman to a girl long grown up and now making her come-out? Yes, we did meet briefly years ago, but I do not believe that is why he asked me to dance tonight."

Her sister grabbed the programme dangling from Margaret's wrist and perused it. Her face turned redder as she dropped it and looked up, aghast. "He signed it *twice!*"

Margaret's belly lurched at the thought. Even she knew what that meant. Mama had told her many of the rules of Polite Society years ago, usually when she bragged about Dolley. For a gentleman to ask to partner with a lady was an honor, but for him to request two dances from the same lady during a single evening signaled his interest in that particular lady. Not only to her—but to the very *ton* itself.

Why had the Duke of Westfield singled her out for such a tremendous honor?

"He never asked anyone during my come-out Season to dance twice—and he was one of the best-looking men that year. I would easily have wed him if he had not been a lowly viscount."

"You did not know he was an heir to a duke?" she asked.

"Two others stood between him and the dukedom," Dolley said bitterly. "If I would have had an inkling he would become Westfield as quickly as he did, I would have made certain that I became his duchess."

Margaret saw the hatred in her sister's eyes, placed there simply because a man had asked to dance twice with Margaret.

"I do not think the duke asking me to dance should upset you so much, Dolley," she said, trying to placate her sister. "You have been wed these past nine years and have produced two wonderful children. You are a marchioness and quite wealthy. What more could you ask for?"

Her sister's eyes narrowed. "I could have been a *duchess*," she hissed.

In that moment, Margaret felt extremely sorry for her sister, who had been given everything in life. Instead, she was jealous and hateful and wanted even more beyond her grasp.

"Well, you do not have to worry about me becoming a duchess," she said frankly. "You know the only reason I am making my come-out is in order to be introduced to as many members of the *ton* as I can. I have made no secret of how I value my art above all else. I have no wish to wed, Dolley. Even a duke and a former suitor of yours. What I do need is for you to make the rounds and continue to introduce me to as many members of Polite Society as you can. You have told me how pleased you are at the portraits I painted of you and Baxter and those of the children. Continue to drop snippets in your conversation with others regarding my talents. Once June first comes and I can access my dowry, I will even move out of your residence if you so wish. For now, though, I would ask that you treat me with kindness in front of others."

Left unsaid was how Dolley had never done so.

Suddenly, her sister's eyes widened and her hands flew to her mouth, covering it. Dolley wheeled and raced behind one of the curtains. Margaret listened to the sounds of her sister retching into a chamber pot. That could mean only one thing. Dolley was definitely with child once more.

When she emerged, Margaret took Dolley's arm and led her to a basin, where a maid poured water and offered a hand towel. Dolley rinsed her mouth and patted it dry with a cloth provided by the servant. Margaret thanked the maid and led her sister away.

Pausing outside the retiring room, Dolley cautioned, "Not a word to Baxter. I have lost the last two. He was incredibly disappointed in me."

Sympathy filled Margaret. "I am so sorry to hear this, Dolley. Should you not rest?"

"I will go and sit for a bit," her sister said brightly. "These feelings pass quickly." She patted her hair and added, "Besides, I have the usual group of men who gather about and flirt with me. I would not want to disappoint them."

Margaret shook her head as she guided her sister back to the ballroom. The strains of music already sounded from the room. They entered, and she saw dancers participating in a lively country dance. Leading Dolley to where the various matrons sat, she parted ways with her sister and returned to the other side of the room, where more chairs had been placed for the single, eligible women who were not dancing. She joined a couple of those women and spoke to them, learning that one was making her come-out this year and the other had done so the previous year. Both were quite plain and not prone to conversation, so Margaret's focus turned to the dancers on the ballroom floor.

When the next set was ready to begin, a gentleman approached her. She had already looked at his name on her dance card and greeted him with enthusiasm, ready to get out onto the floor. She threw herself into the dance, her first ever in Polite Society, enjoying it immensely. She alternated between dancing and sitting on the sidelines for a few numbers, meeting a few lovely women, two close to her age.

She was engaged in conversation with them when a shadow fell over one and she glanced over her shoulder, finding the imposing Duke of Westfield hovering there. Quickly, all three women came to their feet and curtseyed.

"You are not engaged for this set, Lady Margaret?"

"No, Your Grace, I am not. I am enjoying a brief respite as I speak with my new friends."

"Do you wish to dance?" he inquired. "We could join in."

The idea horrified her. Not only had he engaged her for two upcoming dances, but that would mark her for scandal.

Raising her chin a bit, she said, "That would not be acceptable, Your Grace," and she turned away, seeing her companions both gasp at her having the audacity to now ignore a duke.

Apparently, Westfield was not one to be ignored because he said, "Then we shall stroll on the terrace together, Lady Margaret." His tone brokered no chance of her denying him and she turned back, smiling at him, knowing she could not afford to rile a duke.

"Of course, Your Grace. I would be delighted to do so."

He offered his arm to her, and she placed her fingers atop it. A mild oath escaped her lips, thankfully whispered under her breath. Why did she feel something so electric every time they came into contact? He must feel the same because he gave her a satisfied smile that looked like one a cat wore having gotten into the cream.

Leading her around the edge of the ballroom, dancers whirling by them, they exited an open set of French doors. Immediately, Margaret felt the cool of the evening and appreciated the slight breeze. She glanced about the terrace and noted two other couples strolling there, as well.

"Aren't you looking forward to our dance?" the duke asked.

"If you have forgotten, Your Grace, you engaged me for two dances. And no, I have not forgotten either of them."

"Are you enjoying your first ball, my lady?" he inquired politely.

"Yes, I am. I have met some interesting ladies when I haven't danced."

"Others would think you would be more interested in the dancing and your partners than wallflowers sitting on the sidelines."

"Oh, I do like to dance, Your Grace, though I am a bit rusty."

"Why are you making your come-out so late? You should have done so years ago. I looked for you, you know. You are the same age as my sister, Lilly."

Her heart fluttered a bit at his words. "You searched for me? Even after I told you that I had no interest in such affairs?"

He smiled, a devasting smile so warm that it snatched her heart. She better grab it back soon—else he would run away with it.

And she would be in terrible trouble.

"You did tell me so, but you were a precocious child when you did."

"I wouldn't say that," she said hastily. "I was on the cusp of turning fifteen. Fifteen is certainly not a child. Besides, my father always called me an old soul. He said that I was wise beyond my years."

His gaze bored into her as they stopped at the far end of the terrace. Margaret removed her hand from his sleeve, finding it hard to think when she touched him. The spice of his cologne seemed to surround them, however, and she blinked rapidly a few times trying to ground herself.

"What have you been doing all these years, Lady Margaret? Perhaps practicing with the artist's brush?"

She swallowed, tamping down her emotions and said, "If you must know, I was caring for my ailing parents."

"You mean the mother who disapproved of you?"

So, he remembered even that . . .

"Yes," she said tersely. "Mama was quite happy when Dolley wed her marquess, and her health remained good for three years after that. On the cusp of my come-out, however, she had a rapid decline. There was no one to nurse her but me."

"You put your own life on hold to care for a mother who never cared for you?"

Tears stung her eyes at his astute observation. "I did. Mainly because it was expected of me. Dolley has no tolerance for anyone who shows a sign of ill health. I was the daughter of the household, and so the task fell to me."

Sympathy filled his gray eyes and he took her hand, squeezing her fingers. Something delicious rippled through her, beyond her understanding. Margaret knew she should pull her hand from his—and chose not to. They were at the far end of the terrace, and no one would see them, she surmised.

"I cared for Mama for three years. Until her death."

"Yet you are four and twenty," he pointed out. "Why the delay?"

This time, she could not help it as tears filled her eyes. "Papa fell ill soon after Mama's passing. They had fought like cats and dogs my entire life. I was hoping with her gone that he would finally have some solace. Instead, apoplexy attacked him, leaving him paralyzed and unable to speak."

The duke squeezed her fingers. "Oh, Margaret," he said softly. "I am so very sorry. I recall you said you were quite close to him."

He handed her a handkerchief, and she pulled her hand from his to wipe her eyes.

"We were. I spent as much time with him as I could, but there was also an estate to be run."

Surprised filled his face. "You did so?"

She nodded. "With the help of his steward, of course. Papa and I worked out a system so that I might ask him yes or no questions. He helped guide me in this endeavor." She paused, swallowing. "After his passing, my cousin became the new earl. Once my time of mourning passed, he told me I was no longer welcome in the only home I had known."

Anger sparked in Westfield's eyes. "You went to your sister after that?"

"I did. That is why I am making my come-out at such an ancient age." She smiled through watery eyes. "And yet half of my programme filled this evening. Even a duke signed for a dance."

"Two," he corrected.

"Two," she agreed, deciding not to reveal her ulterior motives in making her debut into Polite Society. This man had no interest in her. That was what she had wanted to share with Dolley. Instead, he seemed to be kind and was most likely humoring his grandmother, who wanted Margaret to come to tea so they could reminisce about the woman that both had loved.

"I look forward to those two dances, Lady Margaret. You made quite an impression upon me at our first meeting."

She chuckled. "I am certain I did. Mama always despised my frankness. I know I did not hold back that day when I warned you off Dolley."

Margaret couldn't help but wonder if her warning had chased this man away from her sister and decided it hadn't. Dolley—and Mama—had been set on wedding a high-ranking peer. As Viscount Browning, that title would not have been good enough.

Still, it pained her if she had caused him to not pursue her sister.

"Did you heed my warning?" she asked. "I do not remember you ever calling on Dolley after that day."

"I had no interest in settling down," he admitted. "I recall telling you that, my lady. I was merely placating my parents, who wished me to have a taste of Polite Society. Why, I cannot fathom, since they rarely paid any mind to me or my sisters. Marriage was not for me then."

She studied him a moment. "But it is now?"

He shrugged. "Since we share the same birthday, you know I am past thirty now. My parents are dead and gone. My two younger sisters have wed. One now lives in Scotland and has no plans to return to England. The other is with child. My grandmother is healthy, but she is eighty and won't be with me forever. I suppose I now find the need to wed and sire children of my own." Westfield chuckled. "If I don't, the dukedom would go to an odious cousin upon my death."

"Well, we cannot have that," she said lightly. "I wish you all the best in your pursuit of a bride, Your Grace. From what I gather, the Marriage Mart is full of viable candidates. Being a duke, you should have no trouble in securing your duchess."

He studied her until she felt her cheeks heating. "And I wish you the same as you seek a husband, Lady Margaret."

She wanted to be honest and tell him that marriage was not to be a part of her future but kept silent. He might find it daft of her to wish to remain unwed in order to pursue her art. As a duke, his opinion would weigh heavily regarding public opinion. If she danced with him and gained the notice of a few people in the process, it might help her budding career. Therefore, she did not want to alienate him in any way. She wanted them to dance and be on pleasant terms.

"Shall we return to the ballroom?" she asked. "I am engaged for the next set."

"Of course."

He offered his arm again but this time, he took her hand and tucked it into the crook of his arm, drawing her closer, so close she could feel his warmth. That odd yet pleasant tingling zipped through her again, making her grow a bit lightheaded, and she clung to him.

Inside the ballroom, he returned her to her new acquaintances and bowed.

"Until the supper dance," he said before strolling away.

Panic filled her. Quickly, she glanced at her card. Nothing had indicated on her programme that it was to be the supper dance, but Margaret knew once it ended, she was obligated to remain with her partner and attend the midnight buffet with him. It must have been one of those unwritten rules of the *ton*, which dance would be designated for supper. One she had not known.

One the Duke of Westfield *had* known.

CHAPTER SIX

M ARGARET ENJOYED THE next dance. At least as much as she could. It was one in which she was constantly in motion, and she found dancing to be quite liberating. Her set of four, however, danced next to another set of four, which included the Duke of Westfield. Their eyes met at one point, and as she turned back, she lost count as her arm brushed his. She turned the wrong way, the misstep humiliating her. She vowed not to look in his direction again and kept to it, finishing the dance with no more mistakes. As her partner escorted her from the floor, she apologized to him for the mishap.

"I wouldn't worry about a small slipup, Lady Margaret. You were a delightful partner, and I thank you for the dance."

He returned her to the spot from where he had claimed her. Already, the Duke of Westfield stood there, waiting for her, since they were finally to partner in the next number.

She told the viscount goodbye and turned, nodding brusquely to the duke. She had no idea how he had gotten here so fast—nor why her heart was beating so quickly.

"Are you ready for our supper dance, my lady?" Westfield asked, a gleam in his gray eyes.

"Supper dance?" she said weakly, still worried about spending so much time with him.

"Yes," he replied smoothly. "The supper dance. You know,

where dancing couples take a brief respite and enjoy something to eat, along with one another's company."

Once again, she told herself he had signed for it merely to please his grandmother.

He offered his arm, and she placed her fingers lightly upon it, ignoring her physical reaction as he began leading her onto the dance floor.

"I hope you will enjoy this first waltz, my lady."

Her fingers tightened as a wave of panic flooded her.

"I cannot waltz!" she declared, withdrawing her fingers and wheeling, moving away from him.

Seconds later, strong fingers gripped her elbow and guided her from the floor. As they reached the sidelines, he turned her so they faced one another and asked, "Do you not know how to waltz?"

Once again, it must have been the code spoken by Polite Society, designating this dance as a waltz.

"No, Your Grace. I do not waltz. Although the dance was known when I learned how to dance many years ago, it was considered far too racy for young misses such as me."

He grinned. "But you are no longer a young miss," he said, mischief in his eyes.

Irritation filled her. "Thank you for pointing out the obvious, Your Grace, but it still doesn't mean that I know how to waltz. I thought a programme would indicate such a number. If I had known, I would not have allowed you to sign my dance card where you did. Please," she urged, "go and find yourself another partner to dance with and take into supper."

"I have seen you dance this evening, Lady Margaret. You are confident and graceful, two requirements for the waltz. I can teach you, you know. Can you count to three?"

Upset, she snapped, "Of course, I can count to three."

His fingers still on her elbow were driving her mad.

"Then it takes two things. One is counting to three. It is a long one, then a quick two-three. One, two-three. One, two-three. I know you have a sense of rhythm, and I promise you will feel the beat of the music and instinctively know what to do."

A part of her yearned to see what this dance was about and perform it herself.

With him.

"You mentioned two requirements, Your Grace. What is the second one?" she asked.

He smiled again, that devastatingly devilish smile which seemed to steal her very breath.

"Why, you have to trust me, Lady Margaret. Let me guide you. I know you can do this," he said earnestly. He paused and then added, "We can stay on the periphery as you learn. Come."

It was a simple command, giving her no option to say no. Of course, she could have denied him but at this moment, she seemed bound under some mystical spell as the musicians took up their instruments.

Quickly, he told her which foot to move first and promised he would not execute any fancy twirls until she had the steps down.

The strains of the waltz began, and he slipped his hand against her back and took her other hand in his, drawing her close. Too close. Her breasts brushed against his broad chest. He radiated heat, which seemed to envelop her. The spice of his cologne made her grow lightheaded. Then they began moving to the music as one. She did stumble twice within the first minute but soon caught on to the quite simple movements. It was an easy dance, in truth, a lovely one if she were being honest.

No, an intoxicating one.

"Move more on the balls of your feet and your toes," he suggested.

Once she did, the music seemed to open up and swallow her—and him—until they became a part of it.

They danced along the edges of that large ballroom, confidence soaring through her with each triple beat. Soon, they were turning, spinning, dancing the seductive waltz.

When the last chord sounded, Westfield held her close a moment longer and then seemed to reluctantly release her. Margaret exhaled a long breath.

As he tucked her hand into the crook of his arm, the duke asked, "How did you enjoy your first waltz?"

She savored it because she had danced it with him. Every waltz that came after this one would pale in comparison. It was not something she would ever say aloud, though. While he had been nothing but urbane and polite this evening, she still remembered the arrogant young man he had been. Being a duke, with all its entitlements and power, she believed his arrogance lingered just below the surface.

Nevertheless, she would be gracious now, and said, "You are an excellent tutor, Your Grace. I thank you for teaching me how to waltz."

He began guiding her along, following the mass now exiting the ballroom in search of the midnight buffet. As they moved with the crowd, he said, "You are an outstanding pupil, Lady Margaret. I knew that you would catch on with ease. It is a good thing we will get more practice at it."

That meant only one thing—that the other dance he had reserved was also a waltz. She recalled his name being the final one on her programme.

"Why did you sign my dance card twice?" she inquired. "Though I did not know, you did know that both numbers would be a waltz. Why those dances—and why twice, Your Grace? You have been a part of Polite Society for many years, even if you have not participated in the Season often. Surely, you understand tongues will be wagging tonight simply because we have partnered twice."

"If I told you I had done so to please my grandmother, would you believe me?"

She desperately wanted to believe him and the reason he gave. Margaret also knew the attention they drew would have her name on the lips of everyone present this evening. That could be a good thing, as far as her painting went.

Smiling benignly at him, she said, "I have no reason not to believe you, Your Grace."

By now, they had reached a large room filled with tables of varying sizes. She listened as people greeted one another and noted Westfield said nothing to anyone as they moved toward the long buffet line. As they passed its head to join the rear, a lord called out, "Here, Westfield, you may go in front of us."

"Why, thank you," the duke said, leading her toward the gentleman and as they slipped in front of him, the duke made introductions and then chatted briefly with this earl, obviously having been acquainted with him from somewhere. His club. School. University. He did not say.

They reached the table, heavy with delicacies, and he turned toward her, claiming a plate for each of them. Her eyes glazed over, seeing the feast laid before them.

"Do you have any favorites, my lady? If you do, I am certain they will be among this spread."

He led her through the line, making suggestions on what to put on her plate, including some things she had no familiarity with. By the end of the line, their plates heaped with food, she had no idea how she would manage to eat even a third of what she had selected.

They left the line, and she wondered which table they might join and who his friends were. Some sat four, others six or eight. The head table held twelve, and she prayed they would not go there. Already, she had felt the eyes of dozens upon them and figured she would be mentioned in tomorrow's newspapers, the lead in the gossip columns.

Much to her surprise, the duke led her to a small table away from the others, one stationed in the corner and seemingly forgotten. A footman hovered nearby and pulled out a chair, which Margaret took.

"Is there anything else you require, Your Grace?"

Immediately, she knew he had arranged for them to sit here,

and her cheeks filled with heat.

"No, thank you. That will be all," he said, taking his own seat not across from her but to her right, moving his chair to the spot.

She concentrated on the food before her, taking a bite of this and that as he made suggestions to her. She thoroughly enjoyed the poached salmon and sugared almonds and finished them, while nibbling at the rest.

As they dined, he talked mostly about his two sisters and how he had watched over them during their different come-out Seasons, seeing that both secured good husbands.

"Had you lost your parents by then?" she asked, assuming he had since he had taken over these family duties.

An odd look crossed his face and Westfield said, "No, my parents were both alive at the time. They were creatures who were consumed by their own self-interests. Yes, you would have thought they would be interested in making certain the two daughters they had produced made good marriages. Their children had never been a priority for them, however. It is why I assumed the lead."

He took a sip of his wine and continued. "Thankfully, provisions had been made for both Deborah and Lilly. They had dowries, but I was the one who negotiated their marriage settlements. My father did his duty by paying for both weddings though my mother told my sisters she had no interest in planning a wedding for either of them. She merely presented the guest list each time, and so Deborah and Lilly planned a day which would be special for them and their betrotheds, with no input from our parents."

"That is far different from Dolley's wedding," she revealed. "Papa did pay all expenses, as custom dictates, but Mama was involved in every aspect of planning the wedding. I remember the hours she and Dolley sat simply deciding upon the wedding breakfast menu, debating one choice over another. The dress fittings, as well, were also long and tedious." She smiled brightly. "At least the ones for the wedding gown and Mama's dress."

His lips twitched in amusement. "Are you saying that little attention was placed upon your appearance?"

"It is no secret how the pair felt about me. I told you so on our first meeting. At least I did have a new gown for the occasion. Not that anyone noticed me."

"Well, I hate to tell you, my lady, but I am certain you were noticed. You yourself have mentioned both your height and unique shade of hair color. Sitting in the front family pew at St. George's Church, you would have been easy to spy."

Her eyes brimmed with tears at the memory. She blinked rapidly, hoping they would not fall. Suddenly, his hand engulfed hers and held it firmly. She glanced quickly at him and then at the room at large, realizing at the angle others sat, this hand-holding would go undetected.

"I did not sit with my family at the wedding," she told him, her throat thick with unshed tears. "Mama said I would be a distraction and take attention away from Dolley for the very reasons you indicated. I was to sit upon the last pew on the bride's side." She bit her lip. "I only entered the church and took my seat after Dolley had paraded down the aisle with Papa. Mama had thought as others turned to watch Dolley in all her glory, that I would prove to be a distraction."

His thumb stroked her softly. The pity in his eyes almost did her in.

"But your father was close with you," the duke insisted. "He was the man in the marriage. An earl. How could he allow his wife to dictate such things?"

"You did not have to live with my mother," she insisted, wanting to defend her father. "Mama could make life miserable for those who did, Your Grace. Papa knew Holy Hell would rain down if he fought her on this. To his credit, once he delivered Dolley to her marquess, he did not join Mama and the cousins at the front. Instead, he moved quietly to the side and skirted the church, coming to sit with me. No one seemed to notice he did so. All eyes were upon my beautiful sister and her handsome groom. All talk was how they were the perfect couple."

"And no one gave you a thought," he said quietly. "Oh, Margaret."

Tears stung her eyes. "You do not have permission to use my Christian name, Your Grace. It is not appropriate."

Fire sparked in his eyes. "Neither is a mother abandoning the needs of one daughter for another," he said roughly.

"I learned to live with it. I did not like Mama or Dolley. They did not like me. We learned to manage. I had Papa, after all."

"You deserved better, Margaret. Much better."

Then the Duke of Westfield raised the hand he held and tenderly kissed her fingers.

She stared at him, her mouth agape. And then she realized it seemed as if the entire room's conversations had all come to a halt as the guests watched this play out.

He lowered her hand to where it was once again hidden.

"Please, Your Grace. Let go," she urged. "Others . . . are watching."

"Are they?" he asked, his lips twitching in amusement.

"They are. Let go now, I beg you."

"Only if you promise me one thing."

Her eyes swept across the room and saw the entire *ton* looked on with interest though they could not hear the conversation taking place.

"What?"

"That you will let me kiss you. Once."

CHAPTER SEVEN

D ANIEL DIDN'T THINK that Lady Margaret could become more appealing, but she did so now, a blush running across her smooth cheeks, bringing color to her face at his audacious statement.

He did want to kiss her. Very much.

He had wanted to from the moment he had spied her across the ballroom this evening when he and Gran had arrived. The fact that Gran had actually met Lady Margaret as a child intrigued him. It seemed fated for them to come together. He already knew his sagacious grandmother would approve of a match between them. She had been taken with Lady Margaret at their first meeting and seemed to be more so even now. Daniel would admit he, too, was taken by the fiery-haired beauty.

Perhaps Gran wouldn't have to peruse the Marriage Mart for his bride after all.

Sympathy had filled him when he had met Lady Margaret on that first occasion. It had turned to anger as she spoke tonight about her sister's wedding and being shuttled to the rear of the church as a black sheep of the family might have been. Despite her love for her father, Daniel thought the man had been weak and foolish to allow his shrew of a wife to control him and push aside such a wonderful creature as their younger daughter. He suspected Lady Baxter now did the same to her younger sister, barely tolerating her presence merely because of their familial connection.

It did not matter. In that moment, Daniel realized Lady Margaret was destined to become his duchess. Yet instinct told him he would have to go about this business quite carefully. She was intelligent, far more so than most women, and because of her past experiences, a bit wary. Even prickly. He would nurture their relationship slowly, counting on Gran to form a friendship with her and bring Lady Margaret into the Judson fold.

Now, however, he was faced with the statement he had made about wanting to kiss her. He would see how she now reacted. It wouldn't matter. Eventually, he would make her his duchess. The thought of this woman in his bed caused his blood to sing.

Her blush remained, but her eyes narrowed. "You are still the arrogant beast you were when I first made your acquaintance."

"Yes, I do recall you mentioning I was arrogant," he said cheerily, knowing he got under her skin with his tone.

"Being a duke has not changed that," she noted. "In fact, I am certain it has made you even more arrogant than before. That is not a quality that appeals to me, Your Grace."

"Lady Margaret, there is a fine line between arrogance and confidence. I like to think of myself as merely being extremely confidant."

She gave a very unladylike snort. "Arrogant and bold," she observed. "Not exactly a way to endear yourself to me. And that is what it would take for me to even consider kissing you."

He was glad she was considering it. It gave him hope. "Have you ever been kissed before?" he inquired politely, as if asking her what her favorite food or color might be.

Her jaw dropped. "You did not just ask me that!"

He smiled, a smile he reserved for when he wished for something impossible. "I believe I did ask you that, my lady. There is no shame in being four and twenty and having never been kissed. In fact, you will most likely have multiple opportunities to kiss gentlemen because it is your come-out Season. They will be as curious about you as you are about them."

"You go too far, Westfield," she rebuked. "I know from what both Mama and Dolley spoke of that nice women do not go about kissing gentlemen. Why, Dolley even bragged to me that the first time she was kissed was after her betrothal to Lord Baxter. That she had snagged a marquess without having to share anything of herself at all with him."

"Pity," he commented. "Kissing can be ever so much fun." He dangled that thought, hoping to intrigue her further.

She wet her lips, not knowing in doing so it only called attention to her mouth.

"But . . . but . . . it is not supposed to be . . . *fun*."

"Who told you so? Whoever it was, they were wrong. Period. Or they were kissing the wrong partner and had no idea just how enjoyable kissing can be."

He assumed she gathered her information from her sister, the beauty who flirted outrageously with men of the *ton*, but most likely had a cold, sterile marriage. From the little he knew of Lord Baxter, the man had held a string of mistresses, both before and long after his wedding to Lady Dolley Townsend. He supposed the couple had the typical *ton* marriage. He had even heard talk at his club of how men did not bother to kiss or pleasure their wives as they did their mistresses.

Suddenly, Daniel knew he would not need a mistress if he were married to this woman. That she would challenge him and intrigue him—not only in bed but out of it, as well.

"I look forward to the chance to change your mind about kissing," he informed her.

She shook her head. "I cannot believe we are even having this conversation, Your Grace. It is totally inappropriate. No, I will not be kissing you. Tonight or any other night. In fact, I do not think we shall dance our second dance this evening. You will need to find another partner to torment."

"Torment? Is that what you believe I am doing to you, Margaret?"

Her eyes sizzled with anger. "Quit calling me Margaret."

"It *is* your name," he pointed out.

"But I have yet to give you leave to address me in such a manner, Your Grace."

"I apologize, Lady Margaret, for acting too familiar. I will wait for you to ask me to call you Margaret. You, however, may address me as Daniel at any time though you might not want to do so in front of others. Only when we are alone."

"We are not going to be alone anymore, Your Grace."

"Oh, but we are, my lady. When we dance the waltz again tonight, true, we will be surrounded by other pairs of dancers. There is an intimacy to the waltz, isn't there? And we do dance it together beautifully."

"I told you to find yourself another partner, Your Grace. I insist."

"That is where you are wrong, my lady. *I* insist upon claiming the dance I have signed for. After all, I am a duke. Along with all the responsibilities that come with the office, I also find that dukes get their way. Every. Single. Time."

He gazed at her steadily, her cheeks heating in another blush. "It would be ill-mannered of you to turn me down after we have already arranged to dance together. You would not want to make a poor impression upon the *ton* this evening, now, would you? By ignoring a duke's simple request for a dance, you would alienate every person in this room."

"You are threatening me?"

"No, Lady Margaret. I am merely stating a fact. If you wish to stay in my good graces—and those of Polite Society—then you will dance with me as we have arranged to do so."

"That is blackmail," she declared.

"No, blackmail indicates a person has done something terribly wrong and that the blackmailer has proof of it and is willing to expose the evidence unless a person dances to his tune. I merely wish to dance a waltz with you, Margaret."

"Bloody hell," she said under her breath, but he caught the

oath. Meeting his gaze, she added, "I suppose I have no choice in the matter. After all, I do not wish to stain my reputation nor that of my sister and brother-in-law. I suppose if I were to be ostracized by the *ton*, they would be, as well. I could never live with myself for hurting Dolley so, no matter how many times she has hurt me. She lives for the Season and being around others. I have gathered her marriage is not a happy one, and I would not pile upon her unhappiness."

Her chin raised a notch. "Yes, Your Grace. I will honor my commitment and dance with you a final time."

Daniel refused to tell her that dance would not be a final time. He expected them to dance upon many occasions in the future, both during this Season and in years to come. Though it was custom for husbands not to dance with their spouses, he intended to buck that tradition.

After all, he was a duke.

MARGARET WAS GLAD she had tremendous powers of concentration, else she would have become a puddle the rest of the evening after sparring with the duke. She had excused herself from Westfield's company and headed to the retiring room, spending several minutes behind one of the curtains trying to collect herself.

It seemed the more she resisted his charms, the more he pushed her. She danced a fine line now between keeping his interest and alienating him. He was correct in saying if she disrespected him that she would lose everything. She had to stay in the good graces of Polite Society so she would dance tonight with him a second time. Not beyond that, though. Hopefully, his slight interest in her would stir up enough talk and bring positive attention to her and make others familiar with her. If Dolley did as Margaret had asked and spoken of her sister's artistic talents, then she might be able to approach a few people about painting their portraits. She had decided to paint at least two without charging any fee whatsoever. That should lure a few skeptical and frugal lords and ladies in. If she did well at those, she prayed the commissions would flow in. Then she wouldn't need to attend balls anymore and could avoid dancing with irresistibly attractive dukes.

She still could not believe that he had asked to kiss her. It bothered her that despite her protests, she was tempted to do so. It was hard to admit, but she had no idea how to go about kissing and had never thought of doing so until Westfield brought it up. If she ever did kiss a man, the duke would be the one she would like to do so with. He had certainly grown into the most handsome man she had ever seen in the time they had been apart. He had been fine-looking as a recent university graduate. Now, he was a fully matured man, at the height of his beauty. She chuckled, never having thought of a man as being beautiful, but the Duke of Westfield certainly fit that bill.

She spoke with many others after the midnight buffet, quickly realizing they only wished to meet her because of the duke's interest. She was friendly and polite to everyone and hoped she made a decent impression upon them. One of her dance partners, an earl, had asked if she already had an understanding with the Duke of Westfield. She had blushed profusely and stammered that she did not. She knew, however, that others had probably jumped to the same conclusion as the earl. She needed to harness the interest in her and use it to propel her budding career.

Glancing up, Margaret saw Westfield stride toward her. He was like a statue come to life, chiseled stone becoming warm flesh. He was tall and broad-shouldered, with impossibly long legs. His high cheekbones and regal nose only set off his sensual lips. She longed to run her fingers through his thick, raven-colored hair.

Perhaps she would kiss him, after all.

Not tonight, of course. There would be no chance to do so. This final dance would conclude the ball, and she would need to find Dolley and Baxter and depart. But if the opportunity presented itself on some future occasion?

She would definitely kiss this duke.

She told herself it would merely be artistic research. That if she experienced even a small frisson of passion, it could be poured into her painting. She would be a better artist for the experience. At least, that was what she told herself.

Greeting him, Margaret placed her hand upon his sleeve. This time, he led them to the center of the ballroom. Every eye would be on them. She determined to make no mistakes and enjoy dancing the waltz with perhaps the best dancer present at tonight's affair.

His arms went about her again, and she tingled from her scalp to her toes at the touch, his hand warm against her back.

"You will do fine, my lady," he assured her. "Remember to follow my lead."

She did as he instructed, the music swelling as they stepped off. They seemed to be made to dance the waltz together, moving as one. He did not hesitate in turning her this time, her skirts whirling. The other dancers became a blur of color, gliding by, as their gazes locked. They remained so, her heart beating rapidly, until the music died. Oh, how she wished he would kiss her then and there. If he did, though, it would lead to scandal. Even a duke would not have the audacity to kiss an unmarried woman in front of hundreds of others. That would mean a forced marriage. Westfield did not seem to be the type to be forced into anything. The last thing Margaret herself wanted was to be wed.

She lowered her lashes, breaking the gaze, and he released her. Still, he took her hand and protectively led her from the dance floor. Being a duke, it seemed the crowd parted for them, merely because of his lofty title, and they exited the ballroom, not a soul in front of them.

"I shall call upon you tomorrow," he informed her as they descended the stairs, a swell of others behind them. "I will then take you to tea with Gran. She thought quite a bit of your grandmother."

"She told you that?" Margaret asked.

He nodded. "Yes, Dorothy, as she referred to your grandmother, was quite dear to her. I'm certain Gran with regale you with stories of them as girls at teatime tomorrow."

"I really wish you would not call upon me, Your Grace."

"Why not?"

"It will give others the wrong impression."

He smiled. "You mean because I danced with you twice this evening, calling upon you would cause Polite Society to believe I am interested in pursuing you?"

Relief filled her. "Yes, you understand the situation perfectly. Please, allow me to get myself to your grandmother."

"No," he said flatly. "I do not trust that selfish sister of yours to even provide a maid as your chaperone. I *will* call upon you tomorrow afternoon, Lady Margaret, and escort you to my grandmother."

They had reached the foyer, the entire *ton* descending the stairs behind them, seeing them together.

Then the duke raised her hand to his lips and kissed it tenderly. "Until tomorrow afternoon, my lady."

He strolled off and within seconds, Margaret found the swarm about her. She knew others eyed her with interest—even speculation—and she gazed about in search of Dolley or Baxter. She spied her sister, who waved gaily to her.

That was not a good sign.

Dolley was never happy to see her. Margaret realized her sister put on a happy face for the surrounding *ton*.

And that the carriage ride home would be a dismal one.

CHAPTER EIGHT

I T SURPRISED MARGARET when Dolley arrived with her lady's maid in hand. Margaret had gone upstairs to her bedchamber to change her gown in order to receive callers this afternoon.

It had also astonished her that Dolley had not berated her in the carriage on their way home from the ball last night. She knew her sister bristled with anger but decided she did not want to air any grievances against Margaret in front of her husband. She did feel sorry for Dolley. Her sister's marriage seemed to be one that made her deeply unhappy. Baxter was cold and aloof, and she rarely saw the couple together. If she were to ever wed, Margaret would hope she would at least be friendly with her husband. Dolley and Baxter seemed to live completely separate lives, not even coming together to visit with their children on a daily basis.

Dolley now swept into the bedchamber, her lady's maid trailing, and said, "I will tell you which gown to wear and how to dress your hair. You will not embarrass me."

So, that was what this was about. Margaret might have known that Dolley wouldn't care how her sister looked simply for her own sake, but how any callers might view her and judge Dolley accordingly.

Dolley went to the wardrobe and looked at the various gowns, selecting one and handing it to the maid. "Press this immediately," she ordered.

"Yes, my lady," the servant said and left the room.

Now that they were alone, Dolley said, "You drew an immense amount of attention to yourself at the ball last night. Why, you were even mentioned in the newspaper gossip columns today. Everyone in the *ton* noticed that you danced with Westfield twice. How could you let that happen?"

"I am innocent of whatever accusation you are leaving unsaid," Margaret replied, determined to stand her ground. "You were with me when Westfield came over with his grandmother. He signed my programme. I had no idea he did so twice. That was his decision—not mine," she said firmly.

Dolley sighed, clearly exasperated. "That may be the case, but you should not have dined at a table by yourselves, away from others."

Frustration bubbled up within her. "Who am I to tell a duke I am not going to sit at the table he has chosen? I was led to the table, and a footman seated me. Why are you upset by whom I danced with or where I ate my midnight supper? If I didn't know better, I would think you were jealous of me."

Her sister laughed, bitterness obvious. "Why you?" she demanded. "You, who towers over others and stands out with that garish red hair of yours. I simply do not understand why the Duke of Westfield would single you out as he did. There were numerous, attractive girls making their come-outs. Fresh-faced, sweet young things."

"Not a dried-up prune such as me?" she challenged.

"We will make the best of this situation. Because of the attention you have drawn, I expect a good number of callers this afternoon."

Margaret noticed her sister did not refer to any visitors as suitors.

"You will look your best today," Dolley declared. "I will not be shamed by the likes of you. As for His Grace, you are to decline any further invitations to dance with him. Do not question me on this."

She had no idea how she was supposed to stop any gentleman from signing her programme. Especially a duke. No one told a duke what to do. What Dolley asked for was the impossible. For now, Margaret would ignore her sister's instructions. Another ball wouldn't happen for a couple of days. By then, she doubted the Duke of Westfield would have any interest in her. Why worry about something that might never happen?

Dolley eyed her. "Will Westfield be among those who arrive this afternoon?"

She nodded. "He is to escort me to tea if you recall. His grandmother asked me to come and visit with her."

"Will the duke stay for tea with you?" Dolley asked sharply.

Margaret had not even thought that far ahead. She had tried to put him off conveying her and having lost that battle, she had not thought beyond arriving for tea.

"In truth, I have no idea, Dolley. I doubt a duke wishes to stay and listen to his grandmother reminisce about her good friend from more than six decades ago. I gather Grandmama and the duke's grandmother were close as girls and made their come-outs together."

Dolley snorted. "He would be bored to tears. Yes, I doubt Westfield will stay."

She thought her sister tried to convince herself of that and wondered whether or not the duke would remain with them during tea—and if he did—should she share that information with Dolley?

Definitely not.

The lady's maid returned with the pressed gown and helped Margaret to change into it. She then dressed Margaret's hair in a fashion that flattered her. Dolley nodded her approval and told Margaret to come to the drawing room in a quarter-hour in order to greet any visitors who dropped by.

She went and sat in a chair by the window and watched as people moved down the street. She had no idea who might call upon her this afternoon. She supposed the vast majority of their visitors would be there for Dolley. Her sister enjoyed the Season because of the many social affairs and relished the afternoons when a bevy of gentlemen called and fawned over her. Margaret might never understand the *ton*. Men and women wed and barely spoke to one another afterward, while husbands continued seeing their mistresses and wives flirted outrageously with gentlemen who weren't their husbands.

She had even overheard talk last night in the retiring room of how once an heir and spare were provided women also broke their marriage vows and took lovers within the *ton*. The thought had shocked her. Part of her did not even wish to paint people of such low morals yet the members of Polite Society were the ones who possessed the wealth and inclination to have their portraits made. Margaret had yet to ask Dolley if she had begun mentioning anything to others regarding Margaret's artistic bent.

She wondered if she would have any callers today and supposed a few might turn up, curious about her since she had danced with a duke twice. She hoped that Westfield would come very late during calling hours because she did not want others to see him here and the gossip spread even further, linking them together. She did, however, look forward to having tea with the Dowager Duchess of Westfield and possibly learning new things about her beloved grandmother.

Vacating her bedchamber, she made her way to the drawing room, surprised when she entered because the room was filled with flowers. She supposed Dolley's admirers had sent them.

The drawing room was empty, save for a lone maid who was plumping cushions on a settee. She smiled at Margaret and came toward her.

"Such lovely bouquets, my lady," the servant said. "Lady Baxter said to save the cards accompanying them." The maid reached into her apron's pocket and removed a thick stack of cards.

Margaret looked at her blankly. "I do not understand."

"Why," the maid said as she handed the cards over, "these are for you, my lady. They are from various gentlemen you met at last evening's ball."

Stunned, she gaped at the cards in her hand.

"I knew you would prove to be quite popular, my lady. I know I shouldn't say so, but we have talked about you often in the servants' hall and hope you find true happiness with a gentleman this Season."

The maid smiled brightly at Margaret, and she smiled weakly in return.

The servant walked to what had to be the largest bouquet Margaret had ever seen and said, "This one is from the Duke of Westfield himself. Why, not even Lady Baxter has ever received such a fine floral arrangement."

At that moment, Margaret realized how Dolley would feel about not only this bouquet, but any of the others Margaret had received. Quickly, she handed the cards back to the maid.

"Put these in your apron, please, and then take them to my bedchamber if you would. I will look over them later."

"Yes, my lady." The maid then slipped the cards into her apron and left the drawing room.

Margaret studied the huge arrangement, filled with tulips, roses, snowdrops, and crocus. She then strolled about the room, knowing from the number of cards the maid had given her that a majority of these flowers had been sent to her and not Dolley. She regretted not flipping through the cards before she returned them to the maid so that she might see who had sent them. She had excellent recall regarding names and faces and learned names easily last night, putting them to faces with ease. She had seen a few of those names mentioned in the gossip columns in today's newspapers. Yes, she had asked for those newspapers once Baxter and Dolley had finished with them. She was surprised now that Dolley had not ordered them burned because of the prominence Margaret had played in today's columns.

Dolley breezed into the drawing room, wearing a fresh gown, her hair elaborately dressed high upon her head. Coming to

Margaret, she said, "A few of these arrangements are for you."

Nodding, Margaret said, "Yes, a maid told me so. I asked her to put the cards in my bedchamber."

Dolley winced, seeing she had not pulled one over on her sister.

"Will Baxter be joining us this afternoon?" she inquired.

"No, my husband is at his club, as usual. He prefers being there when others call." She patted her hair. "He knows I am quite popular, and I believe he is somewhat jealous of the number of gentlemen who choose to call upon me, an old, married woman."

Wanting to smooth things over between them so no hostility remained before their visitors arrived, Margaret said, "You look beautiful, Dolley. Baxter is a fortunate man to have you as his wife. I think your beauty has only grown over the years."

"Thank you," her sister said, for what Margaret might actually be the first time in their relationship.

The butler entered the drawing room at that moment, announcing their first guests. Soon, Margaret was swept up in a series of conversations. Dolley was always present, making herself a part of the circle surrounding Margaret, but she felt sorry that no one seemed to be paying any attention to her sister.

These men had all come for Margaret.

Most of the conversations skimmed the surface, with such safe topics as the weather and last night's ball being discussed. She did more listening than talking, knowing from conversations between Dolley and Mama that men preferred dominating a conversation.

Still, she did interject every now and then, asking a question or making a comment of her own. She did not mention her art. She knew to bide her time, wanting to establish solid relationships with others before working that into the conversation.

A good number of gentlemen asked if she enjoyed the flowers which they had sent, and she always replied with a sweet smile that she appreciated them very much.

She saw immediately the pattern was for a caller to arrive and stay a quarter-hour or so before taking his leave. A handful stayed for half an hour before they departed, and Margaret supposed those were the ones who might be more interested in her than others. Every now and then, her eyes went to the door, wondering if she would see the Duke of Westfield lurking there. He never arrived. A part of her felt relieved, knowing he had not come and been seen by the many callers, and yet disappointment filled her at the same time.

After the last visitor exited, however, the butler came to her and said, "My lady, His Grace is waiting for you outside."

"Oh!" she exclaimed. "Why, thank you for letting me know. I must go and freshen up a moment, but I will be downstairs immediately afterward."

Dolley came to stand next to her. "You were quite the success, Margaret," she noted. "I do not think a single gentleman came to call upon me. They were all here for you."

Pity filled her, seeing how dejected Dolley was.

"I believe it was a tribute to you," she said. "You are immensely popular within the *ton*, Dolley. I think they came and paid a bit of attention to me in order to honor and please you."

Though Margaret did not believe her words, Dolley certainly did, a smile lighting her face.

"You are right," her sister exclaimed. "They would know I wish to see my sister successfully launched into Polite Society. Of course, they paid attention to you. It was a compliment to me."

Placated, Dolley actually smiled genuinely. "You must tell me about your tea with the dowager duchess."

"I shall do so," she promised.

Several minutes later, she arrived in the foyer, and the butler greeted her.

"His Grace is once again outside," he informed Margaret.

His words confused her, but she smiled politely and left the townhouse. Standing in front of it was the most elegant carriage she had ever seen. A set of four, matched bays with beautiful lines stood before it.

Suddenly, the vehicle's door opened, and the duke bounded down the stairs. For a moment, her heart skipped a beat. He was far too handsome for his own good. She could not let his good looks affect her.

"Good afternoon, Lady Margaret."

He offered his hand and helped her up the stairs which a footman had placed next to the entry. She entered and deliberately sat in the center of one seat, which would force him to sit opposite her. He followed her inside and saw the situation, biting back a smile as he sat opposite her.

Looking across at him, though, she decided this might not have been the wisest idea, for she would be forced to look at him the entire time. If they had sat side by side, she could have stared straight ahead as they conversed. She took in his tight, fawn-colored breeches, which outlined shapely, muscular legs, and glanced away.

As the carriage pulled away, he said, "I hope you appreciate my subterfuge."

Her gaze returned to him. "I beg your pardon?"

"You didn't wish for me to interrupt your many callers and so I didn't. I had my coachman park down the street from Baxter's townhouse and sent a footman to inform your butler I would be waiting for you outside once your visitors departed."

The butler's words now made sense to her.

"Once it seemed the last of them left, I had the carriage pulled around."

"Thank you for your thoughtfulness, Your Grace."

"Daniel," he prompted. "We are, after all, alone."

Margaret shook her head. "I would prefer things remain formal between us, Your Grace."

"Do I not have any say in the matter?" he asked, his head cocked to one side as he studied her.

"No, I do not believe you do. You are a gentleman and should honor a lady's wishes," she said primly.

He laughed.

"What is so funny?"

"Sometimes, I think your name suits you. Margaret. It is grand and fitting a woman of your confidence. But you are many women within one, I believe. You are witty and often make me want to laugh. You snap at me at times, revealing a bit of a temper." He paused, his gaze intense. "Perhaps I shall call you Maggie. Or Meg."

She shuddered. "If you do, I shall not answer to either of those. I am not one for nicknames, Your Grace."

Then he smiled, that smile that held sunshine and warmed her to her very toes.

"I know. Red."

Confused, she echoed, "Red?"

"Red," he confirmed. "That shall be what I call you in private."

CHAPTER NINE

DANIEL BURST OUT laughing as Margaret sputtered, "Red? Red? No, no, no. I refuse."

He could not recall when he'd had so much fun. Once, he had been a carefree rogue, lighthearted and loving life. Then, with his grandfather's death, the heavy mantle of the title smothered him, blanketing him in heavy responsibilities that choked the life out of him.

Margaret made him feel alive again. He wanted to enjoy time spent with her. Be playful and tease her, as he was doing now.

It convinced him that perhaps life did not have to be so dismal. That even a duke could laugh once in a while and enjoy a bit of fun.

Especially if he had the right woman by his side.

Giving her a sly smile, Daniel said, "I am afraid you cannot refuse, Red. As I mentioned, I am a duke. There are very few of us, and we seem to manage to get our own way. If we err, Polite Society finds a way to forgive us. If we speak an opinion, they hang upon our every word."

He shook his head. "No, I have bestowed the pet name upon you. It is quite fitting. And much more amusing than Margaret."

Fire sparked in her moss green eyes, deepening their color. "Then I will also award a moniker upon you, Your Grace. One which will definitely let you know how I feel about you."

"I cannot wait to hear it, Red."

"Quit calling me that!" she shouted, crossing her arms in front of her. "You are conceited. Cocky. Smug. Totally full of yourself."

"I would prefer assured. Self-confident. Assertive. Composed."

"Presumptuous," she fired back. "Impudent. Insolent. Brazen. Cheeky."

"Unruffled. Cool-headed. Even level-headed. Come on, Red. We can do this all day."

She snorted. "I have no intention of wasting my day with you."

Daniel shrugged. "Seeing as how you are riding in my carriage and about to come to tea at my house, you *will* be spending time a good portion of your day with me Then, of course, I will need to see you home. Whether you consider all this a waste or not remains to be seen."

"I would rather walk than ride in your beautiful carriage and sit across and have to look at your devilish smile," she proclaimed.

"You like my smile?" he said, awarding her with one.

"I did not say that, Westfield. You are twisting my words."

He would like to twist her in his arms and bend her to his will.

But teasing her would have to do for now.

"Very well, Red. I will not speak for you, nor will I interpret your words, incorrectly or otherwise."

Her chin shot up, and she glared at him for a moment before she turned and looked out the window. Daniel couldn't help but wonder what was going on in her head. Certainly not what he was thinking about. His thoughts turned to the fire within her. She would be a passionate woman in bed. Of that, he was certain. He knew she had been sheltered, having cared for her ailing parents all those years. Knowing she had never been kissed—and he would be the first to do so—pleased him tremendously.

Unless some rogue beat him to it first.

The thought of another man holding Margaret in his arms, much less kissing her, stirred anger within him. Why, if he didn't know himself better, he would think he was jealous. Perhaps he was just a little bit. He had left his carriage for a short time and walked to the square where Lord Baxter's townhouse sat, crossing to the small park in the center. Daniel had counted seven gentlemen leaving, knowing every single one of them had been present to call upon Margaret. It had bothered him so much that he had returned to his vehicle, his mood sour. The moment he had seen her, though, the dark cloud had lifted.

Oh, he was going to have to kiss her soon.

The carriage slowed and then rumbled to a halt.

"We are here," he announced.

She turned toward him, her face now composed, the hot fire now faded from her cheeks. "I hope you will not be joining us for tea, Pestfield."

"Pestfield?"

"Yes," Margaret said smoothly. "I think it rather clever. Pest comes from the Latin *pestis*. Specifically meaning plague. Pests are also things which are destructive in nature. And," she smiled brightly, "they also are another name for one who is a nuisance. You have pestered me to no end, *Pest*field."

Admiration for her filled him. "I will admit that it is rather clever on your part. But Red is a pet name. One implying affection."

Her eyes narrowed. "I will have you know, Pestfield, that I am no one's pet. Find yourself another lap dog to annoy."

By now, the door had swung open, and Margaret stood, taking the offered hand of a footman. Daniel watched, getting a small glimpse of a rounded derriere as she bent slightly before coming to her full, glorious height and descending the stairs.

His future duchess was both sharp and spirited—and he liked that.

He followed her out and manage to snatch her hand, bringing

it to the crook of his arm and holding it there in place. She tugged briefly. He held firm. Sighing, he saw she had given up this small battle, probably plotting ways to win the war now seemingly begun between them.

One which he looked forward to engaging in.

Hampton greeted them. "Good afternoon, Your Grace, Lady Margaret. Her Grace is in her sitting room. I will take you to her at once."

"That won't be necessary, Hampton," he told the butler. "I will escort Lady Margaret to my grandmother. Return to your duties."

"Very well, Your Grace."

Daniel led Margaret from the foyer, saying, "It isn't often Gran entertains in her sitting room. Guests are usually directed to the drawing room."

She said nothing.

They reached the room, and he tapped lightly on the door, hearing Gran's voice bidding them to enter. Opening the door, he brought Margaret inside and closed the door behind them.

Gran rose, reaching out her hands. Daniel released his hold on Margaret in order to allow her to take his grandmother's hands in hers.

Surprisingly, the older woman pulled Margaret close, kissing her on both cheeks.

"My dear Lady Margaret, how good of you to come to tea today."

"I was so pleased to be asked, Your Grace," Margaret replied. "I lost Grandmama when I was ten. We were extremely close. I have missed her, especially as the Season has approached. I could have used her sage advice at a time such as this. And I look forward to stories you might tell me of your shared pasts."

Margaret, still holding Gran's hands, glanced to Daniel. "I'm certain His Grace has better things to do than listen to reminiscences of a woman he never knew. I realize dukes have many responsibilities, and he should see to them instead."

She smiled sweetly at him—but Daniel saw the look of triumph in her eyes.

Before he could protest, Gran said, "I agree, my lady. Westfield, you always have plenty to do. I will keep Lady Margaret company during tea. I will send for you once we have finished so that you might escort her to Lord Baxter's home."

"Of course, Gran," he said gallantly, thinking Margaret had scored twice, with her clever nickname for him and now pushing him out the door so she wouldn't have to be with him during tea. "I hope you ladies enjoy a wonderful teatime. Do let me know when you have finished."

Daniel took his leave, going to his study, thinking of where and when he would kiss Lady Margaret Townsend.

MARGARET BREATHED A sigh of relief as the dowager duchess indicated for them to sit together on a settee.

"Would you pour out for us, my dear?" Her Grace asked.

"I would be happy to do so, Your Grace."

She did so, asking how the dowager duchess took it, adding the two cubes of sugar and dash of cream before placing the cup in its saucer on the table in front of the older woman. She had noticed the slight trembling in her hostess's hands as she held them and was happy to take over the simple domestic duty. Then she poured a cup of tea for herself.

"Dorothy would be so proud of you." Smiling, the dowager duchess added, "And a bit vain about you, as well. You are the very likeness of her, you know. Your fine bone structure. Your eye and hair color. Even your height and frame are a match for hers at the same age."

"Tell me about the two of you," Margaret urged.

"Oh, we knew each other as girls. Our parents were friendly, and we were thrown together often. Dorothy and I played dolls together. Read the same books. Favored the same flavor of cakes. Our governesses became friends and would meet up in Hyde Park with us in tow. Dorothy and I would walk along the Serpentine a short distance ahead of them, sharing all kinds of secrets."

The dowager duchess took a sip of her tea and returned her cup to the saucer. "Our mothers took us to the same modiste to have our come-out wardrobes prepared." She smiled. "Dorothy had very particular ideas about the various gowns she wished to wear, often making suggestions not only for herself but for me, as well. Sometimes, in order to get her point across to Madame, she would take a pencil and sketch something for the modiste. Oh, she had a wonderful talent."

The last words were said with a sigh, and Margaret knew something had changed between the women.

"If you were such close friends, what happened?" she asked. "I do not recall Grandmama mentioning you. Or really anything about her come-out Season."

The old woman shook her head sadly. "I did not like the man she became betrothed to. He was quite domineering. Now, I understand that wives are supposed to submit to their husbands. The Bible is quite clear on that. But he was a cruel man. I told Dorothy she was making a mistake. She had always loved to sketch people, and he forbid her from doing so."

"What?"

"Yes. He did not feel it appropriate for his future wife to waste her time on what he termed a meaningless little hobby. Soon, he began to tell her what foods to eat and which friends to see." She paused. "*I* was one he demanded that she avoid."

"Why?" Margaret asked, her heart heavy for both this woman and her grandmother.

"It seems I had expressed an opinion which he believed to be wrong and thought I would sway her. She shared with me that the earl thought I would be a poor influence on her. My heart broke when she ended our friendship at his insistence. We finished out the Season and never spoke again until that day we came across one another."

"The day we were in the bookstore."

"Yes," the dowager duchess confirmed. "By then, many years had passed. We saw one another at *ton* events, of course. Always nodding politely to one another but never conversing. I married the duke, a dull man who bored me to tears, but I made good friends with others. None, however, as good as Dorothy had been."

The older woman clasped Margaret's hand. "Your poor grandmama always looked so unhappy. Her husband isolated her from others. She told me that day at the bookstore how she regretted what had passed between us and if she could go back and change things, she would not have wed him."

Things became clear to Margaret. "My grandfather had died shortly before that day in the bookstore. I remember thinking how Grandmama used to always be sad. Then when he died, she began smiling all the time. I suppose she was like a caged bird who had been released."

"She indicated that to me that day," the dowager duchess confirmed.

"We spent much of our time together the next five years," she revealed. "Papa assumed his father's title, and we moved to the country. Grandmama moved to the dower house, but I saw her every day. She is the one who encouraged my art."

The old woman's eyes lit with interest. "You draw as she did?"

Margaret nodded. "She taught me all I know. How to hold a pencil and charcoal. How to create shadows for depth. What angles were best. I began drawing people. Eventually, I moved on to paints. She taught me about mixing them. Even after her death, when I was ten, I have continued my art. I painted the portraits of every servant we have and beyond."

She decided she would confide in this woman. "I have a strong desire to become a portrait painter, Your Grace. I wish to paint others in Polite Society."

"Are you any good?" the dowager duchess bluntly asked.

"I believe I have both the talent and patience to be successful. Now that I am making my come-out, I hope I can share with others my dream and take on a few commissions. I wouldn't accept any payment for the first few portraits I do. If those who sit for them are pleased, though, I pray they will spread the word and that I might be able to pursue my art."

She paused, sadness filling her. "As Grandmama was unable to do so. I shall right a wrong done to her by the man she took as her husband. The portraits I paint will speak for the both of us."

The dowager duchess beamed. "Then I must be your first subject, Lady Margaret."

CHAPTER TEN

M ARGARET WAS STUNNED by the dowager duchess's words. "You would do so for me?"

The older woman patted Margaret's hand. "Who better than I to be the first portrait you paint of a member of the *ton*? After all, I knew Dorothy well. What better way to honor her than to allow her granddaughter, to whom she passed on her talent, to be the artist who paints me?"

She kept silent about the one she had done years ago of this woman's grandson. It had been her first attempt at painting an aristocrat.

"I would be most honored to paint your portrait, Your Grace."

"When others learn you have done so, they will flock to your door, Lady Margaret," the dowager duchess assured her. "Why, I think I will give a party in order to unveil your work. It will be a small group in attendance, some of the most influential members of Polite Society."

Laughing, Margaret said, "I have yet to even sketch you, much less paint this portrait of you, Your Grace, yet you are already planning such a gathering?"

The dowager duchess arched her brows. "When you are my age, you cannot sit about and waste time. You must act. For you never know what tomorrow might bring." She clapped her hands together in delight. "Oh, we must discuss this and plan what I should wear and where you will paint me. How quickly do you work?"

"You are peppering me with questions, Your Grace. Please take a moment and slow down," she cautioned.

"I am merely excited by this, my dear. I did have my portrait done shortly after I wed Westfield. I had just discovered I was with child. Though my body does not show so, the artist captured the bloom in my cheeks."

"You never had another one commissioned after that?"

The dowager duchess sniffed. "Westfield was not interested in me. Only in me providing him his heir. Once I did so, he didn't give a fig about me. It was quite all right, though. I had wonderful friends and enjoyed time with them, as well as my children. Westfield took no interest in them, especially the girls. When he passed, his title went to Daniel, my grandson, since Daniel's father was already gone. Daniel is already a better duke than Westfield ever was."

She found her cheeks heating at the mention of the current duke.

The dowager duchess studied her with interest. "Might you be interested in my grandson, my dear?"

"No, Your Grace. I am not interested in any man. The only reason I agreed to make my come-out so late was to be properly introduced to members of the *ton,* in order to find future clients to paint."

The dowager duchess's brows knit together. "So, you have no wish to wed? You do not want children?"

Margaret swallowed. "Though it would be delightful to have children of my own, I do have a wonderful nephew and niece." She bit her lip. "I fear that no gentleman would wish for his wife to be a portrait painter. Look at my own grandmother's choice of a husband. Why, he did not even allow her to sketch. What husband would allow me to work at my art?"

"As long as you warm his bed, that should not be a problem,

my dear."

Heat flooded her cheeks. "Your Grace!"

The old woman shrugged. "It is true. You are of a different generation than I was, my dear. If you wish to pursue your art, why not? As long as you provide an heir, you should be allowed to do as you wish." She paused. "*If* you marry the right man, of course."

"You are a most enlightened thinker, Your Grace. I do not think many men of the *ton* would agree with your point of view, however."

The dowager duchess sighed. "Perhaps you are right. We are ahead of our time. Still," she mused, "if you did wed my grandson, you would be a duchess. Much like a duke, a duchess can do no wrong in society. She sets the tone and pace."

Margaret shook her head. "No, Your Grace. I am not marrying your grandson or any other gentleman of Polite Society. If my portrait of you proves to be a success, then I will be swarmed with commissions. I would have no time to devote to a husband or a family."

The dowager duchess studied her. "You would give up a chance at happiness for your art?"

"Were you happy with a husband?" she countered. "You have indicated you were not. Neither was my grandmother. And my poor father was downright miserable in his own marriage."

"How so?"

"Mama's parents arranged with Papa's parents for them to wed. They despised each other on sight and never changed their minds. Mama disliked Papa and all his relatives, especially Grandmama. She lumped me in with that side of the family since I so strongly resembled Grandmama."

"She was cruel to you?" the dowager duchess asked, sympathy in her eyes.

"She was. She put forth all her efforts into Dolley, my older sister. Dolley was blond and petite and beautiful as Mama herself. She lived through Dolley."

"Did your mother's feelings affect those of your sister toward you?"

Margaret nodded. "Dolley has never liked me. She is only tolerating me because our cousin, who assumed Papa's earldom, did not wish for me to be there. She also knows that I will come into my dowry come June. I shall take control of it and live off it until I establish myself as a portrait artist."

"My, you have such plans, Lady Margaret. It seems you have put a great deal of thought into them." The dowager duchess smiled. "Let's talk about my portrait."

They spent the next half hour discussing what the dowager duchess should wear and where she wished to be painted. Margaret made several suggestions regarding the color of her gown and even told the older woman she could wear a gown in a style she favored. Margaret could then change the color in the portrait itself to one that would flatter the dowager duchess.

"You can watch me mix the paints and help choose which color to make your gown if you wish."

"That sounds delightful. Do you have any ideas what the background might be?"

They talked of the dowager duchess's love of music and books, as well as her roses, which she had tended to herself until recently.

"Pruning them is simply beyond me these days. But roses would make for a most suitable background, don't you think?"

"I will sketch you and can add any background I choose. I will need to see the gardens, however, in order to choose the appropriate background for your picture."

"Daniel can help you tour the gardens," the woman said airily. "He knows where my favorite blooms grow."

The last place Margaret wanted to be was alone in a garden with the sinfully handsome Duke of Westfield.

"We can save that for a later time, Your Grace. For now, I will need to do some preliminary sketches of you from different angles."

"Do I sit for those?" the dowager duchess asked, eager as a young girl.

"You can, but I don't believe that will be necessary after all the time we have spent together this afternoon. Once I have done several sketches, I will decide which angle is both the most flattering and yet most representative of you. You can have a say in this if you choose."

The dowager duchess sighed. "I suppose you will paint me, wrinkles and all."

"A few wrinkles would be appropriate," she said diplomatically. "After all, not many women attain your age."

"I suppose being eighty should be celebrated. Yes, that is what this portrait shall be—a celebration of my eightieth year of life, come to life on canvas. I am glad I have decided to do this, Lady Margaret."

"Please, call me Margaret," she encouraged.

The dowager duchess smiled. "Then Margaret it shall be," she agreed. "Now, when shall I sit for you?"

In her mind, the sooner this occurred, the better. Actually, Margaret never had others sit for her. She merely referred to her completed sketches. Perhaps the *ton* would expect to sit for their portraits. She might as well try it that way with this first commission and asked, "Could we start tomorrow morning, Your Grace?"

Distaste flittered across the dowager duchess's features. "I rarely rise before noon, Margaret, especially once the Season begins. And you will need to be home to visit with your callers during the afternoons. Why don't you come again for tea tomorrow, and we can start our session then?"

She saw that would have to work for now. Though she preferred morning light, she might also have a hard time rising when keeping the late hours of the Season. She might simply go back to her method of working from sketches. That would be something she could work out with the dowager duchess later.

"Then I will see you tomorrow at the same time," she promised, thinking it would be interesting to spend more time in this woman's company.

"Let me ring and let a servant know that we have finished so that Daniel might escort you home."

"That isn't necessary, Your Grace. I am eager to stretch my legs after all this sitting. Walking also helps me to think. My brother-in-law's townhouse is not far from here. I can walk to it easily."

The dowager duchess frowned. "Without a chaperone?"

Margaret chuckled. "It is not as if I am straight out of the schoolroom, Your Grace. I will be five and twenty, come the first of June." She rose. "Thank you for a lovely tea and for this wonderful opportunity to paint you."

"I look forward to it myself, my dear."

She said her goodbyes and left the sitting room, easily finding her way back to the townhouse's foyer. A footman sitting by the door quickly came to his feet.

"You are leaving, my lady?" he inquired.

"Yes, thank you."

The servant opened the door for her, and Margaret stepped outside into the late afternoon sunlight, a light breeze stirring the air. She moved the length of the townhouse and continued down the pavement, happiness filling her. It had been wonderful to hear about her grandmama in her youth, though it saddened Margaret to hear how the longstanding friendship between the two women had come to an end. Still, Grandmama's friend had thought enough of her to extend an offer beyond her wildest hopes.

She was to paint the Dowager Duchess of Westfield.

Having tea with the dowager duchess and establishing a strong connection with her would most likely make Margaret's dreams come true, knowing the old woman wielded great influence among the *ton*. If the portrait came out to the dowager duchess's liking and the party she gave proved a success, then Margaret's career as a portrait artist would be secured.

Suddenly, a firm hand gripped her elbow, stopping her progress. She had not thought she would be accosted on a Mayfair street even if she were alone. Swinging her fist, she turned and slammed it into her attacker.

"Bloody hell, Red!" the Duke of Westfield roared.

He released her, his hands going to his face, gently touching his eye where her punch had landed.

Horror filled Margaret. She had struck a duke. And not just any duke. One who was now turning red in the face, bristling with anger.

"I am so sorry, Your Grace," she told him several times. "At least it is only your eye, which may blacken a bit. It *could* have been your nose. I could have broken it. That would have been terrible."

She quit babbling as he glared at her.

"You are going to make this up to me, Red."

"Of course, Your Grace," she told him.

Wondering exactly what she would have to do.

CHAPTER ELEVEN

D ANIEL WAS RELIEVED he had caught up with Margaret, in spite of the blow she had landed to his eye. He had fortunately glanced out his window in time to see her passing along the pavement, unescorted and fiercely independent. She had told him she would see herself home, but he had not thought Gran would allow her to do so. Quickly, he had hurried after her, obviously startling her. She certainly packed a punch, and he wondered what it would be like if she ever graced Gentleman Jackson's boxing rings.

He did not want to ask her for a kiss again. He had already established that and wanted her to think of where and when it might come.

Instead, he told her, "You will partner with me at cards this evening."

She looked at him blankly. "Cards are played at a rout?" Then understanding dawned in her eyes and she said, "I am sorry, Westfield. My sister and brother-in-law accepted an invitation to a rout tonight. Not the card game to be held at Lord and Lady Rawlins' residence. Dolley is abysmal at cards, and she said Baxter plays them often enough since he heads to the card room at the beginning of every ball. I am sorry, but I will have to be your card partner at another time."

"You will attend the event I do this evening, Red. No ifs,

ands, or buts."

Her jaw dropped. "How am I to do so? Dolley turned down that invitation for the three of us. Even I know card parties are exclusive and only a small portion of the *ton* are invited to them. I cannot turn up uninvited, much less unescorted by a chaperone."

He touched his eye tenderly once more, knowing he would be sporting a shiner by tonight's event. Then taking her hand and placing it upon his arm, he proceeded down the pavement with her to Baxter's townhouse.

"You will have a most acceptable chaperone in my grandmother, Red."

He could feel the annoyance bristle from her as she said, "That is simply unacceptable, Pestfield."

So, she was back to calling him the annoying nickname she had bestowed upon him.

"There is no need for your grandmother to chaperone me," Margaret insisted. "As it is, I am not even supposed to dance with you again. Having Her Grace serve as my chaperone—even arriving with the two of you—would set tongues to wagging."

"Your sister has forbidden you from dancing with me?" he asked. Daniel felt her stiffen slightly. "She has made trouble for you."

"If she weren't already wed to Baxter, I would think she might actually be jealous of me for having danced with you. Dolley got the marriage she and Mama wanted. To a man of high rank and wealth." She paused and then added, "If Dolley had known, however, that you were to be a duke one day, she would have set her sights upon you. I know it."

Left unsaid was how Lady Baxter did not want her sister to have him. If indeed Margaret wed him, she would outrank her selfish sister.

"I don't see how Lady Baxter can keep you from dancing with me, much less seeing me at *ton* events. No one denies a duke a dance or the pleasure of his company. A word from me, and Lady Baxter could become a social outcast," he threatened.

She stopped in her tracks. "Please, Your Grace. Do not give her the cut direct. It is true that Dolley has been unkind to me my entire life—but she is my sister. She lives for the adulation of Polite Society. One day her looks will fade and the many men who now swarm about her will fade away, their eyes focused on younger, more beautiful women. I would not see her ostracized by you and Polite Society."

Daniel thought Margaret kinder than she should be, but he nodded. "All right, I will not disparage Lord and Lady Baxter in any way. I will, though, dance with whomever I choose to do so. No marchioness will dictate my dance partners to me."

He propelled her along the pavement again, adding, "The only woman in my life who dares order me about is Gran."

A soft smile graced Margaret's very kissable lips. "Your grandmother is quite formidable. She has been most kind to me." Hesitating a moment, she added, "I am to paint her portrait."

A feather could have knocked him over. "You will?"

"It is what I have always dreamed of doing. Art has given me solace and reason for being. I would like to earn my living as a portrait artist."

"Earn your living? What about marriage?"

"I believe I told you many years ago, Your Grace, that I really didn't have an interest in marriage. My goal has always been to paint others."

He did recall her mentioning this, but the idea of a woman in Polite Society earning her keep baffled him.

"You have no desire to wed?" he asked.

"That is correct, Your Grace."

Daniel sighed inwardly. This just complicated matters. He wanted Margaret Townsend as his duchess. No other woman would do. Even worse, Gran—who was supposed to be aiding him in his hunt for a bride—was now encouraging Margaret to be even more independent than she already was.

They arrived at the Baxter townhouse, and he said, "My carriage will arrive at half-past eight. Do I need to send a note to

Lord and Lady Baxter that informs them that my grandmother will accompany you to the card party this evening?"

She nibbled her lower lip in thought, causing a frisson of desire to ripple through him.

"Much as I would like to think that I am capable of handling Dolley and somehow placating her, I believe she would forbid me to accept your invitation if the note came from you. Unless she received word from the dowager duchess herself. *Not* you, Your Grace. You are a prickly subject with her."

"Then expect a message to arrive within the hour. Act surprised when it is received."

A slow smile spread across her face. "I can do so, Pestfield."

He returned her smile. "Until this evening, Red. And I hope you will prove to be a good card player. I hate to lose."

Margaret beamed at him. "I am better than good, Your Grace. You will see."

>>>×<<<

MARGARET WENT TO the dining room, her thoughts swirling. She was ecstatic to have the Dowager Duchess of Westfield's support and looked forward to painting the old woman. She knew it must be the painting of her life in order to impress the *ton*. Though the dowager duchess's word commanded respect, Margaret would have to prove to be talented enough in order for commissions to result.

She also experienced a slight . . . giddiness. Thinking of the Duke of Westfield made her feel so. He seemed interested in her, but she had quelled it. At least she hoped she had, by announcing to him her intent never to wed. Of course, a man such as Westfield would look upon that as a challenge. She did not think he wished to wed her, in particular, but she did know he would do his best to steal a kiss from her. She anticipated that moment and hoped to learn from it.

Entering the dining room, she saw her sister and brother-in-law already present and greeted them as a footman seated her. Dolley made no mention of an alternate plan for Margaret this evening, and she supposed the note had not arrived after all. Perhaps Westfield had had a change of heart and merely toyed with her. Or the dowager duchess refused to be involved in his scheme.

Dolley talked as they ate, neither Baxter nor Margaret finding a need to respond to the relentless gossip she revealed.

Then a footman appeared with a silver tray, and she saw it bore a note. The footman passed it to the butler, who then presented it to Lord Baxter.

The marquess said, "What is this?" and accepted it, breaking the seal and skimming the contents. "Hmm."

"What is it, Baxter?" Dolley asked. "Who is it from? What does it say?"

Her brother-in-law looked at Margaret as he answered his wife. "It is from the Dowager Duchess of Westfield. She wishes for Lady Margaret to accompany her to a card party this evening."

He passed the parchment to his wife, who read it, frowning. She turned to Margaret. "Did you know of this?"

Playing innocent, she shook her head. "No, Dolley. The dowager duchess mentioned she was attending a card party this evening, and I told her our plans were to go to a rout."

"Why would she wish for you to accompany her?" Dolley mused. "What did you speak of at tea today? I had forgotten that you had gone."

Margaret knew Dolley never forgot anything and that she would quiz her sister about the tea outside of Baxter's hearing.

"Mostly, she reminisced about her girlhood and come-out Season. The dowager duchess and Grandmama were great friends from the time they were young. I heard many stories of them."

Dolley waved a hand dismissively. "Who cares about things

in the long-ago past? Anything else?"

"There is a piece of good news," she revealed.

"What?" her sister asked anxiously.

"Her Grace spoke of Grandmama's sketching. When I shared with her that I also had a bit of talent, she pressed me to discuss it further. I shared with her my desire to become a portrait artist to the members of the *ton*."

"What is this?" the marquess asked. "This is the first I have heard of that scheme."

Margaret knew that wasn't the case because of her eavesdropping. Still, she did not call out Baxter and would let the conversation play out.

Dolley sniffed. "Margaret believes she can paint portraits of others of note. She has asked me to tell others of her talent. I have agreed to do so."

Baxter stroked his chin in thought. "Well, you certainly did well on the ones you did of us and the children. But . . . an artist, Lady Margaret? Aren't they . . . paid for their work?"

"They are, my lord. This is the way I wish to provide for myself. I hate imposing upon you and Dolley any more than I have to. After this Season, I will establish my own household here in town and support myself with my earnings from my art."

Her brother-in-law looked perplexed at such an idea. "Is that wise, my lady? You certainly won't gain a husband by proclaiming your intentions."

"I do not want a husband, my lord. I know that Dolley has made you aware that I come into possession of my full dowry upon my next birthday. I will not need a husband after that. I will provide for myself."

He shrugged and went back to his dinner.

Margaret turned to Dolley. "I will be painting the dowager duchess's portrait. She has promised to give a party and reveal it to a select few."

"A party?" Now, Dolley was interested. "When will you begin painting her?"

"She has asked me to tea again tomorrow. We will discuss specifics at that time."

Her sister smiled brightly. "Then by all means you must go to this card party with the dowager duchess. She is a tremendous force in Polite Society. It would be good for me—for us—to have this connection with her."

Leave It to Dolley to make it all about herself and a connection to a woman of higher rank.

"Her invitation is unexpected, but I do believe I will accept it. We can speak of her portrait on our way there. What gown she might wear. How to arrange her hair. That sort of thing."

"Her note says she will call for you at half-past eight. Baxter and I will be leaving soon after that for the rout." Dolley drummed her fingers upon the table. "I do wish now that I had not declined that invitation. I wonder if I should see if it is permissible for me to change my mind."

Margaret saw Baxter's eyes light with interest. He would certainly prefer to attend a card party over a rout. Margaret couldn't have this, otherwise, Dolley would find out about the duke's scheme.

"Why don't you go ahead and keep to your plans, Dolley? Lord and Lady Simms would be bereft if you canceled at such a late date. You know you simply make every party. Besides, card play bores you."

"That is true," her sister agreed.

Before Dolley could change her mind and insist upon attending the card party, Margaret said, "Why don't you extend an invitation to the dowager duchess? I am certain she would accept coming to tea one afternoon. Spending an entire tea alone with her would give you a chance to truly come to know her."

Dolley beamed. "That is a very clever idea, Margaret. Yes, I shall do just that. Since you will have tea with her tomorrow, I will ask her for the following afternoon. We want to nurture and strengthen these bonds you have made with her."

Relief flooded her. She picked up her fork again and ate a few more bites before excusing herself and heading upstairs to change for this evening's event. She needed to look her best tonight. After all, she would be in the company of a dowager duchess tonight, who might even begin telling others that Margaret would be painting her portrait. Those in attendance, particularly women, always made note of what gown a woman wore. She did not want to appear lacking.

At least that's what she told herself.

A small part of her knew she wanted to appear beautiful and confident.

For the Duke of Westfield.

CHAPTER TWELVE

I F HE WERE escorting any other woman to a *ton* event, Daniel would have gotten out of his carriage and gone inside where she lived in order to greet her. Since Margaret had told him about her sister's jealousy and how she had been ordered not to dance with him, he thought it best to remain inside the carriage and have a footman notify Baxter's butler that the carriage had arrived.

His grandmother did not question his behavior because he had shared the circumstances with her when he asked her to write the note to Lord and Lady Baxter.

"You think she will come?" Gran asked.

"I have no reason to think otherwise," he said coolly, though his heart raced. "You would have received a reply if she wished to remain committed to the other event occurring this evening. Despite Lady Baxter's jealousy of her sister, the marchioness is no fool, Gran. She will see the advantage in having a sister who is close to a dowager duchess and try to use that to her advantage."

His grandmother snorted. "Lady Baxter thinks too much of herself. True, she is quite beautiful, but she has no substance to her. Lady Margaret, on the other hand, is quite intelligent." She eyed him. "Am I still to be searching for a bride for you, Daniel? Or have you found her on your own?"

He didn't want to admit how much he wanted Margaret as

his wife.

"I advise you to keep looking. While Lady Margaret might possibly be a candidate, it cannot do any harm for you to continue to peruse the Marriage Mart for me."

She laughed merrily. "Oh, my dear boy, you do not have me fooled. Margaret Townsend is definitely the one for you."

"If I can convince her of that," he admitted glumly. "She has already told me she has no wish to wed."

"Her art is standing in the way?" Gran guessed.

Daniel nodded. "It means a great deal to her. Even years ago, when I met her while calling upon Lady Dolley, Margaret told me then she wasn't interested in a husband or babies. That she wanted to paint portraits."

"She could do both, you know."

He frowned. "You think so? Gran, no lady in Polite Society—especially a duchess—works for a living."

"Would you not want your duchess to be happy?"

"Of course, I would."

"Then let her be. As a duchess, Margaret can set the tone. If painting makes her happy, she should pursue it. Her grandmother wished to do so, only to have her husband forbid it."

"I did not know that," he said.

Gran nodded. "It is what caused the rift between us. I wanted her to stand up to that bully of a husband. She cowed instead. I had thought Dorothy had more spine to her. It caused an irrevocable break between us. The earl thought I was a bad influence and forbid her from speaking to me, much less maintaining our friendship."

"I am so sorry, Gran."

She patted his hand. "It is all right, Daniel. In a way, Dorothy has come back to me. Through Margaret."

The carriage door opened, and Margaret appeared, looking lovely. His mouth watered seeing the curve of her breasts peeking from the top of the gown.

"Come sit with me, my dear," his grandmother encouraged,

moving over a bit to make more room.

Margaret took the seat and said, "Good evening, Your Graces. Thank you again for chaperoning me to the card party, Your Grace."

"I am happy to do so," the dowager duchess proclaimed. "I plan to share with others our plans. Lord and Lady Rawlins have only invited forty or fifty tonight. By the time the evening ends, we will make certain everyone in attendance knows what you and I are up to."

"I cannot thank you enough for agreeing to me painting you, Your Grace."

"Nonsense, my girl. I was the one who suggested it to you." The dowager duchess paused. "Perhaps you would even consider painting my grandson."

His mouth grew dry as Margaret's gaze flew to him, skimming down and back up, assessing him.

"Let me paint one Judson at a time, Your Grace," she told Gran diplomatically. "Then we can see if His Grace might wish for his portrait to be done."

Yes, Margaret would make one hell of a duchess.

They arrived at the Rawlins' townhouse, and Daniel exited the vehicle first so that he could help both his grandmother and Margaret from it. Though her hands were gloved, he knew his touch affected Margaret because she nervously licked her lips.

He planned on licking those lips sometime this evening. And more.

Much more.

It was the reason he had wanted Margaret to attend the Rawlins' card party. It would be much easier to find an out-of-the-way spot with only a few dozen versus a ball attended by hundreds. Yes, tonight he would see if he and the fiery redhead were compatible in the way which counted the most.

With a woman on each side of him, Daniel led them inside the townhouse, where they were greeted by Lord and Lady Rawlins.

"Oh, Your Graces, it is so good of you to come this evening," the earl toadied. "And I see you have kept a date at Gentleman Jackson's, no less," referring to the shiner Daniel sported.

Sensing Margaret wince beside him, he ignored that remark and said, "I do enjoy card play. Have you been introduced to Lady Margaret Townsend?"

Rawlins smiled. "I have not had the pleasure, Your Grace."

"Oh, you will be happy I begged Lady Margaret to accompany me this evening," Gran said smoothly, making certain for the sake of Margaret's reputation that the pair was made aware of her involvement. "You see, Lady Margaret is going to be painting my portrait."

Lady Rawlins's eyes widened. "Oh, my!" she exclaimed. "How utterly fascinating. I must steal you away at some point this evening, Lady Margaret, and hear all about this."

"I don't believe I have ever heard of a woman who painted others," the earl declared. "You must be quite talented for Her Grace to commission a portrait from you."

"She is simply more talented than any man," Gran declared airily. "I plan to have a small gathering to reveal the finished portrait." She paused. "Perhaps you might be interested in attending it."

Now, both the earl and countess salivated. "It would be our extreme pleasure to do so, Your Grace," Lord Rawlins told them. "Perhaps Lady Rawlins and I also might have Lady Margaret paint us."

"I am not taking commissions at the moment, my lord," Margaret said. "If and when I do, I will be certain to keep you in mind."

They moved from their hosts, and a footman indicated for them to follow him. He led them to a large drawing room, where furniture had been rearranged to incorporate several tables brought in for play, while still allowing groups of chairs and settees available for those not wishing to play or in the midst of a break from table play.

"That went quite well," Gran remarked. "It seems you won't have to paint anyone for free."

Daniel looked to Margaret. "You weren't going to charge for your services?"

Her cheeks pinkened. "I had thought to do a few portraits at no cost, hoping to entice members of the *ton* to seek out my talent."

"That won't be necessary," he said brusquely. "And if you have made that arrangement with Gran, it is now null and void. I will see that you are properly compensated."

"But you have never seen my work, Your Grace. I might do a disservice to Her Grace."

He gazed at her intently. "I sincerely doubt that, my lady."

"Come, let us introduce you around, my girl," Gran said.

After a good half hour of meeting and greeting everyone in attendance, people began moving toward the tables.

"Go ahead and play," Gran told them. "I see two friends I wish to sit with."

Daniel placed his hand on the small of Margaret's back and led her toward a table. He itched to stroke it. Kiss his way down her spine. But he was getting ahead of himself.

Lord Rawlins cleared his throat. "The tables on the right side of the room have been dedicated for whist. The left side of the room will be for Pharo, Loo, and Speculation. Each player will be given thirty matchsticks for betting purposes."

Lady Rawlins cleared her throat, looking pointedly at her husband.

"In accordance with Lady Rawlins's wishes, the matchsticks are merely a tool to place your bets with. They are assigned no value and will not be cashed out in any manner at the end of the evening."

"We see the hen rules the roost in this house, Rawlins!" called out a loud voice, and the group assembled chuckled.

"However," the earl continued, "since a vast majority of you usually play whist, a prize will be awarded to the pair who wins the most matches of that card game by the end of the evening."

Daniel turned to Margaret. "We are going to win that prize," he said softly.

"You don't even know what the reward might be," she whispered.

"It doesn't matter. I always play to win."

"Snacks will be placed upon the sideboard," Lady Rawlins told her guests. "An assortment of cheeses, fruits, breads, and pastries, as well as wine. If a lady prefers sherry or a gentleman wishes to drink port, simply inform one of our footmen."

He seated her at one of the whist tables, and they were soon joined by a plodding earl and a viscountess who claimed she was excellent at whist.

"We shall see, my lady," Daniel said. "I am a more than competent player. I have it on good authority that my partner, Lady Margaret, is quite the player herself."

The viscountess studied Margaret. "Oh, you are the portrait painter. That must be fascinating."

"It is painstaking work, but I find it to be rather rewarding."

"Perhaps I should have my portrait painted by you for my husband. It might draw his attention away from his latest mistress."

Margaret turned beet red.

Daniel accepted the pack of cards from the butler, who brought a silver tray around, disturbing the packets. They drew for high card, and Margaret came up with a king, becoming the dealer. She passed the pack to the earl, seated on her left, for the shuffle. He returned them and as she was the dealer, she took advantage of being allowed the final shuffle before play began.

She handled the cards with surety, her shuffle brisk and her dealing of the cards smooth and efficient. Hearts were the trump suit and within minutes, he realized Margaret had not exaggerated. She was more than proficient, knowing when to lead and when to allow him to take the lead. The thirteen plays saw them take nine tricks.

Lord and Lady Rawlins had circulated among the whist tables and stopped to watch them at play.

"I say, Lady Margaret, you are quite the player," the earl praised.

She smiled sweetly. "I have been gifted with an excellent memory, my lord. Success in whist involves recalling which cards have been played and which still remain."

The viscountess shrugged. "I never can remember what has been played. I ask to review the last trick won, but by the time I look at my hand again, I cannot for the life of me recall what I saw."

"Well, you are the first table to finish a complete round," Lord Rawlins said. He signaled the butler and said, "Mark His Grace and Lady Margaret down for winning a round."

"Yes, my lord," he responded, doing so and handing the duke a token to represent their win.

They played another hand, and the earl grew bored as he and the viscountess lost even worse than before and told the viscountess they both needed a drink. Soon, others took their places and play continued, with Daniel and Margaret winning far more often than they lost. Partners did take respites, however, in order to allow others to play, be it those who had been on the other side of the room engaged in different card games or ones who had merely sat on the sidelines.

When they completed the thirteenth hand and reported their latest win to the butler, Daniel said, "I feel like stretching my legs after sitting. Come, my lady. Let us give others a chance to try and catch up to us."

He offered her his arm and she took it. He had noticed guests moving in and out of the drawing room and led Margaret from it. Lady Rawlins had come around, flitting about as a butterfly, telling guests of more food located in a room off the ballroom and that the gardens were lit in case guests wished to stroll through them.

Both places might be too crowded for what he wished to do

now.

Kiss Margaret senseless.

Daniel moved leisurely down the hallway, having been in this townhouse before for a similar occasion.

"I don't wish to go to the gardens," Margaret announced. "We will be looking at your gardens tomorrow."

Now, that was interesting. "Why so, Red?"

Her nose crinkled. "You are to show me the rose bushes that your grandmother favors. She wishes her favorite flower to be the backdrop to her portrait."

He smiled. "Gran does love her roses. She used to tend to them herself until recently. Now, she bullies the gardeners, barking orders and having them dance to her tune regarding their care."

"Are all you Judsons so domineering?"

"My sisters would demure and say they aren't at all." He laughed. "But they would be lying. They might have soft voices and sweet smiles on their faces—but they both are strong-willed. In fact, I pity their husbands because I am certain Deborah and Lilly run roughshod over them."

"I think I would like them. Very much."

By now, they had reached the library, and he steered them inside, closing the door behind them. The room was lit. Barely. A single lamp glowed in one corner. No fire burned in the grate.

"I don't th—"

Daniel took Margaret's elbows in hand and moved her so her back rested against the door they had just come through.

"Don't think. Just feel," he said, lowering his head until his lips hovered just above hers. He waited a beat, wanting to feel the tension between them before his mouth touched hers.

"But—"

"Hush," he said, his mouth covering hers.

CHAPTER THIRTEEN

M ARGARET'S HEART THUNDERED.

Margaret hadn't known what to expect—but it wasn't this. The duke's lips, soft yet firm, brushed against hers in exquisite tenderness. She felt his immense body heat since they stood so close together, his hands firm on her elbows, holding her gently in place. She was glad to have the door against her back to hold her up because the warm spice of his cologne made her knees grow weak, not to mention his lips on hers.

He released her elbows, and his hands went to cradle her face. Yet the oh-so-tender kiss continued, causing those marvelous tingles to spread throughout her body. He pressed his mouth against hers now in what she had thought would be a kiss. As he did, his thumbs stroked her cheeks. An ache filled her, one of immense yearning. She wanted more from him.

What, she hadn't a clue.

He raised his head, and his eyes blazed with something.

Desire?

She quivered and whispered, "More."

He smiled, that radiant smile that made her want to forget everything.

"With pleasure," he murmured, his mouth returning to hers.

He began kissing her again, this time a little harder, but it was what she wanted. Needed. He slipped one hand to cradle her nape, steadying her, the other moving to capture her waist. He continued kissing her, and Margaret's hands moved to his shoulders, gripping him tightly. She didn't know if it was to keep him from leaving or hold herself up. Perhaps a little of both.

She became aware of him pressing against her, his large body pinning her to the door. He nibbled her bottom lip and then softly bit into it, causing her to gasp. His tongue slid inside her mouth, shocking her. It explored her leisurely, at length, heating her blood. She began to respond and touched her tongue to his, causing a low grown from deep within him. He deepened the kiss even further, her heart now slamming violently against her ribs, so strong that he must feel it because she could also feel his own heart beating out of control against her breast. Both breasts had grown heavy and longed for his touch, whether it be his hands or his mouth. The thought surprised her and yet thrilled her at the same time.

An ache also began between her legs, a place she perfunctori-ly washed without thought. Now, however, it sprang to life, throbbing with need. She also wanted him to touch her there.

Where did these wicked thoughts come from?

His fingers tightened on her nape, his thumb stroking it sen-sually.

Margaret wanted this kiss to go on forever.

He broke the kiss, though, lifting his head. Then he rested his brow against hers as they both caught their breaths.

"We should return to the others," he said huskily.

Reluctance filled her. "No," she said softly. "I don't want to."

He chuckled low and raised his head, his gaze boring down to her very soul.

"You are quite the card player, Red."

"You are quite the kisser, Pestfield."

They both laughed softly, but he still did not release her. Instead, he bent and pressed a final, soft kiss onto her mouth, and then released her. She saw the hunger burning in his eyes and knew it was reflected in her own.

"Shall we go now and win tonight's prize?" he asked lightly.

They might return to the other guests, but Margaret doubted their relationship could return to being the same as before. Not after their kiss. He made her long for things she had never thought she wanted. A husband. Children. A home with a man who would love and cherish her.

She shook her head. A man such as the duke would not believe in love. Why, she did not believe in love herself, having never witnessed it.

Margaret realized her hands still rested on his shoulders though he had put a bit of distance between them. She let them fall away, already missing the hard feel of him.

"You are right. We should return to the drawing room."

He took a few steps back and she moved away from the door, her knees shaking.

"Stay here a moment," he cautioned, opening the door and glancing both ways, then looking back at her and nodding.

She understood no one was in the corridor and joined him, placing her hand upon his sleeve without being prompted. Together, they moved along the hallway and entered the drawing room again.

Lord Rawlins met them and said, "I see you took a break from the game play. In your absence, a few threats have emerged."

The earl led them to his butler, who told them how many tokens had been awarded and to whom. Though they remained in the lead, they had challengers nipping at their heels and must fend them off.

Westfield looked to her, his eyes now full of mischief. "Are you up for another round, my lady?"

She wondered if he meant card play—or kissing.

"I have never backed down from a challenge, Your Grace," she said, hoping he took her meaning.

The duke smiled his sunny smile and said, "That's my girl."

They returned to the tables, playing another six matches

against other couples. Margaret accepted a glass of sherry and sipped it, hoping it would steady her nerves. She pushed all thoughts of the kiss away, knowing she would come back to it later and savor it. For now, however, she wanted to win. She wanted to show this man that she was a worthy partner for him. Drawing upon her tremendous powers of concentration that she used when painting, she did just that.

They won all six times.

The earl and countess thanked all their guests for coming once play had ended and everyone competing for the prize had played the correct number of games. The countess accepted a large vase filled with irises and tulips from her butler.

"This," Lady Rawlins said, "is for our winners this evening—the Duke of Westfield and Lady Margaret Townsend."

Margaret watched as the duke went to accept the prize and then brought it to where she stood with his grandmother.

"Since there is only one, my lady, I think it should go to you. After all, you did carry me at times."

Warmth filled her at his compliment. "I have never won a prize, Your Grace. I will happily accept the vase and its contents."

Westfield signaled a footman and gave the vase to him, saying, "See this is taken to my carriage."

"At once, Your Grace."

They went about the room making their farewells to the other guests, with Lord Rawlins thanking her for making the evening such a splendid one.

The duke escorted them to his carriage, where she saw the footman in the rear cradling the large vase in the crook of his arm. Westfield helped them into the carriage and joined them, once more sitting opposite. This time, Margaret did not mind that he did so. The single lamp inside the vehicle left them in semi-darkness, allowing her to study him more than she could have otherwise.

"You were quite the hit," the dowager duchess remarked. "I only mentioned your portrait painting twice to others. After that, people made a special effort to seek me out and ask about you and your skills."

"Yes, Your Grace," she said. "I had numerous people mention it to me."

"And I told every one of them that Lady Margaret was not accepting any commissions at this time," the duke said. "That she wanted to focus solely on her work for you, Gran." He paused, grinning. "That only intrigued them even more. I would say that Lady Margaret will be able to paint as few or as many as she wishes. And that after only one evening, and with no one having seen her talent on display."

Happiness filled Margaret. She had worried about mixing in Polite Society and even more so about whether any in the *ton* would bite given the chance to have their portraits done by her.

"I will owe all my success to Her Grace for stepping up and asking me to paint her."

The dowager duchess patted Margaret's hand. "Nonsense, my dear. I just helped nudge you along a bit." She smiled. "After all, a dowager duchess does wield a good deal of power in society. I try to use it to benefit others."

They arrived at the Baxter townhouse and this time, the duke left the carriage, helping her from it. He escorted her to the front door and took her hands in his.

A glow filled her as he said, "I did not want your sister to see me earlier, but I do not care now." He raised her hands to his lips and tenderly kissed them. "Might I call upon you tomorrow afternoon, Red? I could then escort you to Gran for tea."

She gazed at him steadily and said, "Yes, Your Grace."

"Daniel," he prompted softly.

"Daniel," she echoed.

She thought he might kiss her and did not want anyone to see such an intimate moment between them. Pulling her hands from his, she said, "Thank you for a lovely evening."

"Thank you for this shiner," he teased, laughing merrily. Then he sobered. "I will see you tomorrow, Red. Until then."

He turned and she watched him move to the carriage. The footman who held the flowers hurried to her, handing her the vase, and she thanked him.

Her focus returned to the duke. He paused beside the coach and raised a hand in farewell. She did the same and then entered the townhouse as the carriage pulled away. She went to her bedchamber, prize in hand, and rang for a maid who assisted her from her clothes and into her night rail.

Slipping under the bedclothes, Margaret lay there and relived every moment of Daniel's magical kiss.

She was in trouble. Deep trouble. She had played with fire—and been slightly scorched. She would have to be very careful and guard her heart before the duke made away with it.

MARGARET ROSE EARLY. Surprisingly, she had slept remarkably well, falling asleep as she pondered over kissing Daniel. No, not Daniel. She refused to use his given name. If she did, it might speak of an intimacy between them.

She had received her kiss from him. He had promised it was coming—and she had been eager to experience it. Now that she had, she saw how bewitching the duke could be. She must stand firm because she had goals in mind, ones which did not involve kissing dukes. She would have to contend with reliving their kiss every now and then. It had been good experience for her, to feel desire simmering in her blood. But no more. She was to be an artist. Hopefully, a highly sought-after one after last night's venture.

After she washed, she sat at the small desk within her bed-chamber and dashed off a quick note to Mr. Dickens. He had been Papa's London solicitor and Margaret had been in contact with him both before and after her father's death. She decided it was time to meet with him face-to-face and discuss the dowry which would come into her possession six weeks from now.

Ringing for a maid, she had the servant help dress her and then sought the butler, asking him to see to the delivery of the note. He assured her a footman would deliver it within the hour.

Making her way to the breakfast room, she saw only her brother-in-law there, recalling that Dolley had revealed once the Season began, she usually breakfasted in her room.

"Good morning, my lord. How was your rout last night?"

He shrugged. "A rout is a rout. People standing about gossiping. I would have rather been at the Rawlins' card party, to be quite frank." He closed the newspaper he was reading and set it aside. "It seems you had a run of luck last night."

She frowned. "How so?"

"The gossip columns report this morning that you and the Duke of Westfield took the prize given for whist."

"That is already in the newspapers?" she asked.

He nodded. "Along with the fact that you are to paint the Dowager Duchess of Westfield's portrait."

She drew in a quick breath. "May I see it, please?"

He signaled a servant, and the footman came to claim the newspaper and brought it to Margaret. She flipped through the pages, coming to the gossip columns, and began to read slowly. What she read pleased her immensely. They reported how Lady Margaret Townsend was to paint the portrait of one of the *ton*'s leading figures, the Dowager Duchess of Westfield, even quoting the dowager duchess, who praised Lady Margaret's talent.

This would do it. All London society would be reading this, whether at their breakfast tables or in their boudoirs. Her name would be on the lips of most everyone at tonight's ball. Satisfaction filled her.

And yet the excitement she thought would come with such news seemed to ring hollow within her. She frowned. It was Westfield's doing. He had distracted her from her goals. She couldn't let images of him fill her head. She needed to remain focused on what she wanted to do. How she wished to live her life.

It wouldn't be with a duke. Especially an arrogant one who kissed extremely well. He would be the kind of man who would wed and bed his bride and get her with child before immediately returning to his mistress.

The thought of Westfield having a mistress angered her. No, she couldn't be jealous. Could she? They had no understanding whatsoever. She wasn't even sure if she liked him all that much. Better to think of other things.

Margaret ate her breakfast, the marquess returning to his newspaper. Then the butler brought in the morning's post. To her surprise, the majority of it was addressed to her. She excused herself, taking it with her to her bedchamber. In solitude, she read through each note. Every one of them expressed interest in having her paint the writer or a member of his or her family. She should be thrilled.

Yet doubt now plagued her.

What if she wasn't as good as she thought? After all, she had no formal training in art, merely what Grandmama had passed along to her and her years in the country, practicing on servants. She was a bit rusty, having done no painting during her parents' long illnesses, although she had painted Dolley, Baxter, and the children recently.

What if she made a fool of herself?

She refused to give in to such musings. Grandmama had been an artist. So was Margaret. She would paint the Dowager Duchess of Westfield with certainty and ease. Painting portraits was her calling. She was meant to do so.

Arranging the letters she had received in two stacks, Margaret separated them by the people she had met and those she had yet to be introduced to. Of those she had met, she placed them in the order of interest she had in painting the particular person mentioned within the letter. As she came to know the others, she would slip them into the first stack, until the two blended together as one.

A knock sounded upon her door, and a maid entered, bearing a letter.

"For you, my lady. It just came, separate from the morning post."

She accepted it and dismissed the servant. To her delight, it was from Mr. Dickens, who was eager to visit with her. He told her if she had any time today, he would be happy to see her. Margaret retrieved her favorite bonnet and placed it upon her head and gathered her reticule. She decided to look in on Dolley before she left and went to her sister's rooms.

Dolley was sprawled upon a fainting couch, looking miserable. As Margaret came toward her, Dolley's eyes widened and she bent, retching in the chamber pot at her feet.

"I despise being with child," her sister said, wiping her mouth with a cloth. "This time it better be a boy. Then I am done with Baxter." Her eyes flicked over Margaret. "I hear you were quite the success at the little card party. That everyone wishes for you to paint them."

"The Dowager Duchess of Westfield was most kind. With but a few sentences of praise, word spread that I was painting her and how pleased she was that I was doing so. Several at the Rawlins' party discussed having me paint their portraits."

"I suppose that is a good thing," her sister remarked.

"I believe it is. I have long dreamed of doing this very thing."

Dolley's eyes narrowed. "You won at cards with His Grace."

Margaret felt heat rise in her cheeks. "I did not know he would escort us there. His grandmother insisted we partner together."

"You could not refuse the dowager duchess, I suppose."

"No. Fortunately, His Grace is excellent at whist." She left out that she was, as well.

"Did you tell her about tea with me?"

"No. I thought it best for you to extend the invitation yourself. After all, this is your home. You are the marchioness."

"I will write to her now," Dolley declared. "Where are you

off to?"

"To see Mr. Dickens." When her sister looked blank, Margaret added, "He was Papa's solicitor and now mine. I wish to discuss my dowry with him, as well as ask his advice on which bank to set up an account. If I am to paint members of Polite Society, then I will be receiving funds from these commissions. I need financial advice and an institute in which to store my earnings."

Her sister flicked her wrist, waving a hand that Margaret knew was dismissing her. She made her goodbyes and promised to return for calling hours this afternoon.

Downstairs, she asked the butler if one of the maids or footmen might accompany her to her appointment with Mr. Dickens. He called for a maid and then had a footman stop a hackney cab since the marquess had already left in the carriage for his club.

Margaret and the maid entered the cab and within twenty minutes, they had arrived at Mr. Dickens's offices. She paid the cab driver and entered with the maid in tow. A clerk greeted them, and the maid was left to wait on a bench as Margaret was escorted to Mr. Dickens's office.

He rose as she entered, a jovial smile on his face, his bald pate shining. "My dear Lady Margaret, I was delighted to receive your note. Please, have a seat."

She did so and he said, "Have you come to discuss your dowry?"

"I have. I would also like some advice from you."

Quickly, she outlined her situation and how she would be painting the portraits of members of the *ton*, beginning with the Dowager Duchess of Westfield.

"I will need to establish a relationship with a bank."

"I have just the bank and banker, my lady. Once we have concluded our business here, I would be happy to escort you there."

They talked over the terms of the dowry and how it was to go to her husband if she wed before the coming of June first. If not, control of the monies would revert to her.

"When you do wed, my lady, you will have no dowry to present to your husband—unless you wish to designate all or a portion of it and turn it over to your betrothed."

"I have no plans to wed, Mr. Dickens. None at all. And if by some miniscule chance that did occur, I would insist upon remaining in control of my money—both this dowry and any commissions I receive from my portraits completed."

"I see." His rubbed his chin in thought.

"I would also like to seek my own quarters," she announced. "I have been staying with my sister and her husband. I do not wish to be an inconvenience to them."

"Your sister can be quite demanding," he said diplomatically.

"She can. I would prefer to have somewhere of my own, which would include space for my studio. I wish to paint from home. I need to lease a place where I could use the top floor as my working space. It would need a good deal of natural light."

"That might prove difficult now, with the Season going on," he said. "Places are let rather quickly and little will be available."

"I do not wish for a grand house, Mr. Dickens. After all, it will be only me. And a handful of servants, I suppose."

"Let me look into it for you, Lady Margaret. Is there anything else we need to discuss?"

"Not at this time. Might we go now and see the banker you are recommending?"

He rose. "I think it a splendid idea."

The solicitor escorted her and her maid to the bank, where Margaret set up an account. Mr. Dickens explained the situation regarding Margaret's dowry and how a large deposit would be made to her account six weeks from now, on her twenty-fifth birthday.

Mr. Dickens saw her and her maid home to Mayfair, telling her he would be in touch with her regarding the leased property.

As she and the maid entered the townhouse, the girl asked, "Will you be leaving us, my lady?"

"I most likely will."

"You will be missed," the servant said. "You're a favorite in the servants' hall."

"That is kind of you to say."

"You are the kind one, my lady." The girl paused. "If you have need of help, I would be happy to go with you."

This maid had helped dress Margaret a few times and done a good job. She would definitely need someone to do so once she left Dolley's, as well as someone to cook and clean for her.

"I will think on it," she promised. "Will you help me change my gown now? It is almost time for afternoon callers."

"Of course, my lady."

"What is your name?" she asked as they went up the stairs.

"Molly, my lady.

Molly helped Margaret change into a mint green gown, pinning a few stray locks of hair which had escaped. She thanked the servant and then made her way to the drawing room, her belly filling with butterflies.

"Stop," she told herself, knowing it was because Daniel was coming. Westfield. Not Daniel. And he wouldn't arrive until just before it was time to leave. She wouldn't see him for another two hours or so, close to the end of the time when callers were leaving.

Until she entered the drawing room and found him already there.

CHAPTER FOURTEEN

DANIEL GLANCED AROUND the large drawing room. Every surface was filled with a bouquet. He knew they all had to be for Margaret. He should be delighted that she had become popular in so short a time. Many who made their debut into Polite Society barely caused a ripple. Others were a flash in the pan, their stars burning brightly and then flickering out even before the Season ended. Others endured, however, making brilliant matches and setting the pace within the *ton* for years to come.

Lady Margaret Townsend definitely fell into the final group.

Their kiss had made a lasting impression upon him. He rarely kissed a woman. Even when he had a mistress, which he currently did not, any kiss with her was cursory. He had always believed himself immune to kissing.

Until last night.

He could have kissed Margaret all night long, until the sun came up—and he would have gone on kissing her far into the day. He had teased her, telling her kissing was fun, but he hadn't truly believed it.

Now, he most certainly did. And he planned to repeat his actions with her as soon as humanly possible.

Though the side of his face was sore and his eye both black and swollen from her punch, Daniel's step felt lighter than it had since he had taken on the heavy mantle of Duke of Westfield. Gran had begged him to set aside his duties and enjoy being young and having a title and wealth. He had hoped he could do so until he became more familiar with the estate. The longer he was Westfield, the more he saw how much there was to do. Daniel wasn't a man to foist his responsibilities upon another. True, he did have a business manager and a solicitor. Stewards at all five of his estates to manage the daily tasks. In the long run, though, he did more because he knew it was expected of him. That, and the fact that others depended upon him.

It had caused him to grow glum and sober by the time he turned thirty. Margaret coming into his life brought a lightness to his being. He enjoyed their verbal sparring and looking at her beauty. He appreciated her warmth and intelligence.

He also was impatient to have her in his bed.

As a lady of virtue, however, she would not come to it willingly. No, he would have to propose marriage to her. To a woman who didn't wish to wed. One who wanted to follow her dreams and have a career of her own when women in Polite Society simply did not do something so dashedly bold.

Could he pledge himself to a woman that might love her art more than she did him?

He cursed under his breath, thinking love had no place in this equation. He didn't believe it existed. He'd had no example of it in his family and had never witnessed it among his friends or acquaintances in society. Yet a part of him yearned so for Margaret that it caused him to be one mass of raw ache. Daniel did not think he could be whole without her by his side, in his life, arguing with him, cajoling him, kissing him.

Making love with him.

Was he in love with her?

Gran would probably tell him he was if he described his feelings of restlessness and despair. He did want to offer for Margaret. Desperately. Yet he knew without a doubt she would turn him down.

How could he make her see they had a future together?

Even he wasn't certain about that. Yes, he could see himself marrying her—but could he allow her to gallivant about town, painting portraits, when she should be at home seeing to his needs?

He chuckled to himself. Just using the word *allow* would send Margaret into a frenzy. She would berate him for thinking he could exercise such power over her, even if he were her husband. Truth be told, he did not want to see her tremendous spirit broken. He wanted her just the way she was. Daniel thought she wanted him, too. He had seen the raw desire in her eyes last night. Though it was obvious she had never been kissed, somehow within moments she had become an expert at it. Their mouths had melded even as he had longed for their bodies to join together, as well.

He decided to bide his time. By God, he would woo Red. Continue plying her with kisses until he broke through the barrier that surrounded her. He would insist she continue to paint. He would let her do anything she desired to do. After all, she would be a duchess. No one would dare say a disparaging word about his duchess—or he'd have their head.

Lord Baxter entered the room, one eyebrow arched in a quizzical fashion.

"They told me you were here," the marquess said. "You do know, Westfield, that proper calling hours start ten minutes from now?"

"I do," he agreed cheerfully. "I merely wanted to make certain I had a place to stand. From what I gather, you are anticipating a large crowd."

Baxter shook his head. "It's those damned newspapers. They print whatever they wish, and we have to live with it. The chit does have a bit of artistic talent. She painted both Lady Baxter and me and our two children."

Daniel gazed at the marquess steadily. "She is not a chit, my lord. She is Lady Margaret," he said coldly.

"Of course, Your Grace." The marquess looked properly cowed, realizing with but a few words that Daniel might have him and his wife ostracized from Polite Society.

"Do you have your portraits on display?"

"Not yet. They are being framed. That costs a small fortune, I will tell you. But they will most certainly hang in the gallery at my country estate once that has been completed."

He decided he would ask Margaret if she had any other portraits she had painted with her. He would enjoy seeing her work. It might give him an idea of what she would do when she painted Gran. He was glad this was being done. A portrait of her existed from decades ago and hung in the portrait gallery at his country seat. Gran had been a woman of great beauty, barely in her twenties when the portrait had been completed. Daniel would see that they hung side-by-side once Margaret finished her version.

He sensed the door opening and glanced toward it. Margaret rushed in, wearing a gown of palest green, her hair dressed in a fashion he had not yet seen on her. She stopped in her tracks when she spied him.

"Oh!"

She swallowed, her cheeks flushing with color. She nibbled on her bottom lip, and he suspected it was her only bad habit. Still, it was one which made him aware of her lips and how much he wished to brush his against hers.

"As you see, my lady, our first caller is early," the marquess said. "I was entertaining him."

"Thank you, my lord." She came toward them and curtseyed to Daniel. "Your Grace. How good of you to come. I was not expecting you until the end of calling hours."

He grinned, happy to see her. "I was afraid I might not find a spot in Baxter's drawing room if I delayed. You still are coming to tea with my grandmother today, aren't you?"

"I said I would. I always keep my word."

"As do I," he replied, wishing Baxter would leave them alone and knowing he wouldn't.

"Oh, Your Grace!" Lady Baxter swept into the room, all smiles, and came straight to him, offering her own curtsey. "How wonderful to see you." She glanced to her husband. "How good of you to keep His Grace company, Baxter."

"He has the two of you now to entertain him. I am off to my club."

When he had gone, Margaret asked, "Whatever do men *do* at their club? Baxter spends an inordinate amount of time at his."

"Most likely the same thing women would do if they had a club of their own to go to," he replied.

A faraway look appeared in her eyes. He could almost see the wheels turning in her head.

"What a lovely idea, Your Grace," she said.

"I wrote to your grandmother today," Lady Baxter interjected. "I asked her to come to tea tomorrow. I do hope you can accompany the duchess, Your Grace."

He doubted Gran would care to come to tea with Lady Baxter, knowing she did not hold the woman in high regard. Still, she would probably accept the invitation since it came from Margaret's sister. He also wondered why the marchioness was suddenly wishing to cozy up to Gran, especially when she had forbidden Margaret to dance with her grandson.

"That is very thoughtful of you, my lady. I would be happy to do so." He turned to Margaret. "Perhaps we might even go for a drive through the park afterward?"

Daniel saw he had caught her off-guard. So did her sister, who replied, "Margaret, do you have another engagement after tea tomorrow?"

"I will need to consult my diary," she said primly.

He coughed, covering the laughter that bubbled up from within him. Margaret might be the death of him—but he would meet it happily—especially if he had spent a lifetime in her company beforehand.

The butler entered and announced the first callers of the afternoon. Soon, the drawing was swarming with guests. At first,

Daniel stood in a small circle surrounding Margaret, but he had better manners than to continually remain by her side. Besides, he needed to give her a chance to spread her wings a bit and mix in Polite Society, hoping he would compare favorably to the numerous callers who populated the drawing room.

Finally, calling hours concluded. Daniel watched the last swain depart and then moved to rejoin Margaret and her sister, who waved a fan furiously and looked a bit pale.

"Sit down, Dolley," Margaret suggested. "Or would you rather go upstairs and lie down?"

"I may do so," Lady Baxter agreed. "A cup of tea and a nap would be welcomed before tonight's ball."

"I will see you this evening, my lady," Daniel said gallantly, and the marchioness took her leave.

"I must collect my bonnet and reticule," Margaret said, her shaking voice betraying her nerves.

She turned to go, but he caught her wrist and pulled her toward him, their bodies close, their faces even closer.

"What are you doing?" she whispered.

"It is only us now, Red." He moved toward her, intending to kiss her.

She shoved him away. "Anyone might come through that door and see us. Any moment a servant could walk through in order to straighten the room or dust or some other such activity."

He caught her hands again, lacing his fingers through hers. "Would that be so terrible?"

She sniffed. "You are not the kind of man who would wish to be trapped into a marriage, Pestfield. I am certainly not the kind of woman who would be forced to enter one under such circumstances."

But he saw her weakening. She licked her lips, as if anticipating what might come next.

"You are right," he agreed, not wanting a servant to come across them and find them in an embrace. He didn't want Margaret to be forced into wedding him. He needed her to come to him willingly.

"I am glad you see it my way," she said stiffly.

Was that disappointment in her eyes?

"I will make it up to you," he promised, releasing her hands.

She eyed him with suspicion. "What does that mean?"

It meant that he planned to kiss her in the carriage. He had not brought his phaeton or curricle, where he would be occupied driving it. No, he had brought his carriage.

Because he was going to kiss Margaret Townsend the entire way home.

CHAPTER FIFTEEN

MARGARET EXCUSED HERSELF, telling Daniel that she needed to collect her bonnet and reticule before they departed, and she would meet him in the foyer in ten minutes. As she hurried up the stairs to her bedchamber, she pondered this afternoon.

Though Daniel had not stayed by her side the entire time, she was aware of his presence every minute. Even as she spoke to others, she had felt his gaze upon her. She had done her best not to let it unnerve her.

It surprised her that she had received even more bouquets today than yesterday. Though she had not been at a largely attended event the previous evening, that did not limit the number of gentlemen calling upon her at the Baxter drawing room this afternoon. Margaret supposed she was gaining a bit of notoriety, first by having danced with a duke twice in one evening and then partnering with him again in cards at his request last night. She would be hard-pressed to have found a single visitor who had not read the gossip columns in today's newspapers. Because simply everyone seemed to mention the fact that she would be painting the portrait of the Dowager Duchess of Westfield.

She had to give the old woman credit. By inviting Margaret to do so and then mentioning the commission to a handful of others, it had brought ample attention to Margaret as an artist, separate from being the daughter of an earl and a lady making her come-out into society. She needed to commence with the portrait as soon as possible so that it might be completed. Then, the dowager duchess could hold her party for others to see the work. Once they did, Margaret was confident she would be able to book a few sessions with other clients, carefully selecting those to paint. She would also need to discover which members of the *ton* remained in town once the Season ended. She would like to set up those appointments so that by the time the majority of Polite Society returned to London next spring, they would hear about— and hopefully see—her works on display.

Reaching her room, she quickly freshened up, washing her hands and securing a stray curl. She had enjoyed circulating about the room this afternoon and felt she had done so with ease, greeting their guests, even as she wondered how many of them viewed her as a novelty and if there were a few who might actually consider pursuing her. She told herself she would not be prickly with them as she had been with Daniel, telling him up front that she had no intentions of marrying. Rather, she would try to get to know those who called upon her over the next few weeks. Not because she wanted to wed any of them, but because it had been so long since she had been around others. Caring for her parents had been isolating, as well as the year she had spent mourning Papa's death. It simply felt good to be out and about in the company of others again, even though it proved a bit exhausting.

Placing her bonnet atop her head and tying its ribbons, she reflected upon a conversation she had overheard. As she listened to one viscount who, in all honesty, was very nice but exceptionally boring, she nodded vaguely and eavesdropped on the two lords to her left.

Because they had been discussing Daniel.

One had remarked that he was surprised to see the duke present in the drawing room, while the other had mentioned that

Westfield had both danced and played cards with Lady Margaret. The first then noted that the duke rarely was seen at any *ton* affairs, much less two nights in a row.

His companion had revealed that he had known Westfield at school and considered him quite fun-loving and lighthearted during those years. It was only after he gained his title that he had sobered considerably. Both men noted they never saw him smile.

She had wondered about their conversation. True, Daniel could be a bit solemn at times, but he also smiled quite a bit around her. He was also argumentative, though she knew it was all in good fun as he teased her. Besides, he was searching for a bride. That was why he had returned to the Season this year. Still, it bothered her that he had seemingly not had any fun since he had come into his title. She hoped the woman he chose for his duchess would make him happy.

As she slipped her reticule onto her wrist and left her bed-chamber, she ignored the flare of jealousy at the thought of him having a wife, which was absolutely ridiculous. Of course, he would wed. He must in order to produce an heir to the dukedom. She had no intentions of wedding him or any other gentleman.

So why would that bother her so?

Rejoining him in the foyer, Margaret stepped outside with Daniel and saw his gleaming black carriage awaiting them. A sudden thought filled her with dismay.

"I am new at this and neglected to summon a maid to act as my chaperone, Your Grace. I must return inside and see if one is available to accompany us."

He clucked his tongue. "Come now, Red. We are only going to be traveling a few blocks."

"It does not matter if it is a few blocks or to Bristol," she bristled. "It would be one thing if we were in your curricle and others could see us. Quite another to be inside a carriage, all alone. I refuse to be gossiped about."

Daniel smiled, his eyes twinkling at her. "Oh, Red, I think there has been plenty of gossip about you. Most of it good, thanks to my grandmother, if the number of callers you had today was any indication. Still, I understand your concerns." He sighed. "Go collect your maid."

"Why don't we simply walk?" she questioned. "It is not but a few blocks to your townhouse. I am a country girl at heart and have always enjoyed a bit of walking." She paused. "After all, we have walked from your residence to here once before."

"Very well. I will dismiss my driver."

Margaret watched him give a brief word to the coachman, who nodded and tipped his cap to the duke. He stepped back as the carriage pulled away. He joined her, offering his arm, and they set off in the direction of his townhouse in companionable silence.

He did not make any effort at conversation, for which she was grateful. In truth, she felt exhausted after having entertained others for the past two hours. He seemed to realize that. She relished the feel of his arm, however. If anything, this man was all hard muscle, something she had come to appreciate. She noted the shiner she had given him yesterday and decided she should ask for forgiveness once more from him.

"I did want to apologize once more and tell you how sorry I am for blackening your eye."

"I startled you. No need for apologies."

"I am still mortified to have done so. Lord Rawlins mentioned something about a gentleman in connection with it?"

"Gentleman Jackson. He is a former professional boxer who now runs a gymnasium for men of the *ton*. Many go there and take boxing lessons from him or one of his assistants, as well as spar with partners. It was easier to let Lord Rawlins think that I had somehow let my guard down and received my shiner while sparring there." He grinned at her. "Instead of admitting that my lovely female companion had landed the blow."

They arrived at his townhouse, and he led her inside, where the butler told them tea would be served once more in the dowager duchess's sitting room.

As he led her there, Daniel said, "You and Gran aren't chasing me off this time. I intend to get a proper tea in me today. I won't say a word and interrupt your hen party of two, but I do plan to have a slice of cake, along with a sandwich or two."

"It is your home, Your Grace. You may have tea in whatever room you wish."

He burst out laughing. "That was not your attitude before. Of course, you and Gran were hatching your scheme."

"It is not a scheme," she insisted. "I am merely painting her. It is what I do."

"Would you ever consider painting me?" he asked.

Should she admit she already had?

"You should wait and see how Her Grace's portrait turns out and then ask me again after you have seen it."

They reached the door to the sitting room, and he stopped. "I do not have to see your work to know you are immensely talented, Red. I would be honored for you to paint me."

Her throat thickened with sudden emotion. His confidence in her was surprising and yet very humbling.

"Thank you, Daniel," she said quietly. "I appreciate your kind words."

Though her father had always encouraged Margaret in her art, he had not seemed to place much faith in it. He had looked upon it more as a hobby and had not understood her desire to make it her life's work. Her mother, on the other hand, had openly scoffed when Margaret painted their servants. She had told her younger daughter no good would come of wishing to paint people. To have Daniel's faith in her, sight unseen, was quite moving.

As they entered the sitting room, she saw the dowager duchess smile fondly. Though she had only known this woman a few days, she already had warm feelings regarding her.

Margaret went to the settee and sat beside the dowager duchess, who took her hands and squeezed them.

"I am delighted you could come for a second day in a row and have tea with me." The dowager duchess paused. "I see Westfield will be joining us today. I promise not to live strictly in the past and recount stories from long ago."

He bent and kissed his grandmother's cheek, taking a seat. "You know I love to hear stories from you, no matter what decade they concern."

The teacart arrived then and once more, Margaret was asked to pour out for them. She did so and they began talking comfortably, as if they had all known one another for many years.

Finally, their talk turned to the portrait.

"When will you begin this project, Lady Margaret?" Daniel asked.

She appreciated that he addressed her formally and reminded herself to do the same, although he was becoming Daniel to her more and more.

"I have already begun a few sketches of Her Grace," she shared. "I will show them to her if she comes to tea at Baxter's tomorrow."

"The invitation form Lady Baxter surprised me," the dowager duchess said. "We have never been on friendly terms."

Margaret chuckled. "It seems my sister is eager to strengthen the connection between herself and a dowager duchess. She also asked His Grace to tea, as well."

The woman looked at her grandson. "I did not realize you would be included in the invitation. Lady Baxter made no mention of that."

"She asked me this afternoon when I called upon Lady Margaret. I told her I would be happy to escort you to tea." He looked to Margaret. "I also asked Lady Margaret if she might wish to drive with me in Hyde Park afterward. Did you have a chance to consult your diary?"

Her cheeks heated. "It might prove to be an inconvenience, Your Grace. Naturally, you would bring Her Grace in your carriage. You would have to then see her home before returning for me. My understanding is the point of driving through the park during the fashionable hour is to be seen, which means you would need to have an open air vehicle. By the time all that coming and going occurred, I fear the park would be deserted."

"I am always one to find a solution, my lady. My carriage will convey Gran to your brother-in-law's residence tomorrow. I will follow in my curricle. That way, the carriage can take her home and the two of us can leave immediately after tea for the park. That is, *if* you are available, of course."

She saw no way to wriggle out of his invitation and so graciously said, "I am glad you thought of a solution so quickly, Your Grace. I would be happy to accompany you on a drive tomorrow afternoon."

He smiled, and the smile reached his eyes, unlike many people. She liked that about him.

She liked him . . .

Once again, Margaret knew she was treading upon dangerous ground where the duke was concerned. She could not let him have the upper hand, much less bully her into following his agenda when she clearly had one of her own.

"I have decided the perfect background for my portrait would be my roses in the garden," the dowager duchess interjected. "Lady Margaret needs to see them, though. We are done with tea, Westfield. Why don't you escort her to the gardens now and show her the best of my rose bushes?"

She turned to Margaret. "You might even want to bring your sketchpad the next time you visit me, my dear, and capture my roses. Are you comfortable drawing flowers since you specialize in people?"

"When Grandmama put a pencil in my hand, flowers were the first thing I sketched. She would take me on long walks about the estate, and I drew both flora and fauna before I ever did people. The hardest thing will be to capture the exact shade of your roses. Have no fears, Your Grace, for I enjoy that part of the artistic process. Mixing colors for a gown is very similar to doing so for flowers."

The dowager duchess patted her hand. "That is good to know. Go now and tour the gardens and see what you think."

She and Daniel rose and he led her to a set of French doors nearby, saying, "It will be quicker to go this way, my lady."

Opening them, he gestured for her to step outside, and she did so. He slipped her hand through the crook of his arm, and they leisurely strolled toward the gardens, which were a stone's throw away.

"Gran has always loved her flowers. Unlike most women of the *ton*, she enjoyed digging in the dirt, actually planting them herself. She pruned her rose bushes each year and even cut flowers from them, arranging the roses herself. Nowadays, however, she is too infirm to accomplish those tasks. Instead, she accompanies a gardener a few times a week, pointing out what needs to be done and indicating which blooms he is to cut. She still arranges them, though. It is something she has always enjoyed."

They entered the gardens, and Margaret saw how well-tended they were. They passed a wide range of flowers and shrubbery in vivid colors before they reached the center of the gardens. A large gazebo stood in the middle, roses surrounding it, their sweet, intense scent wafting over her.

"Oh!" she exclaimed. "This would be a marvelous setting for your grandmother's portrait. Why, I could paint her sitting on that bench, the trellis behind her, roses surrounding her. Go sit there for a moment if you would."

They stepped into the gazebo, and Daniel moved to the stone bench, plopping down.

Waggling his eyebrows, he asked, "Shall I pose for you?" and then did so, looking stern, then mischievous, then downright silly as he crossed his eyes and twisted his mouth.

Margaret laughed, enjoying seeing this playful side of him.

"Quit wiggling about," she ordered. "Sit up. Your grandmother has excellent posture. So should a duke."

He did so.

"Now, turn your knees slightly to the left."

He followed her instructions again.

"Drop your right shoulder slightly. No, not like that." She paused. "And tilt your chin up slightly."

He didn't seem to follow directions well, and so she moved toward him, thinking to correct him and then step back to see the pose.

When she reached him, she took his chin in hand. "Like this," she said, her heart beginning to beat faster. She had removed her gloves before tea began and had neglected to replace them before this stroll. Her bare fingers brushed against his chin, feeling a bit of stubble. His valet must have shaved him quite early this morning and would most likely do so again before tonight's ball.

Daniel reached up, his fingers fastening around her wrist. Butterflies exploded inside her belly as their gazes met.

Gently, he tugged on her—and Margaret suddenly found herself on the Duke of Westfield's lap.

Chapter Sixteen

D ANIEL HAD LOST his opportunity to kiss Margaret repeatedly in the carriage, thanks to her being so skittish about her reputation. He could not blame her. While Polite Society forgave rogues—and especially dukes—almost any transgression, a woman was quite a different matter. Already, Margaret was flouting convention by trying to paint portraits. She walked a fine line of being an interesting novelty and a scandal. He would avoid placing her deep within a scandal around others.

Now, however, no one was nearby. He intended to convince her they were meant to be together. A need had grown within him, causing his desire for her to flare into something he had never experienced before. He needed Margaret Townsend to want him.

Because he wanted her . . .

The moment she fell onto his lap, Daniel went to work, knowing his powers of persuasion were strong. Both his hands held her waist, and his mouth sought hers, no softness about this kiss evident. It was born of greed and need and desire. His lips met hers and he knew this woman was for him.

He kissed her over and over, licking and nipping until she opened to him. When she did, she tasted of the honeyed sweet bun she had eaten at tea, along with a sweetness that was hers alone. His tongue mated with hers, and a fierce possessiveness swept through him, knowing he was the only man who had ever kissed her.

He would be the only man who ever did so.

His thumbs arched upward, grazing her ribs, brushing the bottoms of her beautifully rounded breasts. The thought of those breasts enticed him, and he broke their kiss, hearing her sound of protest. Daniel trailed his lips down the long column of her throat until he reached the rounded globes peeking from the neckline of her gown. His tongue traced over them, and she wriggled a little on his lap, causing his cock to swell. He brought an arm around her waist in order to anchor her and then his fingers slipped into her gown, freeing one breast. He saw the rosy tip beckoning to him, and his mouth was upon it, his tongue swirling around it.

Margaret moved restlessly, her arms going about him and pressing him to her breast, causing him to smile. He allowed his teeth to graze across the nipple, and she sucked in a quick breath, followed by a long sigh. Her fingers crept up and pushed into his hair, gripping his scalp as he feasted upon her breast. The little noises she made from the back of her throat told him he was doing everything right. He broke the contact and heard her small protest as he slipped her breast back into her gown, quickly removing the other one and devouring it. Her fingers tightened against his scalp, kneading him like a kitten as it drank from its mother.

He sucked and laved her breast, thinking it the most delicious thing he had ever tasted. But he wanted more of her. Needed more of her. He intended to take full advantage of this time alone with her and brand her as his.

Once more, he slipped her breast back into place and kissed his way up to her mouth again. This time, she opened readily for him and kissed him back, no longer satisfied to sit back. Instead, she was a more than willing participant. Because of that, he decided to take things a step further. His arm still held her secure in place on his lap so he allowed his free hand to go exploring. It slipped under her gown, and he stroked her shapely calf. She murmured something, but he kept moving his fingers up and down lightly, reaching her knee and then her thigh. He moved to her inner thigh, knowing how sensitive the flesh was there, and felt her shiver in delight. His fingers danced along the smooth skin, moving higher and higher until they reached her core. Daniel felt her stiffen as he toyed with the curls nestled there. He took a finger and slowly stroked the seam of her sex, causing her to gasp.

Margaret broke the kiss, her eyes wide as she gazed at him. Once again, he caressed the slit the entire length, smiling at her.

"What are you doing?" she whispered.

"I am going to give you pleasure. Pleasure you have never known, Red." He hesitated, afraid to ask, but knowing he should. "Do you trust me?"

"I do," she said immediately, causing a glow to light within him.

"Kiss me," he urged, wanting her to take the lead now.

"All right," she agreed, lowering her mouth to his.

He let her be the aggressor now. She had learned her lessons well, teasing his lips open and plunging her tongue into his mouth. She explored him without apology, and he began stroking her core once more. This time, he pushed a finger inside her and stroked her deeply. She gasped into his mouth but continued kissing him. He thought that an excellent sign.

Daniel had always tried to please women he coupled with, but never more so than in this moment with this woman. He continued his caresses as they kissed passionately, pushing a second finger inside her and finding the beautiful bud that would help her passion explode. He only wished his mouth were there instead of his fingers.

And told himself soon . . .

Margaret began moaning softly, her hips moving now, meeting each stroke. Her juices flowed freely, and he knew she was on the cusp of paradise. Her whimpers became louder and as he pressed hard against the bud, he muffled her cries with a deep kiss and felt the orgasm rip through her body. Wordlessly, he encouraged her to ride out the waves of pleasure, and she did so with enthusiasm. Her trembling finally ceased. He slipped his fingers from her, gentling his kiss, and finally breaking it altogether.

Her eyes were glazed, her jaw slack, her lips swollen from the many kisses they had shared.

"What . . . *was* that?"

"That, Red, was me satisfying you. It is called an orgasm."

"Orgasm," she echoed softly. "Why does no one speak of this? I had no idea my body could respond in such a way."

That let him know she had never discovered how to pleasure herself. Once more, he felt a smug satisfaction that he had been the one to introduce her to this.

Boldly, she looked at him and asked, "Can I do that to you?"

If he had taken a sip of brandy at that moment, he would have spewed it out.

"Surely," she continued, "if women can experience something so glorious, men should be able to do so, as well. You have given me a precious gift, Daniel. I would like to return it to you."

"Perhaps another time, Red." He thought her generous to think of him—then something occurred to him. He thought to warn her and said, "This is not something to speak of with anyone. It is something that occurs in private between a man and a woman. That is why you have not heard it discussed over tea."

She nodded solemnly. "I understand. I know if anyone had come across us, I would be ruined—and you would have been forced to wed me. From what I gather, even being seen chastely kissing a man can cause a woman's downfall."

She cocked her head, studying him a moment. "I don't think you would know how to give a chaste kiss, Daniel. The ones you bestow upon me cause a tremendous fire within me. It feels as if my blood has heated to a boiling point and wants to spill from me."

Margaret leaned close and softly pressed her lips against his.

"Thank you for kissing me. For touching me. I have never been kissed before I met you and obviously never done—this—before you. I will never do so again, but these sweet memories will stay with me a lifetime."

"You are still determined not to wed?" he asked.

She nodded. "I wish to devote myself to my art. I know of no man in Polite Society who would give his wife such free rein as to be an artist. One who accepts payment for her work. It would be too scandalous."

Daniel wanted to say that he would and hesitated. He didn't know if he wanted his duchess to have such independence. He had thought he would be able to let Margaret forge her own path, but now doubt filled him.

Bloody hell.

He did not think of himself as one who conformed to the *ton*'s code. He hadn't for many years, playing the rogue while he was a viscount. With the dukedom coming to him, however, he had played by Polite Society's rules. Perhaps too much so. Could he make Margaret his duchess and give her such tremendous freedom? He wanted her more than he had any other woman. But he knew there were limits as to what even he might be able to manage. He would have to give this some thought before he made any kind of declaration to her.

Resting his hand on her thigh, he said, "You have seen the roses now and know where you wish to paint Gran. Perhaps we should return to the house."

He stood, bringing her with him, reluctant to release her but knowing he must. He set Margaret on her feet and then kissed her softly on her swollen lips. They would need to avoid Gran. If she saw Margaret, she would know exactly what they had been up to and demand they wed.

Margaret smoothed her gown and asked, "Do I have any stray locks that have come loose?"

"One," he told her, tucking it behind her ear, loving the feel of her red, silky tresses. He could picture them spilling about her, fanned against a pillow as she gazed up at him.

Daniel pushed the thought aside and took his time leading her back to the house.

"Thank you again," she told him. "For showing me something about myself. About life. About what can pass between a man and a woman. I am eager to reflect on these new feelings, and I know they will find their way into my art."

"Is everything about art to you?" he asked, curious about the passion she felt for it.

Her face glowed with wonder as she breathlessly said, "Oh, yes. It is hard to explain, I suppose, to someone who has no interest in art or talent for it. There are times when it consumes me. An idea strikes—and I simply must get it down. Through a sketch. With my brush and paints. I am the one who brings it into existence. Who gives it life. Who can allow it to shine for others to see."

"You do feel strongly about your art."

Her eyes twinkled now with mischief. "I most certainly do. It is the way I can express myself. *Be* my true self. Show others how I view the world and life. Art is about beauty. Truth. It should evoke an emotional response within us. Teach us. It is transformative in every way that matters."

Her words moved him. Margaret was so passionate about art, something he had, for the most part, ignored his entire life. Yet hearing her speak of it made him long to see what she saw. Experience what she did. Her point of view let him know just how limited his own had been.

By the time they returned to his grandmother's sitting room, her color was no longer high, and her lips looked almost normal. It did not matter. Gran was not present.

Margaret collected her bonnet and reticule and without asking, they strolled to the Baxter townhouse.

At the door, he asked, "Will I see you at tonight's ball?"

"We will be there."

That was all he needed to know. Lady Margaret Townsend

intrigued him more than any woman Daniel had ever met. Both her looks and intelligence appealed to him, as did her passion for her art. If she could feel so strongly about it, he believed he could unlock that passion in other areas, particular ones which occurred in the bedroom between lovers. He determined to claim two dances again tonight so that every gentleman of the *ton* would know he intended to make this woman his. He didn't require time to mull over the situation.

He was a duke. A leader in society. One who set the pace which others followed. If his duchess wanted to paint to make herself happy, he would do everything in his power to see that occurred. No thinking was necessary on his part. Only action.

"Until tonight," Daniel said, raising her hand and kissing her fingers.

CHAPTER SEVENTEEN

M ARGARET WENT TO her bedchamber. She needed time to be alone.

Time to think about the Duke of Westfield.

And what he did to her.

She shut the door and moved across the room, discarding her reticule and removing her bonnet, then sitting in a chair. It wasn't merely how he had touched her. It was what now churned within her, filling her with thoughts of him, a constant barrage of images of him in her mind.

She wanted to be with him. Forever. Knowing that was impossible, as he needed a certain kind of woman who would make for a perfect duchess, she would settle for one night.

One night . . .

Would he accept her offer?

She hoped so.

Margaret felt herself changing in subtle ways, all thanks to Daniel. She wanted to please him. Make him laugh. Help him toss off the serious mantle he wore around others so they could see what a kind, humorous man he truly was. She yearned for his kiss. His touch. At the same time, she knew he desired her. That knowledge brought a certain confidence to her, one she might never have experienced if she had not met him.

Though she had no idea where they might be able to arrange

a night together or how it could come about, she trusted he could solve that small problem. The Duke of Westfield could do whatever he put his mind to. She wanted to experience hours alone with him, exploring his large, muscular body. She wanted her blood to sing at his touch. She longed to make him soar to the heavens as she had during what he called an orgasm. Margaret wanted to put a smile on his face—and carry him within her heart until her final day.

She still hadn't changed her mind about marriage. She didn't believe it was for her. And Daniel would most certainly have to wed in order to produce the next little duke.

She would ask him tonight. Somehow, she would pull him into a corner and whisper her request.

And look forward to a night of learning. Feeling. Doing. Her one night with Daniel. Not the Duke of Westfield. Just Daniel, a man who had infiltrated her heart like one of England's finest spies embedding himself among those who supported Bonaparte.

HOURS LATER, MARGARET descended from the Baxter carriage and accompanied her sister and brother-in-law into Lord and Lady Strumbull's townhouse.

"Strumbull will forgive me for skipping the receiving line," Lord Baxter said. "He hates them even more than I do. I am off to the card room." The marquess parted from them.

Unlike before, when others called out greetings to Dolley, this time Margaret was the one recognized and addressed most often. She could tell her sister was miffed at the attention Margaret drew.

"Remember, you are not to dance with the Duke of Westfield," Dolley hissed into her ear as they waited in the receiving line.

"What?" she asked, confused by the remark. "But Dolley, you

said you liked the connection. You even asked His Grace to tea tomorrow."

"Tea is one thing. And yes, I am encouraging a friendship between myself and the dowager duchess. You painting her will be helpful in that regard, but Westfield is a rogue, Margaret. One who will try to steal kisses from you. If you are caught with him, you would pay the price." Dolley frowned. "He would not offer for you."

A blush filled her cheeks as she stubbornly said, "I believe he would, Dolley. He is a good man."

Anger flared in her sister's eyes. "I know what's best for you. Stay away from him."

"You are jealous," she stated flatly. "That is wrong, Dolley, and you know it. You have a husband and two beautiful children, with another on the way."

Distaste filled her sister's face at the mention of her condition. "You are not telling me anything I do not know already. But *I* should have had the duke. Not you."

"You won a marquess, Dolley. A fine title of your own. The admiration of all of Polite Society. You have wealth and properties and every material item you might desire." Margaret paused. "You know I wish to paint others. Do you think a duke would put up with a wife who did so? Of course not. He would forbid it. Ignore the little attention His Grace has paid to me. I have no plans to encourage him to offer for me."

Relief filled Dolley's face. Margaret didn't know where this jealousy stemmed from. Dolley had always been the prettier of them. The more popular. Even if Margaret was searching for a husband, she would have her choice of a handful, not the huge numbers who pursued Dolley during her come-out Season. The only thing she could think of was that Dolley did not wish for Margaret to outrank her.

They greeted Lord and Lady Strumbull and then made their way into the ballroom. She glanced around quickly. The room was about half full, with no sight of Daniel or his grandmother.

They ventured to the left and within moments found themselves swarmed with gentlemen. Some flirted with Dolley and asked her to dance, but a good majority of them begged Margaret for a dance, passing her programme about until it was returned to her, every dance claimed. She smiled brightly.

And wondered how Daniel would react.

After what had passed between them in the gazebo, she was certain he had planned to request a dance from her. He had specifically asked if she would attend tonight's ball.

She carried on several conversations with those around her, both men and women now, but she knew the moment he entered the ballroom. Her gaze lifted and met his as he stood in the entrance, his grandmother on his arm, as they came toward her.

"Ah, Your Graces," Dolley said breathlessly, dipping into a curtsey, which Margaret copied. "Isn't it a delightful evening for a ball?"

"I suppose so," the dowager duchess agreed. "Then again, I always enjoyed dancing and thought every night a perfect one for a ball."

"Speaking of dancing," Daniel said, "might I claim a dance from you, Lady Margaret?"

She swallowed. "I am afraid it is too late to do so, Your Grace. You see, my dance card has already filled."

Fury burned in his eyes a moment, but his features remained schooled. "I regret that I arrived too late. I suppose I should have asked for you to reserve a dance for me."

"Oh, I don't think that appropriate, Your Grace," Dolley said. "However, I have room on my programme." She handed it to him, presuming he would sign it.

"I think not, Lady Baxter," he said, returning the card to her. "I would not want to keep you from your many admirers." Turning to his grandmother, he said, "Gran, we should get you settled."

Margaret didn't have to look at her sister to know she was

seething. "We shall see you at tea then tomorrow, Your Graces," she said, linking her arm through her sister's.

"Yes, tea tomorrow," Dolley echoed. "I am delighted you will be joining us."

After the pair departed, several told Dolley how jealous they were, saying the Dowager Duchess of Westfield rarely accepted invitations of any kind.

"We have formed quite a special relationship," Dolley told the group around them. "The duchess and I are very close."

Margaret groaned inwardly. She hoped her sister would not be caught in her lies.

It came time for the dancing to commence, and her first partner claimed her. The next few hours continued in a blur. She danced. She smiled. She made inane conversation, speaking about the same few, safe topics over and over. Some of her partners were accomplished dancers. A few were far from it. Several were quite good-looking. A couple were plain but nice.

Not a single one of them held her interest.

Because none of them were Daniel.

She always seemed to sense wherever he was in the room. She tamped down the jealousy filling her when she saw him dancing with a beautiful partner. He danced every dance this evening and seemed to be having the time of his life—while she was becoming more miserable by the moment. Margaret had known she would not enjoy the Season before it even began but had considered it a necessary evil in order to build the relationships needed to pursue her career.

What she hadn't counted on was falling in love.

She denied it, telling herself she was wrong. This wasn't love. It was merely desire she felt for this man. A natural thing for a woman to feel. Still, she would keep this knowledge close, sharing it with not another living soul.

The supper dance finally arrived, and she danced it with a tall, lean lord who was a marvelous dancer. Margaret gave herself over to the dance, losing herself in the very waltz which Daniel had taught her a few nights ago. Yet all the magic she had felt in his arms seemed to have vanished, despite the skill of the man she partnered with.

The music ended, and her partner led her into the grand hall where a lavish buffet was spread out upon numerous tables.

"Would you care to go through the line together, Lady Margaret?"

She realized he was speaking to her and quickly smiled. "Of course, my lord."

As they moved toward the line, she tried to recall his name. She had danced with so many different gentlemen this evening, she hadn't a clue whose company she now kept. Surreptitiously, she glanced down, trying to turn her programme.

"It is Lord North, my lady. Viscount North."

She quickly glanced up, seeing mirth sparkling in his eyes. "I am sorry," she apologized.

"No need to do so. You have no doubt danced every number this evening. It is your come-out Season, and there are many faces to come to know, much less putting names with them. I am not offended in the least. I am simply pleased that you agreed to dance with me."

"You are very smooth on your feet, my lord," she complimented.

He laughed. "I will tell my mother you said so. She insisted I take dance lessons years ago, though she first taught me how to dance herself before I began formal lessons. Mama was my first partner and favorite one—until perhaps now."

The gleam in his eyes told Margaret he was interested in her. It caused heat to rise in her cheeks. "Then I will tell your mother what an excellent job she did as a teacher. Who is she?"

"Your hostess tonight. Lady Strumbull," he replied.

"Ah. You favor your father," she noted. "In both looks and your height."

"He would be pleased to hear that," Lord North told her. "I am his only son. We are quite close."

Margaret decided she really liked him and found talking with him a pleasure. They went through the buffet and then joined another couple at a table. She had thought with him being the only son of the household that they would spend the time at the head table. Instead, she saw several couples close to Lord and Lady Strumbull's age had joined their hosts.

Once they finished supping, the viscount said, "Would you care for a brief stroll before the dancing begins again?"

"I would. Thank you."

He led her outside, where several couples moved along the terrace. They discussed his parents' country estate, and she told him a little bit about where she had grown up before the conversation turned to politics, which she enjoyed discussing.

"You are very easy to talk with, Lady Margaret. Most of the women of the *ton* only speak of fashion or gossip about one another. I have found our conversation refreshing. I wonder if you might wish to—"

"Lady Margaret? My grandmother wishes to speak with you," a familiar voice said.

She glanced over Lord North's shoulder and saw Daniel standing there.

"Is Her Grace all right?" she asked.

"She is. But you know Gran. When she wants something, she wants it immediately. I will wager it has something to do regarding her portrait." He looked to the viscount. "Would you excuse us, Lord North?"

"Of course," he said.

Margaret thought the viscount a bit perturbed by being interrupted, though, and wondered what he was going to ask her.

"Perhaps we can continue our conversation tomorrow, my lord?" she asked.

"I would be honored to call upon you if you are agreeable," Lord North said.

"Please do so," she encouraged.

The viscount smiled. "Then I will see you tomorrow afternoon, my lady."

Daniel slipped Margaret's hand through his arm. "Come along, my lady," he said brusquely, leading her away.

She didn't say anything as he led her across the terrace and through the open French doors. They continued through the ballroom and out it, down the corridor.

Suddenly, he pulled her into an alcove, the curtain falling behind them, and his mouth was on hers, stealing her breath. The kiss was demanding, possessive in nature. His arms held her close, so close she could feel his heart hammering in his chest.

The kiss did not satisfy the hunger for him in her. Instead, it only made it burn brighter. She answered its call, needing him more than she should.

He broke the kiss, his forehead resting against hers. "I did not like seeing you with North. Or any other man tonight."

Margaret kept silent. She would not reveal that she, too, had been jealous.

He kissed her again, swiftly, and then framed her face with his hands. "Why didn't you save a dance for me, Red?"

"It was impossible to do so. My programme was passed around and then returned to me, completely filled."

"I wished we could have waltzed together tonight," he said huskily, his lips grazing her ear.

"I have a suggestion. Actually, a question to ask." She swallowed, drawing upon her courage. "You have ... made me curious about . . . many things."

He chuckled. "I am happy to quell your curiosity, Red."

"You know I do not wish to be wed, but I feel I need to explore a few things."

"Things?"

"Things of a nature . . . similar to our time in the gazebo," she said, not quite certain how to express what she wanted. Then Margaret decided to just come out and say it in plain English without beating around the bush.

"I would like to spend one night in your bed, Daniel."

CHAPTER EIGHTEEN

D ANIEL ESCORTED HIS grandmother from the carriage to the door of the Baxter townhouse. His knock was quickly answered by a butler.

"Good afternoon, Your Graces. Won't you please come in?"

They stepped inside, and the butler said, "Tea will be served in the drawing room. I am to take Her Grace there. Lord Baxter wishes to have a private word with you, Your Grace, before the two of you join the ladies."

He wondered what Baxter could possibly have to say to him. There was no way the man could know what Margaret had asked of Daniel last night.

As he followed a footman to the marquess's study, he tried to slow the beating of his heart.

Margaret wants me.

He still could not believe that she had asked to spend one night with him. She had given him no reason for her request. He did not think she had changed her mind about marriage. He did believe, however, that he had awakened within her a passion which had been dormant her entire life and that her inquisitive nature demanded that she pursue this encounter. He planned to show her a night she would never forget. One that would change her mind about marriage—and marrying him, in particular.

They arrived at Baxter's study, and the footman rapped on

the door. He entered and after a word from the marquess, the servant indicated for Daniel to go inside. He stepped into the room, finding Baxter seated behind his desk. The other man did not rise to greet him, which irked Daniel. Though he wasn't a stickler for rules, custom demanded that a man of lower rank rise for one of a higher one. Especially a duke.

"Have a seat, Westfield."

Warily, Daniel did just that, knowing his outward demeanor gave away none of his thoughts.

The two men studied one another coolly and then the marquess said, "You are not to have anything to do with my marchioness, Your Grace. Is that understood?"

So, this is what it was about.

"I have no designs upon Lady Baxter. Of that, I can guarantee you."

The marquess smiled wryly and said, "I knew as much. But my darling wife certainly has designs upon you, Westfield. I have my heir off her. She is with child again, though she has yet to tell me. I want my spare before she goes to another man's bed. So far—to my knowledge—she has only flirted outrageously with my fellow peers."

Baxter paused. "You, however, are different, Your Grace. She was interested in you back then and still is today. I was her second choice and always knew it. I overheard a conversation between her and her mother that I wasn't supposed to hear. Dolley pleaded with her mother, saying how taken she was with you. With your good looks and your fortune. The countess would not budge, however. She insisted that Dolley remember the goal for her marriage had always been the highest possible title. Dolley said that left me."

Baxter shrugged. "I knew I had looks and wealth and was one step away from being a duke. I have never forgotten, however, that my wife always wished to be in your bed."

Daniel felt sorry for this man, but then recalled how he still kept mistresses and had probably never given his wife the attention she craved, much less deserved.

"Let me assure you, my lord, that I had no intention of bedding Lady Dolley then nor Lady Baxter now. Her come-out Season was the first I ever attended. I knew I wanted to sow my wild oats for several years. I was not serious about her or any other young lady making her come-out that Season. As for now, I will admit that I am perusing the Marriage Mart and that my grandmother is guiding me in my selection of a duchess."

Daniel didn't know this man enough to know whether he could trust him with the knowledge that he wanted to wed Baxter's sister-in-law. For all he knew, the marquess would tell his wife, though he did not think they were especially close. It made more sense now, the fact that Lady Baxter did not want her sister dancing with him. The chit envied her sister and tried to undermine Margaret in every way. He would find immense satisfaction when he marched back up the aisle at St. George's, Margaret on his arm, bearing his name having become his duchess.

"Thank you for your assurances, Your Grace. I hope you are successful in finding a woman to be your wife. Your grandmother is quite sage, and if she is helping you, then you need not fear. You will make a brilliant match this Season."

The marquess rose. "Shall we go to tea?"

They left the study and went immediately to the drawing room, where Gran sat with Margaret and her sister. Lady Baxter was talking animatedly. Margaret was doing a good job of trying to look interested. Gran, on the other hand, appeared utterly bored.

"Ah, there you are, Baxter. Your Grace. It is about time you came. The teacart just arrived."

As the men seated themselves, Daniel took the chair closest to Margaret, who sat on a settee next to Gran. Margaret gave him a shy smile and said, "It is good to see you, Your Grace. Did you enjoy last night's ball? I saw you danced quite a bit."

"A ball is a ball," he said. "It can be more than that if one finds the appropriate partner. Last night, I did not."

Lady Baxter poured out for them and began chattering again until her husband flashed her a look. She fell silent, giving others the chance to speak. Daniel decided to steer the conversation toward Margaret and her commission.

"Have you the sketches to show my grandmother?" he asked. "You mentioned at tea yesterday that we might be able to view them today."

"I do, Your Grace," she said brightly. "Let me fetch them. They are just on a table the other side of the room."

"I will retrieve them for you, my lady."

She directed him to a table halfway across the room, and he picked up the sketchbook. Curious, he opened it and was startled by the likeness of his grandmother staring back at him. Slowly, he turned the pages, seeing Gran from different angles and in different poses. He reached the last one and returned to the others.

Reclaiming his seat, he said, "You are most talented, Lady Margaret."

"Let me see, Westfield," Gran commanded.

Daniel handed over the sketchbook, and Gran went through it, commenting to Margaret as she did so.

"These are worth framing themselves," Gran praised. "Will you allow me to have these once you have completed my portrait?"

"I would be happy to give all of them to you, Your Grace," Margaret said. "Go through them again and tell me which ones please you the most."

Gran looked to him. "Westfield, come help with this."

He set down his saucer and went to stand behind them, leaning over. He could smell the scent of lavender wafting from Margaret and longed to nibble her neck, proud of the restraint he showed.

As his grandmother leafed through the sketchbook a second time, he paused and picked out the two which were his favorites.

"I agree with you," Gran said. "Shall we mark them in any way?" she asked Margaret.

"No, Your Grace. I will be able to remember which ones you prefer."

"When do we commence then?" Gran asked, eager as a schoolgirl.

"You will not actually have to sit for me, Your Grace," Margaret revealed.

"Why not?" Gran asked, puzzled.

"Most of my practice has been on servants. Mama did not want me to distract them from their duties, and so I learned to paint without anyone formally sitting for me," she explained. "I would do sketches of them, just as I have of you. Since I had grown up with most of my chosen subjects, I knew them quite well. Once I had the pose down that I wished to use, I simply painted from my sketches and memory. I plan to do the same for you, Your Grace. I have seen the rose garden which I will use as the background. If you approve these two sketches, then I will create a third from them, combining the best elements of both. Although we have only known each other a short while, I feel as though I know you fairly well and will incorporate elements of your personality into my painting, as well."

Curiosity filled Daniel. "Where will you work on Gran's portrait, my lady?"

Lady Baxter answered. "The paints Margaret uses have always given me a terrible headache. She has a room at the very top of our townhouse in which to paint, far from everything."

"She worked up there, doing portraits of me and Lady Baxter, as well as our two children," the marquess added.

"Are those still here in London?" Gran asked.

"They are," Margaret said enthusiastically. "Lord Baxter said they will be taken back to his country estate, where they will be placed in the family's portrait gallery. For now, they are still in what I am using for a studio."

She paused and then said, "If you wish to see them, Your

Grace, I would be happy to show them to you. I do have another portrait, though, I believe you would be interested in. I painted my grandmother several years after her death, once again basing it upon sketches I had done of her over the years. I brought it with me. Would you care to see it?"

Daniel spoke up. "I, too, would enjoy seeing your work, Lady Margaret. I am also thinking of having my portrait made and would like to know if you are talented enough to take on the commission."

"We should finish our tea before anyone goes traipsing about the house," Lady Baxter interjected, trying once more to take control of the situation and conversation.

She chattered on for several minutes, Daniel paying no attention to her.

Finally, tea ended and his grandmother said, "I am ready to see the portraits of your family and my beloved friend."

They all rose, and Lady Baxter frowned. "While I suppose it is all right if His Grace accompanies you to the top floor, Grandmama's portrait hangs in my sister's bedchamber. I believe it would be highly inappropriate for His Grace to see it there."

Pride filled Daniel as Gran stared down the marchioness, icily saying, "I find it wholly appropriate, Lady Baxter. After all, I will be present, which ensures nothing untoward might occur. Give your sister and my grandson more credit than that," she snapped.

Lady Baxter looked cowed, and the marquess amused as the three of them left the drawing room.

"You certainly put the marchioness in her place, Gran," commented Daniel.

"I am sorry, my dear," his grandmother said to Margaret. "I simply do not like your sister one whit."

Margaret laughed. "That makes two of us, Your Grace."

They reached the staircase and, he took his grandmother's arm, helping guide her up the flights of stairs until they reached the topmost floor.

"It is this way, Your Graces," Margaret said, leading them

down a long hallway until they reached its end.

She opened the door and indicated for them to enter first. Daniel steered Gran through the entry, immediately smelling paint. He released Gran's arm, and they both moved toward the completed portraits leaning against one wall. The first was of Lord Baxter, capturing his aristocratic air and yet conveying a warmth Daniel had not witnessed. The second painting was of Lady Baxter. In it, Margaret had captured her immense beauty, along with a regal air. The third was of two small children, a boy and girl. Margaret had painted their innocence and sweetness.

Turning to her, he said, "You have captured your subjects well, my lady. The detail is astounding, down to every fold in the material of your sister's gown."

"Thank you, Your Grace," she said humbly. "Painting my niece and nephew was a true joy."

"I believed you had talent before I saw these," Gran said. "Knowing that viper of a sister of yours, I see you truly bring out the best in your subjects."

Margaret chuckled. "I try to provide a true likeness, while infusing it with personality. Dolley is most beautiful, and she treats those who worship her well."

"These should be on display here in town," Daniel said.

"No, Dolley was pleased with my work but that would only draw attention away from her and to me. We have already established, Your Grace, that is not something she wishes to do. While she has shared with a few others about my painting her and her family, she has her limits as to how far she will go on behalf. The portraits will never hang in this house."

"Show me your paints, my dear," Gran said.

Margaret led them to a far corner of the room, near a large window.

"I like to mix my paints here, thanks to the strong, abundant light."

She began explaining how she did so. Daniel listened to her voice and watched her elegant hands as she gestured, not listening to her words. He caught her enthusiasm, though, and knew he wanted her to paint him at some point.

"Shall we go downstairs?" she asked. "I am happy to show you Grandmama's portrait. I am quite proud of it."

Once more, Daniel took Gran's arm and guided her to Margaret's bedchamber. Inside, his eyes were drawn immediately to the portrait hanging on the wall. Both he and Gran stood and studied it at length. He glanced over his shoulder and saw that Margaret was watching them, wringing her hands nervously as she did so.

Gran turned to her. Daniel saw his grandmother's eyes brimming with tears. Margaret came and embraced the older woman, who began to sob. He had never seen Gran cry before and felt a bit helpless.

When her tears subsided, Margaret released Gran and took the woman's hands in hers. "I hope you think it a good likeness of Grandmama, Your Grace."

"It is everything Dorothy was. It is as if I am seeing my old friend come to life again. It pains me to know you shared the same talent with her—and that hers had to remain hidden until her husband's death."

"When did you paint her?" Daniel asked, handing Gran his handkerchief.

"She passed when I was ten, and I did not believe I had the skills at that time to do justice to her portrait," Margaret explained. "I practiced on our servants for the next five years and painted Grandmama when I was fifteen, almost ten years ago."

"That would have been around the time I first met you," he noted.

Her cheeks bloomed with color. "Yes, Your Grace. I believe I had just completed work on her portrait about that time."

He wondered why she would blush at that but did not press her.

Gazing directly at her, Daniel said, "When you finish with Gran's portrait, my lady, I am to be your next subject."

CHAPTER NINETEEN

D ANIEL PONDERED ON where he and Margaret might have their tryst. With a mistress, it was fairly easy. A man either went to said mistress's residence or, if he was her protector, he had purchased a small hideaway for their affair. With a lover from the *ton*, arrangements were made to slip into houses when a husband was to be gone, servants threatened with firing if they spoke to the lord of the house. On some occasions, Daniel had even had his lover come directly to him, knowing his servants would never dare breathe a word of the rendezvous. He had preferred encounters with a willing widow, not having to worry about a husband in those cases.

But with a virginal woman living in her brother-in-law's house, matters grew entirely more complicated. Margaret's every move was accounted for by her sister or servants of the household. She couldn't go anywhere without a chaperone. Season events took up practically every waking hour. Obviously, he had no way of sneaking into Baxter's residence and making love to her in her bedchamber, much less asking her to come to him in the dead of night.

It would take a bit of subterfuge on his part to find a time and place for him to make love to her.

He realized that was exactly what he would be doing. Making love. Before, every encounter with a woman had been merely sexual in nature. For the first time, Daniel wanted to be as emotionally involved as he was physically. He wanted to please Margaret in every way. His own pleasure would be secondary. Everything would be for her. About her. Because of her.

An idea came to him, and he immediately called for his carriage. Within the hour, he sat across from his solicitor, explaining that he might have need of a small house for a period of time. One in a good neighborhood that could be leased for a short while. Though he never made mention of a mistress, that was the unspoken impression he gave.

"I would also wish to see the rental in person. Tour it before I made a decision."

"That can be arranged, Your Grace. I can look into properties to be rented and see that a key is delivered directly to you so that you might peruse the property at your leisure and see if it will . . . fit your needs."

Securing a rental house for their assignation would be perfect. The place would be empty of servants. He could meet with Margaret in complete privacy and then let his solicitor know that he would not be needing the place after all.

Daniel only hoped one time of coupling with Margaret would change her mind and convince her that she should be his.

The solicitor rubbed his chin and thought and then said, "How large would this house have to be, Your Grace?"

He leaned forward. "You have something in mind?"

"I know of one going on the market early next week. It belongs to my wife's sister-in-law, who became a widow two months ago. She is returning to the country. City life is not the same without her husband, who was a clerk. The place is small but neat."

"I would be interested in it," he said. "Send the key when it is available, and I will take a look at it when I have the time."

"I will do so, Your Grace."

Daniel left, knowing the size would not matter. It was the privacy which was of most importance. A clerk's house would also be nowhere near the more fashionable parts of London, minimizing the risk of Margaret being seen. He smiled, feeling all the chips were falling into place.

A garden party was scheduled for that afternoon. He escorted his grandmother to it, quickly searching for Margaret once they arrived. He saw her in a group of two other women and three men. A frisson of jealousy rippled through him as she smiled at one of the men. Daniel gritted his teeth when he saw it was Lord North, the gentleman she had been with on the terrace.

Why should it bother him that she gave a smile to another man?

Because . . . he was in love with her.

It didn't matter when it had happened. Only that it had. Daniel had convinced himself that he wanted Margaret physically. That her intelligence and grace would make for a perfect duchess. Still, he had wanted to hold himself emotionally at arm's length.

And found that impossible.

"Will you see me to my friends, Westfield?" Gran asked. "That is, if you can quit staring at Lady Margaret long enough."

"Is it that obvious?"

"You have fallen for her, my boy. I am pleased you have done so. Her sister might be a terrible gossip and superficial, but Lady Margaret Townsend is her grandmother made over." She pursed her lips a moment. "Must I go on searching among the *ton* for a bride?"

His grandmother had suggested a few ladies for him to dance with at the previous ball. He had been bored by every one of them. Daniel realized now that even then, Margaret had seeped into his heart and no one could hold a candle to her.

"No, Gran. I have made my choice." He hesitated. "If only she will choose me, in return."

She patted his arm. "She will. It may take a bit of persuasion on your part, but she will come around."

Daniel led her to her friends and spent a few minutes chatting with them, all the while keeping an eye on Margaret and the people she was speaking with. After a suitable amount of time, he excused himself and headed in her direction.

"May I join you?" he asked, sliding into the circle she was a part of.

Of course, a duke was a welcomed guest anywhere he went.

He was pleased to see that Lord North was engaged in conversation with one of the other ladies, and they soon paired off. Others did, as well, until he was left alone with Margaret.

"You certainly ran everyone off," she commented drolly.

He was taken aback. "You think I caused them to leave?"

"I most certainly do. Did you see how they quickly melted away, Pestfield?"

She had not referred to him that way in a while. Daniel wasn't sure if that was a good thing—or bad.

"Our names have been linked in the gossip columns," she continued. "And that is despite the fact we did not dance even once at the last ball."

"You believe they are giving us an opportunity to speak alone and further our acquaintance."

"Yes. Exactly."

He smiled charmingly, seeing that it did affect her. "I have begun plans for our rendezvous."

Her face lit up. "You have?" Then she frowned. "I know you said you would find a solution. I am eager to hear it. I thought about it at length and could not come up with a way to . . . spend time alone with you." Her cheeks pinkened.

"I spoke with my solicitor, who is looking for a small house I could rent. I have asked that the key be sent to me when it becomes available. I will look it over and get back to him, telling him that it will not suit my needs." His gaze locked on hers. "Before I do so, however, you will visit this property. We will have it to ourselves . . . for the night you requested."

He noticed the slight tremor that ran through her. Desire flickered within him. Daniel wanted to touch her again. Make her scream his name. Kiss her everywhere. He swallowed, reining in his feelings, which tried to gallop out of control.

"I will keep you posted."

"How will I be able to sneak away to this place?" she asked.

"I am working on that, as well, Red."

"Don't call me that," she chided.

"Then don't call me Pestfield. Truce?"

"Agreed."

Offering her his arm, he said, "Shall we take a turn about the party? We could also explore the gardens."

Her cheeks spotted with color. "I know what you do in gardens, Your Grace. Particularly when roses are nearby. We better stick to the party. Agreed?"

Daniel nodded, leading her to various small circles, introducing her when an introduction was called for. It seemed she knew quite a few people at this early date in the Season and that everyone seemed familiar with her and the fact that she was painting the Dowager Duchess of Westfield's portrait.

The afternoon passed quickly, mostly because he never left Margaret's side. She was quite witty and easy to converse with. She had a sympathetic ear and was a good listener, a quality not found in many of the self-centered members of the *ton*. Daniel's admiration for her seemed to grow with each passing day.

As the party ended, he asked if she might be at the musicale he had agreed to attend.

"No, Dolley is keen on attending a rout this evening."

He wished he already had the leased house key in hand. It would have been the perfect opportunity. Knowing now that she would not be in attendance, he decided to skip the musicale and go to the rout instead.

Daniel returned her to Lord and Lady Baxter, kissing her hand. "I hope to see you very soon, my lady."

With that, he went in search of Gran.

MARGARET RETURNED FROM the garden party with a burning desire to work. She had caught the Dowager Duchess of Westfield at a certain angle and wanted to incorporate it into the two sketches that had pleased both the dowager duchess and Daniel. She went straight to the top floor, where her paints, charcoals, and pencils awaited. Soon, she was lost in sketching.

After a few attempts, she got on parchment exactly what she wanted.

It would be how the dowager duchess would want to be seen.

Still restless, she put her sketchbook aside and paced the room as a caged tiger might. Then she realized what she had left to do.

Sketch Daniel.

Once more, she took up her pencil and the sketchpad and furiously began to draw. She completed one sketch and began another of him, then another, losing all track of time. By the time Molly entered, Margaret had moved on to charcoal sketches of the duke.

"I have been looking for you, my lady," the maid said. "You did not come to dinner, and it is time to dress for the rout."

"I will not be attending the rout."

The maid flinched, and Margaret knew the girl did not want to deliver the news to Dolley.

"I shall go and speak to my sister myself, Molly, and inform her of my plans."

Relief swept over the servant's face. "Thank you, my lady. Would you care for anything to eat?"

Margaret realized she was hungry, having missed dinner, and nodded. "Bring a tray up here if you would in half an hour. By then, I will have spoken to my sister myself."

She went downstairs to Dolley's rooms and quietly slipped in. Her lady's maid was dressing Dolley's hair, piling it high atop her mistress's head in elaborate coils. Her sister's gaze met Margaret's in the mirror.

"You are not dressed, Margaret. Do so at once."

"I will not be attending the rout this evening, Dolley."

"Why not?" snapped her sister.

"I have begun working on the final sketches for the Dowager Duchess of Westfield and wish to prepare her canvas. I will begin painting at first light tomorrow."

Confusion filled her sister's face. "You would miss a rout . . . to . . . work?"

"It does not seem as work to me," she explained. "Also, the dowager duchess is eager to have me commence. Remember, she wishes to hold a small party once I have completed her portrait."

"I assume Baxter and I will be invited to this party. I did mention it to Her Grace."

"Of course, you will, Dolley," Margaret assured her sister, hoping the dowager duchess would agree to such a request. "The sooner I finish the portrait and members of Polite Society see it, the sooner I should have other clients. I know that will give me a chance to relocate to a small place of my own and allow you and your husband the privacy you deserve."

Dolley smiled and then an odd look crossed her face. She called, "The basin!"

Her lady's maid dashed for and brought it quickly to her mistress, which Dolley retched into.

Once she stopped, Dolley barked at the maid, "Get rid of that at once!"

"Yes, my lady." The servant left with the basin.

Dolley's nose crinkled in disgust. "I cannot stand to be around it."

"Have you told Baxter that you are with child?"

"No. I suppose I should. Oh, I do fret when I begin growing large again. I despise losing my figure."

"Isn't it worth it, to bring a new life into the world? You already have two darling children."

Dolley said, "This one better be another boy. Then my duty to the marquess will be done."

Boldly, Margaret asked, "Would you then take a lover from

among your admirers in the *ton*?"

Her sister smiled. "I plan to do that very thing. Hopefully, it will be the Duke of Westfield."

Shock rippled through her. "The duke is not seeking a lover, Dolley. He is perusing the Marriage Mart with the help of his grandmother. He wants a wife. Not a lover."

And yet he had agreed to become hers for one night.

Dolley waved a hand dismissively. "Men such as Westfield are always looking for a lover, whether they are wed or not. I want him—and I want you to stay away from him."

Ignoring the comment, Margaret said, "I am off to work now."

She returned to her makeshift studio and soon after, Molly brought something for her to eat. Margaret took her time, chewing her food thoughtfully, wondering why Dolley was so obsessed with Daniel. She hoped it was not because he had expressed a slight interest in Margaret. She had no wish to compete with her sister, knowing it could only lead to further animosity between them.

Especially if Daniel rejected Dolley.

She finished eating and moved to the portraits she had painted this spring, propped against the wall. Behind the one of the marquess was her portrait of who was then Viscount Browning. She slipped it from behind the one that blocked it, moving it so she could study it. Daniel had been younger then by a decade, already a man but not the commanding presence he was now as a duke. After several minutes of studying his portrait, she returned to her sketches. By the time she finished, she had seven done in pencil and three in charcoal, all portraying what Daniel looked like now. Margaret was eager to paint him as he was and show the contrast between the man then and the one he had become.

She would start his grandmother's portrait tomorrow morning.

And then paint Daniel himself.

CHAPTER TWENTY

MARGARET ROSE BEFORE dawn, thanks to the fact she had not been out until the wee hours of the morning at the previous evening's affair. She preferred morning above all other times, when the world was fresh and new and ready for her to leave her mark upon it. She dressed herself without ringing for a maid, not needing to don the usual, many layers. This morning she would be working with her oil paints, and so she slipped into her chemise and a simple gown. She would cover it with an old smock which she wore when she painted.

Her belly grumbled, however, and she decided to go down to the kitchens in search of a cup of tea and perhaps some bread and jam. Quickly, she twisted her hair into a simple chignon and pinned it into place before leaving her bedchamber.

The house was silent as she descended the stairs. When she reached the bottom floor, the night footman sitting by the door greeted her.

"Good morning, my lady. You are up rather early."

"I plan to paint this morning in the studio on the top floor which Lord Baxter has been gracious enough to allow me to use," she told him. "I wanted to be up and capture every bit of the light I could. But first, I am in search of a fortifying cup of tea."

She went straight to the kitchens, where Cook sat sipping a cup of tea. The old woman rose and greeted Margaret.

"Good morning, my lady. You are up and about rather early."

"I will be painting this morning, Cook, and am in need of a cup of tea and a bite to eat."

"Let me take care of you, my lady."

Soon, Margaret carried a tray upstairs with her tea and two slices of warm, fresh bread slathered in strawberry jam. She had insisted upon carrying the tray herself. Once in the studio, she ate quickly and finished her tea, setting it aside, ready to take up her brushes.

As she donned her smock, she had a clear vision of how she wished to paint the Dowager Duchess of Westfield and so mixing the colors did not take long. She did not know how much time had passed when she sensed the door behind her opening, vaguely wondering who might be visiting her so early. Turning, shock filled her as a disheveled Daniel raced toward her. His fingers latched onto her shoulders, and his mouth came down in a bruising kiss. She felt swallowed whole by him as he devoured her. The kiss went on, its fierceness overwhelming her. Then Daniel finally gentled and broke it.

"Where were you last night?" he demanded, searching her face.

"Why, I decided to stay home and work on your grandmother's portrait," she told him, secretly pleased that he had missed her. "I knew the two sketches she had liked best. I caught her at an angle during the garden party, which I thought was flattering and revealed more of her. I wanted to get it on paper and then start at first light on the actual portrait itself."

She paused. "Why are you here, Daniel? It is so early." Her eyes swept over him. "You look terrible."

She took in his unshaven faced, the stubble darkening his cheeks somehow making him seem even more attractive than usual. He wore a wrinkled shirt and coat but no cravat or waistcoat were in sight. His hair, thick and abundant, stood up as if it were an unruly child who refused to obey a parent.

"I was worried about you," he admitted. "You had told me you would be at the rout. When you did not come, I feared the worst."

"You should have asked Dolley about me," she told him. "She knew why I stayed home."

He shook his head. "I had no wish to address your sister, even in trivial matters." He hesitated and then added, "When we came to tea yesterday, Lord Baxter asked to visit with me privately."

"I had wondered why your grandmother had arrived without you. Then you turned up with Baxter, and everything seemed fine."

"The marquess informed me that your sister had designs upon me. He begged for me not to take her to my bed. Apparently, she had a tendre for me back in the day and now intends to make me her lover. I want no contact between us and promised Baxter this would never happen."

As Margaret took in such astonishing information, she heard a small plop and glanced down, seeing a drop of paint from her brush had landed upon his boots.

"Oh, dear! We must clean this at once."

She pulled away from his grasp and set down her brush, quickly gathering an old cloth. Dropping to her knees, she wiped the small bit of paint from his gleaming Hessian boot and looked up, smiling. "Your boot has been saved, Your Grace."

He leaned over and clasped her elbows, helping her to rise. Wordlessly, they gazed upon one another until his mouth descended upon her again.

The kiss was achingly tender, unlike any he had ever bestowed upon her. She needed for him to stop kissing her—because deep within her soul, she admitted to herself that she had lost her heart to this man. It would be ever so painful when she saw him wed to another woman. Already, she seethed with jealousy, watching him dance with a pretty female. Seeing him with his wife would destroy her.

Margaret broke the kiss and stepped away from him. She turned to face him, relieved to have put distance between them.

"You must go at once, Your Grace," she said formally. "It would not do for you to be seen leaving here, especially in your current attire."

She realized he was not looking at her. Not listening to her. Instead, he stared over her shoulder.

Margaret wheeled, realizing he had spied his portrait. She turned to face him again as he took steps toward her and then passed her, coming to stand in front of his likeness. Reluctantly, she joined him.

"You painted me," he said in awe, wonder in his voice. "All those years ago."

"You made quite an impression upon me," she said softly. "I had recently finished my grandmother's portrait, the first that was not one of a servant, and my confidence had soared, seeing the likeness. I believed in myself and my talent. I had no chance to paint anyone except servants. Then—I met you. While you and Dolley were driving through Hyde Park, I was furiously sketching you from memory."

"Do you still have those sketches?" he asked.

"I do," she admitted.

"I would like to have them. I would also like this portrait. I will pay you for it, of course." He turned and faced her, one hand cradling her cheek, his thumbs caressing it tenderly. "And when you finish Gran's portrait, you must begin mine."

She did not tell him that she had already completed the sketches of him and had in mind exactly how she would paint him.

"How long will it take for you to finish Gran's portrait?"

"It depends upon how soon you leave me, Your Grace," she said lightly, trying to keep her emotions hidden.

"I can take a hint," he told her, smiling. "Seriously, though, how long?"

She shrugged. "It is difficult to say, simply because my time is not my own these days. I skipped last night's rout because I had a need to work. I may have to miss other *ton* affairs, as well, in order to complete your grandmother's portrait in a timely fashion."

Suddenly, he beamed at her. It was as if she were awash in

warm sunshine.

His other hand came to frame her face and he said, "That will be the way we can be together. You can say you are working on Gran's portrait and skip some event. Your sister will not think to check your bed when she comes staggering in from some ball or card party."

He kissed her swiftly and then stepped back. "I am still working on the place we can meet. For now, I will leave you to work." He paused, tenderness in his eyes. "Thank you for painting me all those years ago, Red. It is interesting to see how I appeared to a young girl on the cusp of womanhood. I am eager to see how I will appear now—once you complete a second portrait of me."

Softly, he brushed his lips briefly against hers and then left the room.

Margaret knew she must never let he Duke of Westfield know how she truly felt about him.

With grim determination, she pushed all thoughts of him aside as she picked up her paintbrush and began again.

DANIEL RECEIVED A note from his solicitor early that afternoon. He had slipped from the Baxter townhouse as it had begun to stir, hoping it was only the footman who had admitted him who had known of his presence in the household. The servant had explained to Daniel that Lady Margaret was already on the top floor where the nursery was located, working on a painting. Since he and Gran had been to the room Margaret was using as her artist's studio, he knew exactly where to find her. He had slipped a gold sovereign into the footman's hand as he departed, asking the servant to keep his visit to Lady Margaret a secret. Knowing how servants gossiped, though, he was unsure if that would occur. If word reached Lord or Lady Baxter of Daniel's early morning visit to Margaret, it could ensue in a scandal.

Of course, if the marquess demanded that Daniel wed his

sister-in-law, he would be most happy to do so.

Still, he wanted Margaret to know that she had a choice in the matter, which was why he hoped the footman would keep his mouth shut regarding a duke's early morning visit.

He returned his attention to the note, which had contained a key and an address. In it, his solicitor explained that the small house had become available sooner than expected, with his sister-in-law moving out more quickly than previously planned. Daniel was free to view the property at his leisure and let the solicitor know if it would suit his purposes.

Tonight, he had promised Gran that he would accompany her and her friends to the opera. Other small affairs were being held about town, as well. Tomorrow night, however, another grand ball would take place.

That was when he would make love to Margaret.

He would need to get word to her that she needed to plead work—or even a headache—tomorrow night. In fact, he thought he would send word to her now, instructing her to make certain she went to whatever event Lord and Lady Baxter were slated to attend this evening. Margaret's sister had excused her from last night's rout, but if she missed tonight's event, then it would be more difficult for her to also skip the ball. With the bulk of the *ton* attending tomorrow night's ball, there was less of a chance for them to be seen making their way to their rendezvous.

Removing parchment from a drawer, Daniel penned a quick note to Margaret, hoping she could read between the lines and ascertain that he wished for her to attend tonight's social affair.

Then he worried that she might not even see it, especially if a servant placed it in her bedchamber and she remained upstairs, working on Gran's portrait.

He decided he must call upon her this afternoon in order for her to know she was to meet him tomorrow evening. No, he should send his carriage for her. No, that wouldn't do. Margaret couldn't be seen getting into his ducal carriage, unaccompanied. He would have to find another way to get her there.

"Bloody hell," he said aloud, never having stooped to such

subterfuge in order to see a woman in private. He supposed there was an advantage to having a mistress who was available whenever he wished, no questions asked.

Yet something deep in his soul told him his days of keeping a mistress were behind him. He had yet to make love to Margaret—and already, he found her endlessly fascinating. She would be all the woman he needed. After all, he was in love with her. He had swans on his country estate in Sussex. His gamekeeper had told him that the swans mated for life.

Daniel's very bones told him it would be this way for him and Margaret.

Always.

He checked his pocket watch and found he would have time to stop by the house for let before he called upon Lady Margaret Townsend. Quite a crowd had gathered during his last visit. She was proving to be popular.

Which was why he wanted to make love to her as soon as possible and offer her marriage.

Daniel called for his carriage and while waiting for it to be prepared, sent for his gardener. The man appeared at the open door to Daniel's study looking incredibly out of place.

"Come in," he said, gesturing with his hand. "I need you to hurry to the gardens and clip a handful of the best blooms for me."

"Come again, Your Grace?" the gardener asked, clearly puzzled by the request.

"I am calling upon a lovely young lady and wish to bring her fresh flowers from my garden."

The man's face lit with a smile. "Ah, it is a young lady, Your Grace? Might she become Her Grace?"

"I hope so," he said fervently, realizing just how much he wanted Margaret in his life. "Be quick about it. My carriage will be ready soon."

"At once, Your Grace."

By the time his butler summoned him to the waiting carriage, the gardener stood beside it, colorful tulips wrapped in tissue paper, along with a few pink roses.

"I hope these will do for your young lady, Your Grace," the gardener said.

Daniel smiled conspiratorially. "I hope so, too."

He gave the address to his coachman and climbed into the carriage, setting the bouquet beside him. It took half an hour to reach the small house, which was in a decent neighborhood. Leaving the flowers in the carriage, he entered the rental using the key his solicitor had provided.

The place was as neat as a pin, with a small drawing room, dining room, and kitchen downstairs, all smelling fresh, with no dust in sight. He supposed someone had been in to clean after the widow left. Moving up the stairs, he found two bedchambers, one slightly larger than the other. Both beds had linens on them.

He chose the larger of the two rooms and proceeded to turn back the covers. The quality was not quite what he was used to, but he doubted he would be thinking about bedclothes when he had a naked Margaret writhing beneath him.

The thought made his cock stir.

He poked about the room and returned downstairs, finding the cupboards bare. The solicitor's sister-in-law had left the furniture and linens but obviously taken her dishes and pans with her. He would send his valet here tomorrow afternoon with a hamper filled with wine, bread, and cheeses. If anything else came to him in the meantime, he would also make certain it awaited his and Margaret's arrival.

Daniel locked the door and told his coachman to take him to Lord Baxter's townhouse. He wouldn't stay long, just deliver his simple bouquet and pull Margaret aside briefly to explain that she must go to whatever event with the Baxters this evening because she would be skipping the next night's ball in order to spend it with him.

He climbed inside the vehicle and closed his eyes, picturing a naked Margaret and all the things he would do to her tomorrow night.

CHAPTER TWENTY-ONE

M ARGARET PAUSED AND studied the work before her. Even she was surprised with how much she had accomplished during this first, lengthy session. Not having known any other artist beyond her grandmother, she did not know the pace at which one worked. Because she usually painted servants and Mama would not let her pull them from their duties, Margaret had learned to rely upon the sketches that she made of her subjects. She sketched them from every angle, both in person and by memory. Then when she stood before her canvas, she had an excellent idea how to portray them in their portrait, and her brush seemed to fly across the canvas as she worked.

Though she had not painted for a good while beyond the portraits she had done for Dolley's family, everything came back to her, including various brushstrokes she used, from the dowager duchess's hair to the folds in her gown and the roses behind her. At this rate, Margaret would finish the portrait most likely in two-or-three-days' time if she kept up her current pace. She doubted that would occur, though, with all the social obligations she faced. She could not put off seeing visitors, especially ones who had been thoughtful enough to send her flower arrangements. She had already skipped the previous evening's affair and doubted she could continue to do so, else she'd draw Dolley's wrath.

Just then, the door flew open and Molly rushed in.

"There you are, Lady Margaret. You must come downstairs at once. Her ladyship is looking for you. It is almost time for morning calls to begin."

Margaret's belly growled noisily and she burst out laughing. She had forgotten to stop to eat anything beyond the bread and jam she had consumed many hours ago.

"Come quickly, my lady," the maid urged.

"But I must clean my brushes," she explained. "If I do not, they will become worthless."

Molly grabbed Margaret's elbow and began pulling her from the room, saying, "You can trust me and tell me what to do with them. I promise that I will return here and clean them however you tell me. For now, though, we must get you properly attired. The drawing room is once again filled with bouquets, all for you." The servant paused and added, "Lady Baxter is not pleased."

Margaret could imagine the tirade her sister must be on, not having received a single bouquet from her many admirers.

They reached her bedchamber and as Molly stripped Margaret of her smock and old gown and helped her dress anew, Margaret explained what to use to clean the brushes and how to set them out to dry. She had Molly repeat the instructions back to her, not wanting to sacrifice any of her brushes. The girl was clever and repeated verbatim what Margaret had said. When the time came for her to leave this house, she decided she would definitely ask Molly to come with her.

"You don't have time to do anything with your hair," Molly said, "but this simple style suits you. You do have paint on your face, my lady, and on your hands."

The servant took one of Margaret's hands, holding it up and inspecting it. "Even under your nails!" she gasped.

Quickly, water was poured from a jug, and Molly helped soap Margaret's hands, scrubbing at them with a small brush, removing all traces of paint. Next, she attacked Margaret's cheek and finally stepped back, assessing her work.

"You're as right as rain now, my lady. The gentlemen will be eager to see you. Especially that Lord North. He sent the biggest of all today's bouquets."

Margaret liked Lord North. He was interesting and intelligent, as well as remarkably good looking. She almost thought that Daniel might have been jealous finding her on the terrace with him.

"Did the Duke of Westfield happen to send flowers?" she asked.

"No, my lady. I am the one who collected the cards again today. I didn't see his name on any of them. Does that disappoint you?"

In a way, it did—thought Margaret would never have admitted it to anyone.

Even herself.

She supposed he was already losing interest in her since she had agreed to couple with him. Once they did so, she would be old hat to him, and he would toss her aside, perusing the Marriage Mart with renewed interest.

She didn't care. She wanted to be with him. Wanted to explore the feelings and emotions churning within her. Especially since she would not wed, she believed she owed it to herself to try to make love with a man at least once in her life. She assumed Daniel had done so many times over the years and would be quite skilled at this. She might be simply another conquest to him—but he would be her one true love for all time.

She pushed these feelings aside, knowing it would do no good to dwell upon them. She was an artist. It was good to experience a wide range of emotions. Eventually, she would not travel in the same social circles that he did with his duchess. She doubted after she left her brother-in-law's townhouse that she would attend any *ton* events. The invitations that had been extended to Dolley and Baxter had been generous enough to include her. Once she left their household, it would be a different matter. Still, though, everything depended upon the portrait she now painted. If she did an outstanding job and the Dowager Duchess of Westfield was pleased with the outcome, word of it would spread throughout Polite Society. She believed she would have plenty of clients in the months and years to come.

"Hurry, my lady," Molly urged. "You go to the drawing room and I'll go to your studio. Trust me," the maid said. "I will follow your instructions to the letter. Your brushes will be fine."

"Thank you, Molly," Margaret said.

She entered the drawing room and saw Dolley and Baxter standing at the far end, along with two other gentlemen, both whom she recognized as they turned, looking over their shoulders at her, giving her a smile.

Dolley's look was murderous.

She joined them. "I am sorry I was delayed. How delightful of you to call upon us this afternoon," she told their two visitors.

The next hour passed swiftly, with callers coming and going. She forced herself not to look at the door, much less think of Daniel. It wasn't as if he had to call upon her every afternoon. She did not expect that. Surely by now, his grandmother had suggested a few ladies of the *ton* as marriage partners. After all, Margaret had seen him dance every dance at the previous ball.

She tamped down the jealousy that rose within her just as the butler announced Daniel's name. Her heart quickened upon hearing it and slammed against her ribs as the duke entered the drawing room. Gone was the stubble from their early morning encounter, as well as the wrinkled shirt and coat. In its place, he wore a shirt so snowy white, it was almost blinding. His cravat was expertly tied and his coat of deep gray only enhanced his gray eyes.

He crossed the room and greeted her and then Dolley before saying a word to Baxter. The other callers seemed to melt away from their circle. Dolley batted her eyelashes flirtatiously at him, causing anger to fill Margaret.

"Come, my lady," the marquess said. "You look a bit

peaked."

"I am feeling quite well, my lord," Dolley said evenly.

"Come anyway," Baxter demanded. "I believe you have something you wish to share with me."

Margaret supposed her brother-in-law had figured out that he was to be a father again. She could not understand why her sister had not already informed her husband of her delicate condition. The couple moved away, leaving her alone with Daniel.

"I am going to speak quickly and then leave, Margaret," he said, low. "The small house I told you about has become available earlier than anticipated. I already have the key and will be waiting for you there tomorrow evening."

"How am I to get there?" she asked. "I am supposed to attend a ball with Dolley and Baxter. And I am coming along swimmingly with your grandmother's portrait. I hate to leave that."

"You need to attend whatever affair you have promised to go to this evening," he cautioned. "You have already missed one last night. If you are also to miss tomorrow night in order to be with me, then I suggest you attend whatever commitment you have for this evening."

He glanced around and then his gaze fell back to her. He gave her the address, telling her the door would be open and she was to enter without knocking.

Then he said, "During tea tomorrow, mention you have a headache. When it is time for dinner, ask that a tray be sent up to you since you are still feeling poorly. Whatever you do, pick at the food and send most of it back."

She grinned. "What if I am hungry?"

"I will take care of your hunger." His eyes darkened, and Margaret knew he wasn't talking about food—but her hunger for him.

"Tell your sister whatever it takes to make her believe you are unwell. Once she and Baxter have left for the ball, the house will settle down. The servants will retire to their own hall and enjoy time to themselves for a few hours."

"There is always a footman stationed at the door," she pointed out. "How am I to slip past him?"

"You won't. Go to Baxter's study. I was there recently. You can leave through one of the windows there. I will have a hansom cab waiting for you a block to the east. It would be too conspicuous to convey you in my carriage."

Her brows arched. "You seem a master of subterfuge, Your Grace."

"Quit looking so appealing," he said. "Or else I might kiss you right here."

Heat filled her cheeks. "You wouldn't."

"Don't tempt me." He smiled brightly at her and took her hand, bringing it to his lips for a brief kiss. "It was a pleasure seeing you again, Lady Margaret."

She understood their conversation had reached its conclusion. "Thank you for calling, Your Grace."

Daniel retreated and once more, Margaret found herself surrounded by other callers who had remained at a distance, giving a duke time alone with her, even if it was in a room full of others.

She listened as best she could—but her thoughts kept returning to their assignation tomorrow night.

And how her life would be forever changed.

⇥⟫⟪⇤

Margaret came to tea the following afternoon knowing she looked tired. She had attended the social event the previous evening, seeing Daniel from afar, but deliberately not speaking to him. She did talk at length with his grandmother, though, telling the dowager duchess how quickly the portrait was progressing.

Arriving home earlier than when at a ball, she went to bed immediately and then rose well before dawn so that she would once more be ready to work in her makeshift studio. She had remained in it until Molly once more sought her out, forcing her to step away from her brushes and return downstairs to dress for any visitors.

Dolley asked a few callers to stay to tea, all gentlemen who had no interest in Margaret but were among Dolley's constant sycophants.

She allowed tea to go on about her, remaining silent throughout it. When their visitors finally left, her sister turned to her.

"Is something wrong? You didn't utter a single word during tea."

Margaret winced at the sharp tone and raised her hand to her brow. "I have had a headache building all day."

Dolley snorted. "It is probably those paints which gave it to you. Their scent is so strong. I do not see how you can stand to be around them for hours at a time."

She actually adored the smell of her paints but refrained from mentioning it. Instead, she said, "The pounding has only gotten worse. I believe I will lie down for a while and see if it helps."

"That is a good idea. I am going to do the same before dinner." She frowned. "The nausea was terrible this morning. I retched so loudly that even Baxter came from his suite to check on me."

"I am glad you told him you are with child."

Dolley shrugged. "There was no need to hide it any longer. I merely wished to make certain of my condition before I shared it with him. He hopes for another boy, of course. So do I."

Margaret excused herself and went upstairs. Though she itched to go to her studio, she wanted to continue to play the role Daniel had given her. When Molly arrived to help her dress for dinner, Margaret pleaded a headache and asked for a tray. After the maid brought it upstairs, she made certain to only eat a few bites as Daniel had instructed. Molly retrieved it and that was when Margaret told the servant that she would not attend this evening's ball.

"Would you please let my sister know?"

"I will, my lady. Is there anything I can bring you?"

"No. I think a good night's sleep will remedy things."

Margaret doubted she would get any sleep tonight.

"Let me help you to undress, my lady," Molly said, helping peel away the layers and placing Margaret in her night rail before she left.

The hardest part was the waiting. She made sure she was in bed with the bedclothes pulled up to her chin when a light tap sounded upon her door. Feigning sleep, she sensed the door open because it created a slight draft. Then she inhaled the heavy perfume of her sister, who came to stand next to the bed.

In a surprising gesture, Dolley bent and brushed her lips against Margaret's brow before she left the room.

When Dolley was gone, Margaret left her bed and went to the window, barely parting the curtains. She saw the waiting carriage, and then her sister and brother-in-law appeared and climbed inside it. The vehicle departed.

She flung off the night rail, leaving it on the bed. She had to dress simply, pulling a chemise over her head and then an unadorned gown, followed by her stockings and shoes. It would feel odd to leave the house without her corset, but she had no way of getting into it on her own. She found her cloak and draped it about her shoulders, tying it at her throat. At least now she didn't feel so exposed.

With care, she blew out the candle at her bedside and slipped from her bedchamber. It was as Daniel predicted. She saw not a servant in the house stirring as she crept down the servants' staircase and entered the kitchens. No one was present, though she did hear laughter coming from the servants' hall. Quickly, she left the kitchens and headed to Baxter's study, again not seeing a single servant. She wondered if some tried to sleep while the marquess and marchioness were gone, knowing they would have to rise and care for them once they returned from their evening of fun.

Entering her brother-in-law's study, she closed the door and moved to the windows, pushing a foot out slowly, feeling around her with each step until she reached the other side of the room. Margaret slipped behind the drawn curtains and found the lock. She slid it and then pushed open the window before stepping through it. The ground was less than a foot beneath her and she eased onto it, leaving the window slightly ajar. No servant would have a reason to enter the marquess's study and find it open.

Margaret pulled her cloak about her, lifting the hood to cover her hair as she moved toward the pavement in front of the townhouse. Stepping onto it, she turned and headed for the hansom cab she saw. As she approached, the driver climbed from his perch.

He did not call her by name, which pleased her.

"Are you headed to visit a friend?" he asked.

"I am." She gave him the address Daniel had given to her.

"That is the destination I was told to convey you to," he nodded purposefully.

The coachman helped her into the hansom cab. Though it was exposed in the front, she knew the members of Polite Society would all be headed toward a glittering ball being given this evening, while she would be going in the opposite direction.

They encountered little traffic and within twenty minutes, they had arrived. Again, the driver descended from his perch and aided her from the vehicle.

He pointed down the street. "I will park there so that I might see you when you come out. I will see you get home properly."

"Thank you," she told him.

She watched him take up the reins and flick his wrists. The hansom cab pulled away. Trepidation filled her. Margaret took a calming breath and moved to the front door and pushed it open.

There was no turning back now.

CHAPTER TWENTY-TWO

TURNING FROM THE door, Margaret saw a lamp on a table. Her eyes swept over the small, tidy room as she untied the cloak and placed it on a wooden chair.

Then Daniel stepped from the shadows, causing her heart to flutter violently in her chest. He was so incredibly handsome, wearing the black evening clothes that he would have worn to tonight's ball. She appeared dowdy by comparison.

He moved toward her, his gray eyes steady as he drank her in.

"You are no longer experiencing a headache?" he teased, his hands coming to rest on her shoulders, his fingers massaging her.

"It seems to have vanished all on its own," she replied, placing her palms on the solid wall of his muscled chest.

His mouth moved to hers, covering it, his lips firm and cool. He kissed her gently, without rushing, which she appreciated because nerves flittered through her at what they were about to do. He had all the experience in the world. She had none. Yet he was here with her now and would be in the hours to come before dawn.

Margaret knew she must make the most of their time together.

Her hands slid up his chest, moving over his shoulders, her fingers toying with the hair at his nape. She heard a low noise in his throat as his hands swept down her back, drawing her close to him. The kiss intensified, more demanding now, and her breasts began to ache in need.

Without warning, Daniel swept her into his arms, stealing her breath. She clung to him as he carried her up the stairs. They entered a small bedchamber, flickering candles placed on the floor, casting a soft light against the bed. The bedclothes had been turned back, awaiting them, but Daniel moved to a chair in the corner, the only other piece of furniture in the room. He sat, Margaret now on his lap.

"I have thought of nothing all day but kissing you," he said softly, his lips again seeking hers.

This time, he teased her mouth open, his tongue sweeping inside, causing her bones to dissolve into nothingness. She clung to him, answering his kiss, heat and desire filling her, spilling over. She still worried about her lack of experience in these matters. He kissed her as if they had all the time in the world. She tasted the mint on his breath. Smelled the spice of his shaving soap. Felt the hard muscle beneath her fingertips.

And reveled in it all.

Daniel broke the kiss, his lips trailing along her cheek, his breath warm as he reached her ear. He toyed with the shell of her ear, using his tongue, causing her to shiver uncontrollably. Then his teeth sank softly into her earlobe and she cried out.

He smoothed her hair and then slowly began pulling the pins from it, his face solemn as he accomplished this task. When he had removed all of them, he placed them on the ground and then ran his fingers through her locks. They spilled to her waist.

"A fiery, red cloud," he murmured, his mouth seeking hers again for long, drugging kisses that made her tremble.

He rose and she tightened her arms about his neck as he carried her to the bed and placed her gently atop it. He slipped off her shoes and then pushed her gown up to her knees, untying her stockings and rolling them sensually down her legs, the heat in his fingers scalding her.

Margaret started to scoot off the bed so she could stand and have him remove the rest.

"No," he told her, nudging her back. "You should see what I look like first. It is only fair."

"All right," she said, already breathless as he removed his coat, revealing broad shoulders.

Daniel unbuttoned his waistcoat and shrugged from it, setting it atop the coat. Then he slowly untied his cravat and cast it aside. Now, he wore a shirt of fine lawn, his breeches, and his shoes and stockings. She held her breath as he unbuttoned the three buttons on the shirt and then reached for the hem, pulling it up and over his head, revealing a muscular chest dusted lightly in dark hair.

She licked her lips in anticipation of running her hands over it.

Removing his shoes first, his breeches came next, and he bent forward to pull them down and step from them. Her eyes immediately were drawn to his manhood, which sprang to life from the thick, dark patch of curls between his legs. Finally, his stockings were gone and the Duke of Westfield stood before Margaret in naked glory.

He absolutely took her breath away.

"Thank you," he said humbly.

"Did I just say that aloud?" she asked.

He nodded. "So, you are pleased? You wish to continue?"

Margaret swallowed, finding it hard to take her eyes off such perfection. His broad shoulders tapered into a narrow waist. His belly was flat and ridged with muscle, as was his chest. His arms and legs were solid, hair covering them, as well. All she wanted to do was glide her hands up and down his body.

Slowly, she stood, drinking him in even as she bent to the hem of her own gown. It was a simple one and had been easy for her to slip on, but her fingers shook.

Daniel clasped her elbows, raising her. "Allow me."

She nodded wordlessly and stood rock still as he lifted her gown from her and set it aside. Capturing the hem of her chemise, he lifted it, too, causing her to squeeze her eyes tightly shut.

"Open your eyes, Margaret," he commanded.

She did—and his gaze immediately told her that he was pleased with what he saw.

Moving toward her, he wrapped his arms around her, gathering her to him. Soft breasts rubbed against hard muscle as his mouth descended to hers. His hands slipped to her buttocks, kneading them, stroking them and her back. His mouth devoured hers as his hands continued to roam her body, as if he were memorizing each curve. Her body heated at every touch—but his was like an inferno, raging out of control.

Margaret broke the kiss, breathless, panting. She caressed his cheek, seeing desire burn in his eyes.

"I am ready to make you mine," he growled, his voice low as he threaded his fingers through hers and pulled her toward the bed.

She knew his words didn't mean there was any permanency between them, only that for this night she became his.

One glorious night.

He settled her on the bed, climbing in beside her, propping one hand under his head as his hand glided along her body slowly. She luxuriated in the feel of it moving along each limb. Down her throat. Across her belly.

Then it moved lower, his fingers tangling in the curls hiding her womanly core. Her gaze flew to his, and she saw he was watching her carefully, a satisfied smile playing about his sensual lips.

"I am going to watch you, Margaret. I want to see your face when your orgasm arrives."

Her body already knew how to respond to this kind of touch, thanks to their encounter in the gazebo. Those precious minutes together were what had convinced her there was a world she had no familiarity with and that to be an artist in every sense of the word, she would need to experience physical pleasure on the deepest level.

She was only glad this would happen with Daniel. She couldn't imagine herself opening up to anyone else.

He teased the seam of her sex, gliding a finger up and down it in a maddening fashion before inserting a finger inside her. She caught her breath and waited for the wonderful rhythm from before, the one that caused the immense pressure to build inside her until she wanted to shout at the top of her lungs.

This time, though, he pinned his gaze to hers. Margaret could not look away, even as she began whimpering, her hips rising with each touch.

"Do you like this, Red?"

"You know I do," she said breathlessly. "Else I wouldn't have asked for this one night with you."

He increased both the pressure and speed and she gasped, her breathing now shallow and rapid. She felt as if she danced upon a dangerous precipice, knowing any moment that she would fall over the edge. That he would push her. That she would be awash with pleasure.

It happened when he touched the tip of her. She heard him murmur something about her sweet pearl before she was lost in a wave of sensation, her cries loud. This time, he did not muffle them since they were alone.

Gradually, she fell back to earth, sated, so limp she could not even lift a hand to brush her hair from her face. Daniel did it for her, lifting the stray curl and rubbing it between his fingers, kissing it, and then smoothing it. He kissed her a long time, her body heating again.

His lips then journeyed from her mouth downward, his tongue licking and teeth nipping a sensual path as he hovered over her body. Margaret reached up and caressed his chest, playing with the flat discs and his nipples. He growled low in his throat, continuing his march down her body.

She began to grow nervous as she realized where his final destination was and pushed up on her elbows.

"I don't want you to do that."

He stopped kissing her and met her gaze. "How do you know what I am going to do?"

She nibbled her already swollen bottom lip. "I have an idea."

He grinned. "I have a wonderful idea." He searched her face and said, "I have asked you this before, but it seems I must do so again. Do you trust me?"

By all that was holy, she did.

It was herself she didn't trust. She knew now that what she gave Daniel tonight was more than her virginity. It would be all of her. Her heart. Her soul. Her very essence. She should ask him to stop. Leave before she was lost.

Her mind warred with her body.

Her body won the argument.

Sighing, she fell back into the pillows, hearing his chuckle even as his lips reached their final destination.

He paused and said, "You'll enjoy this, Margaret. I promise."

He pushed her legs apart, his hands moving her so that her knees were bent. Then the feast began—and she was its only course. Daniel's tongue plunged deep inside her, causing her hips to rise. Soon, she bucked as he caressed her with tongue and fingers, sucking, licking, biting, kissing. It was enough to drive her mad.

Then the orgasm came again, shattering her into a thousand pieces. Wave after wave rolled from her as she writhed and cried and laughed in delight. It subsided and she quieted, both her body and mind. She lay limp, unable to move or even think.

Then she felt something against her core, lightly stroking her. Opening her eyes, she saw Daniel above her and realized he was ready to push his cock inside her, his fingers preparing the way. Fear swept through her, seeing how large it was.

"It will n-n-not fit," she stammered.

He grinned. "Oh, it will, Red. And it will feel delicious."

She supposed this act was what gave him pleasure. She had asked if she could make him feel it when they had been in the gardens at the gazebo, and he had put her off. Tensing, she squeezed her eyes shut, not wanting to witness what would happen next.

His caresses continued and soft kisses began. Soon, she hungered for more, and her arms went about him, matching him kiss for kiss as their tongues warred with one another.

Then a sudden pressure occurred, a sense of fullness she had never experienced before. Margaret realized it was because Daniel had pushed inside her, but he remained completely still.

"I want your body to get used to me," he told her.

An urge to move overwhelmed her, and she rocked her hips. "Oh!"

He smiled. "Oh, is right."

She tried it again, feeling that marvelous tingling begin again. He withdrew from her and then sank deeply into her. Quickly, she caught on to the rhythm and they began a dance, a sensual dance of desire. The tempo quickened, and Margaret clung to Daniel, her nails digging deeply into his back, anchoring him to her. Then she cried out in pure pleasure, and he echoed her, sinking deeply into her before collapsing atop her, driving her into the mattress.

They clung to one another, spent, his weight welcome. He rolled, though, bringing her atop him. She nestled her cheek against his heart, sprawled atop him, its beat gradually slowing to a steady rhythm.

It had been heaven. Pure magic.

She didn't know how long they lay this way, only that she never wanted tonight to end.

Margaret remained atop him, his finger tracing her back in lazy patterns, no words spoken. Then he kissed the top of her head. Her temples. Shifted her so that his mouth settled against her neck. Within minutes, they were kissing passionately, the flames fanning higher until she reached the heavens again.

This time he lay beside her, on his back, his arm going around her. Daniel drew her to him and Margaret curled into him, flinging a leg over him and nuzzling his neck before resting her check against his shoulder.

She wouldn't tell him this was the most incredible experience of her life. She would pour it into the portrait which she would paint of him.

This night with this man had taught her so much. With the highs, though, would come the lows of tremendous heartbreak. Reality already seeped into her soul. Margaret realized she hadn't merely given him her heart. She had denied it for too long and couldn't any longer.

She had fallen in love with the Duke of Westfield.

CHAPTER TWENTY-THREE

D ANIEL BASKED IN the glow of Margaret being in his arms. He had never experienced the feelings he had this night.

It was love. Absolutely, definitely, most certainly love.

Somehow, he had thought love made a man weak. Less than he should be. Instead, Daniel felt stronger than ever before with this woman in his arms and in his heart. They would be a formidable team, moving through Polite Society. All he had to do was offer for her now.

Should he do so as their naked bodies were entwined with one another? Or should he be far more proper and wait until they were clothed and sitting in a drawing room?

He had no patience when it came to Red. He wanted to make certain she was his.

Now.

He brushed his lips against the top of her head, the silky locks feeling even better than he thought they would. His fingers lightly danced along her arm, and he thought he would be the most fortunate man in the world to wake up each morning with this woman by his side. None of that separate beds for him and his lady love. They would toss tradition and spend every night together. He could not wait to see her belly swollen with his child inside it. Even now, he might have planted the seed of one inside her. That made him realize they should wed sooner rather than later. He did not think St. George's would be booked for a wedding so early into the Season and then decided he could not wait three weeks for the banns to be read. He needed Margaret now—and that meant a special license. Hopefully, she would not mind a quick wedding.

He wanted to look into her eyes as he spoke and so he eased her away from him until they both faced one another, their heads lying close together on the same pillow. He saw the most beautiful woman he had ever seen and was happy she would be his.

"We have plans to make," he told her.

She smiled lazily at him. "Do you plan to have your way with me again, Your Grace?" she teased.

"We need to talk about our wedding. Where you wish to have it held. I thought if I obtained a special license, Margaret, that I—"

Her hands shot out, pushing hard on his chest, putting distance between them. She sat up, her mouth trembling.

"What is this talk of a wedding?" she asked. "Suddenly, you are telling me about it. Not even asking me if I would consider marrying you. I asked one night of you. Not a lifetime." She drew the bedclothes over her breasts protectively and glared at him.

"I did not think you meant that," he said, dismayed that she would argue with him. "Did you not see how we good we are together just now? We could have that every day—every night— of our lives, Red."

She bristled at the use of the nickname. "My name is Margaret," she said haughtily, her chin rising a notch. "And you are not to even use that, Your Grace. I am Lady Margaret to you. *If* we ever speak again when we run into one another at some *ton* event."

She turned away from him, and Daniel realized he was losing her—and did not understand why. His arm shot out, grasping her upper arm.

"Why?" he asked, a feeling of helplessness filling him.

"Tonight was nothing more than an experiment," she told him. "First and foremost, I am an artist. I wanted to experience a range of emotions. Coupling with a man was an experience I believed would make me richer. Make my paintings better."

Hurt filled him. "You *used* me? I was merely an experiment to you?"

He had been ready to declare his love for her, and yet she was tossing him aside as if he meant nothing to her. Anger replaced the hurt, his damaged pride driving it.

"Who cares about your bloody art?" he spat out. "So, you have a bit of talent and can paint a likeness of others. What does that matter? You could be my duchess and rule the *ton*. I could give you anything you desired. You need never pick up a paintbrush again."

Anger sparked in her eyes. "It matters to me, Your Grace. It is the only thing that matters," she said vehemently. "I don't want to be your duchess. I don't want to belong to you or any other man. I plan to make my own way in the world. I despise everything about the *ton*. The members of Polite Society have no souls. They live only to gossip and indulge in things that will never be important to me."

"But you wish to paint them."

"Yes, so that I might become independent and beholden to no one. Truth be told, I would much rather paint common people. Their lives actually mean something, but they barely make enough to exist. At least by painting people of the *ton*, their families will have a lasting legacy and see their history brought to life on canvas."

He couldn't believe she refused to be his wife. "Then I hope you experienced the full gambit of the emotions you wished to this evening, my lady," he said stiffly.

Daniel tossed the bedclothes aside and went to his clothes, turning his back to her so that she could not see as he fumbled to dress just how crushed his spirit was. As he dressed, he heard her leave the bed and knew she did the same. He finished his task and turned to face her. Her face was void of all emotion and color.

"You said this place was to be let," she said, her voice tight. "What must we do to put it right again?"

"Nothing," he snapped. Wanting to hurt her, he added, "It is in a convenient location. Most likely, I will purchase it and install my mistress here."

His words had the effect he wanted. She flinched. He knew he had wounded her deeply.

Wordlessly, Margaret left the bedchamber, and he heard her retreating down the stairs. He supposed she gathered her cloak about her, and then he heard the door open and close softly.

What had just happened?

Daniel had experienced the best hours of his life with Margaret. He had thought them the start of a foundation they would build upon as they created a life together. He could not understand why she had used him so callously. How she could seem so innocent and naive and yet have hidden how coldhearted she truly was.

He had to accept the fact that she would never be in his life. She would not be his companion and mother to his children. The thought nearly undid him. For the first time, he wasn't getting what he wanted. Everything had come so easily to him his entire life. He had been good at all things academic. Others flocked to him, wishing to be his friend. He'd had looks and wealth, even before his grandfather died and Daniel became a duke. Ever since that had occurred, no one had dared tell him no.

Except Margaret. His Red. The one woman who was different from all the rest. The one who had entered his heart and he feared would remain there a lifetime. He despaired, not ever speaking to her again, much less sharing her bed.

Daniel rushed down the stairs, thinking he would apologize for all the horrible things he had said to her. He flung the front door open and stepped outside, glancing down the street to where he had arranged the hansom cab, driven by his own coachman, to be waiting for her. He saw Margaret being helped into it and then his driver returned to his seat and took up the reins, taking her far away. Out of his life.

MARGARET SAT IN the hansom cab as it went through the deserted streets of London. A coldness filled her, numbing her to her very soul.

She had no idea that Daniel would have offered for her after they made love. She believed he did so out of obligation. That was no way to start a marriage. It was almost as bad as if someone had seen them in an embrace and demanded they wed, lest she be ruined. A forced marriage between them would be terrible—and that is what he had wanted to do—force her to wed him. Merely because he was a duke, he thought he could get his way about everything.

Besides, he had so callously brought up his mistress to her. How could he have coupled with her so passionately tonight and yet had another woman he did so with on a regular basis? Even if Margaret weakened and agreed to wed him, which she knew would be impossible after the harsh words spoken between them, she would be ill every night, wondering if he went to his mistress's bed instead of hers. She could not live like that. Already, he had ripped out her heart and stomped upon it. She knew she would never be the same again.

They arrived at the end of the block Baxter's townhouse sat upon. The driver helped her from his hansom cab.

"I'll watch you go, my lady," he assured her. "Nothing bad will happen to you," he promised.

"Thank you," she told him, already thinking the worst thing that could have happened already had occurred.

As she made her way along the pavement, Margaret realized the worst had yet to occur. It would be when Daniel entered a ballroom, his duchess upon his arm as he beamed at her in pride.

Margaret knew that would be her undoing.

She slipped through the window of Baxter's study once more, closing and locking it before creeping silently through the quiet house. Returning to her bedchamber, she threw off the clothes she wore and then caught the scent of Daniel on her. She brought her forearm to her nose and inhaled deeply. It was as if he had been embossed upon her skin.

Frantically, she poured water from a pitcher into a basin and dipped a cloth into it, scrubbing herself so that all remnants of him would be gone. But she had been so caught up in the moment that she had not thought to ask him what he would do to prevent creating a child. She had heard talk of this but had no clear knowledge. Now, she had one more thing to worry about.

Bearing the illegitimate child of a duke.

She would be ostracized by the very *ton* she wished to paint if that occurred. She prayed no babe would grow within her although a small part of her wished it would. That she would have something of Daniel with her always. Though she had wanted a child, she did not want to bring one into the world and have the *ton* gossip viciously about the babe. She had done the right thing in pushing Daniel away. He would wed a suitable young lady chosen by his grandmother and get his heir off her. Margaret would do what she wanted to do. Paint.

Then why did she hurt so much now?

She tenderly cleaned her sore core, thinking only a short time ago Daniel was inside her. A part of her.

She must push these thoughts aside. If she did not, it would be pure torture and might drive her into madness.

Pulling her night rail over her head, Margaret climbed into bed and brought the bedclothes protectively around her. Images haunted her. Daniel's mouth on her breasts. His hands roaming her body. The dance of love they had performed together when they had joined their bodies as one.

She dissolved into tears, crying herself to sleep.

When she awoke, her eyes were swollen. She resolved to

move on. The first rays of dawn were streaming through her window, and she decided to take solace and refuge in her work. The dowager duchess's portrait was a little more than halfway completed. She would finish it.

Today.

Rising, she washed her face, holding the wet cloth to her eyes in hopes the swelling would subside. Though she longed for a cup of tea, she did not want to see anyone now. After dressing, she climbed the stairs to the top floor and her studio. She began painting, not in a frenzy, but calmly. Each brushstroke soothed her soul. She might never have Daniel—but she would always have her art. She had done the best thing for the both of them. He was free to wed and she to invest herself in her art. Eventually, she hoped she would once more find the joy in it and some bit of happiness for herself.

Determination filled her as she focused on the canvas before her.

CHAPTER TWENTY-FOUR

M ARGARET SET DOWN her brush and stepped back in order to be able to study the completed portrait. She viewed it with a critical eye, as she knew others would, as well. She spent a good ten minutes searching for any imperfections to correct and found none.

It was truly finished.

She had never painted for that number of hours in a row. She had no idea of the time, only that her fingers cramped and her legs were tired from standing so long. Her back and shoulders also ached. But she was exceedingly pleased with the results—and thought the Dowager Duchess of Westfield would be, as well.

Methodically, she cleaned her brushes, her brain simply too tired to think as habit took over. That was a good thing because if she had the energy to do so, she would have wasted her thoughts on Daniel. No, the Duke of Westfield. All familiarity between them had ceased to exist. She must erect a strong barrier around her in order to protect herself from being hurt any more than she already had been.

She finished putting everything back in its place and decided to send the dowager duchess a message that the portrait had been completed. She knew the old woman was eager for this to occur and had again mentioned the party she wished to hold to unveil it when she had last seen Margaret. Unfortunately, that would mean seeing Westfield again. Another ball was to be held this evening, which he would no doubt attend. She would do her best not to look at him—or for him. She would focus on making new acquaintances and put the events of last night behind her.

Returning to her bedchamber, she rang for a maid and dashed off a note to the dowager duchess. Molly answered her summons.

Handing her the note, she asked that it be delivered at once and then for bath water to be sent up.

Molly giggled. "You do need a bath, my lady. You have paint on you and your gown."

Margaret glanced down and saw she had forgotten to place her smock over the gown, which was now stained with various shades of oil paints. Fortunately, it was an old one because it was now ruined. Since it looked too awful to hand down to any of the servants, she would keep it and possibly wear it in the future as she painted.

Molly returned three-quarters of an hour later with several other maids, each bearing buckets of heated water. Two footmen carried in a bathtub, which she assumed was from Dolley's dressing room. The maids poured the water into the tub, while Molly tipped a vial and stirred the water. Margaret caught the scent of vanilla.

Once the tub was filled, the other maids disappeared and Molly undressed Margaret, who sank into the hot water, a long sigh escaping her lips. She rested her head on the back of the tub, simply enjoying the feel of the water for a few minutes until Molly had her sit up in order to wash Margaret's hair. The maid then scrubbed Margaret from head to toe and rinsed away the suds, enfolding her in a large bath sheet and helping her step from the tub.

Molly combed the tangles from Margaret's hair and dressed her in a gown of soft blue.

"I sneaked up to see how the dowager duchess's portrait was coming along," the servant admitted. "You finished it, my lady!" Molly said enthusiastically. "Why, I thought it was the dowager duchess herself, it looked so much like her."

"Thank you for the compliment. I hope the dowager duchess will like it as much as you do." She paused. "And that others in Polite Society agree."

"Why?" the maid asked.

"My goal is to become a portrait artist," Margaret explained. "If the Dowager Duchess of Westfield is pleased, she will let that fact be known. Hopefully, others will then want to pay me to paint them, as well."

Molly thought a moment. "You want to do that rather than go to parties?"

"Very much so. I actually find *ton* events to be rather boring." She hesitated and then said, "My plan is to leave Lord Baxter's townhouse and move to a small place of my own. You know some of this since you accompanied me to Mr. Dickens's offices."

The maid grinned. "Then you will need help, my lady. I said it before. I would be happy to accompany you. I can clean and cook a bit. Take care of you and your clothes."

"You really would come with me?" Margaret asked, suddenly very much hoping that Molly wished to do so.

"Why not?" the servant asked cheekily. "I like you and would be happy working for you."

"You would not miss your position here?"

Molly's nose crinkled. "Not a bit, my lady."

"I need to see my solicitor. I am coming into a bit of money upon my next birthday. Perhaps he will have good news for me. I asked him to look for a place for me to let. I will keep you informed."

Dolley came in, waving a piece of parchment. "This came for you," she informed Margaret, handing it over. "From the Dowager Duchess of Westfield. Naturally, I opened it in case it concerned me."

She sighed inwardly, knowing her sister would never change. It made her want a place to call her own even more so, where she would have the privacy she craved.

"The dowager duchess wishes for you to call upon her for tea this afternoon." Dolley frowned and barked at Molly, "Do something with her hair. It is almost time for callers to arrive."

"Yes, my lady," Molly said quietly, taking up a brush and running it through Margaret's still-damp hair.

Once Dolley left, Margaret said, "A chignon again, please. It is easy and simple to style. I will go straight from here to see the dowager duchess. Would you be willing to accompany me?"

"Yes, my lady."

Margaret went downstairs once Molly had finished and was just in time to greet their first three callers of the day. As expected, the Duke of Westfield was not among them. She knew he wouldn't come after the words they had exchanged. It was hard to believe merely twelve hours ago, she had been lying naked in his arms, enjoying his every touch.

"Margaret?"

She blinked. "Yes, Dolley?"

"I have asked that the carriage be readied for you. If you wish to slip out now, do so. I would not want you to be late for your tea."

"It is because I have finished her portrait," she explained to her sister. "That is why I have been asked to tea. We will discuss it and the party the dowager duchess wishes to give."

Her sister's face lit up. "Oh, I cannot wait to attend."

Margaret left the drawing room and found Molly standing outside it.

"Here is your bonnet and reticule, my lady. I have also checked with the housekeeper, and she said I might accompany you."

She smiled. "I think we will do quite nicely together, Molly," she praised.

They arrived at their destination. Molly said she would wait for Margaret in the carriage. She was admitted and taken to the dowager duchess's sitting room, where a teacart already waited.

"Your Grace," she greeted. "Thank you for inviting me to

tea."

"Where is it?" the old woman asked eagerly. "I thought you would bring my picture with you. Is a footman waiting with it in the foyer?"

She chuckled. "No, Your Grace. I left the portrait to dry. It should be ready in a day or so. You wouldn't want it smeared. Also, I will need to have it framed."

"I will see to that. I have a good eye for these things. Have it delivered to me tomorrow morning. I shall plan my little party for the day after tomorrow. In the afternoon, I think, so others might talk about it that evening. What do you think of holding the party outside in the gardens? Perhaps at the gazebo where my roses are since they are featured?"

Margaret flushed guiltily, thinking of what she and Daniel had done in that gazebo.

"I think it a fine idea, Your Grace. As long as we can see to the framing that quickly. These things usually take more time," she warned.

The dowager duchess waved away the concern. "I am eager to have others see it—and I am a dowager duchess. You would be surprised how quickly things are done to please a dowager duchess." She paused, looking at Margaret steadily. "Would you care to be a duchess one day, Lady Margaret?"

Panic filled her. She wondered if Daniel had mentioned to his grandmother that he had offered marriage to Margaret.

"I would not enjoy it, Your Grace," she said, trying to calm herself. "A woman who is a duchess claims far too much of Polite Society's attention, both in a good and bad way. I wish to remain on the fringe of the *ton* and devote myself to my art."

"I see. Well, pour out if you would, please. I don't want our tea to get cold."

DANIEL DIDN'T BOTHER with a snifter, drinking the remainder of the brandy straight from the decanter. He let it slip from his fingers and drop to the floor.

His head throbbed painfully. He moved from his slumped position and stretched out on the settee. He was too long for it, causing his feet to hang over the end. He had been drinking since he'd arrived home around four in the morning after watching Margaret being safely driven away. He thought he could drink her image away.

That idea failed miserably.

Nevertheless, he continued drinking, all morning and throughout the afternoon. He would be in no condition to attend tonight's ball, where he had thought to dance with every pretty creature he could, hoping to make Margaret jealous. It would be difficult to even stand at this point. He dreaded when Gran would find him, demanding to know why he was soused.

The door to the library opened, and he heard her crossing the room. She moved more slowly these days, which was how he recognized her gait. He waited, eyes closed, sensing her come to stand before him. Then firm fingers tightened about his ankles, lifting his legs into the air. Gran sat, lowering his legs again so that they were settled upon her lap.

"Is it that bad, Daniel?" she asked.

He opened his eyes and raised his head slightly, causing her image to swim. Still, he caught the sympathy in her eyes and lowered himself back on the settee.

"Worse than bad. Rotten, in fact."

"Does it have anything to do with Lady Margaret?"

He let out a long breath. "It has everything to do with Lady Margaret."

"She just left, you know."

Quickly, he sat up, immediately regretting the movement. Nausea filled him. The ache in his head was only matched by the one in his heart. He lowered his head again, trying to swallow the unshed tears clogging his throat.

"Margaret sent a note around, and I invited her to tea," Gran continued. "She has finished my portrait."

Daniel opened one eye and looked at her. "Finished, you say?"

"Yes. I had hoped she would have a footman bring it when she called, but she said she had only completed it, and it still needed time to dry properly. It should be delivered here tomorrow morning, however. I will take care of having it framed and hold a party so that an exclusive group might view her work."

His heart quickened, thinking of Margaret here, yet knowing she would definitely ignore him.

"Will you tell me what passed between you, Daniel?" Gran asked.

"I offered for her—and she turned me down."

"She . . . turned down a duke? My, she is an independent one. I think I like her even more than I did."

He swung his legs to the floor, forcing himself to sit up. "You *like* a woman that refused to wed me?"

"I have always liked Margaret," Gran explained. "It has nothing to do with you. She must have a very good reason not to wish to marry you."

"She said she wanted to devote herself to her art," he said glumly. "She was angry, too, because . . . well, because I told her we would wed."

"You did not ask her if she wished to? Oh, Daniel, you have mucked things up now, haven't you?"

"Whose side are you on?" he demanded, immediately wincing because his volume made his head hurt.

She took his hand. "I am always on your side, my dear boy. I always have been." She smiled knowingly. "I simply understand that Margaret is the one for you. You will have to fight for her."

"She won't have me," he said. "I said a few . . . ugly things. About her art."

Gran frowned deeply. Daniel had not seen her look so displeased in years. If ever.

"*What* ugly things?" she demanded, and he heard the controlled anger in her tone. "Why would you disparage her and her art?" Gran clucked her tongue, shaking her head, anger now sparking in her eyes.

Before he could reply, she said, "Margaret has hopes. High hopes for her art and what she wishes to accomplish. I am doing my best to see that she attains her goals, Daniel. It is the least I can do after what happened to her grandmother. My *friend*."

"What do you speak of?" he demanded.

"I was the closest of friends with Margaret's grandmother when we were girls," Gran explained. "Until she wed a man who despised her talent. He mocked her. Belittled her for wanting to be an artist. He refused to allow her to continue painting and forbid we see one another." Gran's eyes filled with tears. "I had to watch her wither under his domination. Lose herself until she was finally a mere shadow of the passionate, headstrong young woman I had known and loved."

His grandmother's words shocked him.

"I see so much of her in Margaret," Gran said softly. "I wasn't able to stand up for my friend—but my rank in Polite Society gives me quite a bit a sway over other members of it. I will do everything in my power to see that Margaret's talent shines and is not wasted."

"But—"

"No buts, Daniel. I don't wish to hear any excuses from you. You have admitted you said ugly things to her. I'm sure she fired back a few choice phrases at you. That does not matter one whit." Gran paused, finally smiling at him. "You will certainly have to grovel. Even then, she may not take you back right away."

"Who says I want her back?" he said moodily.

"When was the last time you drank yourself into a stupor?"

"I don't know."

"You are despondent over the fact Lady Margaret Townsend

did not fall at your feet. That is a good thing, Daniel. You would not want some simpering miss to be your duchess. You need a woman of character. One with backbone. One who will stand up to you and not always let you have your way." Gran paused. "Do you love her?"

"Yes," he admitted without hesitation.

"Then she is worth fighting for."

It was true. He had never quit anything he had started. Once he wanted something, he went after it, single-mindedly.

He wanted Margaret as his duchess. No other woman would do.

"You are right, Gran." He rubbed his temples. "I merely needed a little pity party—and then a swift kick in the arse from my adoring grandmother. I will find a way to win Margaret back."

"That's my Daniel," Gran cooed.

CHAPTER TWENTY-FIVE

M ARGARET WENT DOWNSTAIRS to breakfast and found her brother-in-law perusing the morning newspapers. He looked up and greeted her.

"I hear we are to see this portrait which you have been working on at a small gathering the Dowager Duchess of Westfield is holding."

"Yes, Her Grace has invited a handful to come and view her portrait. I hope seeing it will encourage at least a few of them to want to have their portraits painted."

He gazed steadily at her. "By you."

It may have seemed a question but sounded more a statement.

"Yes, my lord. I want to paint members of the *ton*. I believe I have made you aware of this fact."

"Interesting," he remarked, going back to reading.

Halfway through breakfast, the morning post arrived and one letter was for her. She opened it, seeing that it was from her solicitor. Mr. Dickens told her that he had found a proper house for her and he believed she should see in person. He asked her to stop by this morning so that they might view it together.

Margaret finished her meal and excused herself, thinking Baxter did not even hear her, being lost in the day's news. She stepped to the butler and asked if Molly might chaperone her as she had a meeting with her solicitor. The butler agreed and asked if she wished for the carriage.

"I suppose I should ask his lordship."

Margaret explained to her brother-in-law why she would like to use his carriage. The marquess was more than agreeable. She thought he wanted her out sooner rather than later and that was why he provided the carriage now.

A quarter hour later, she and Molly were off to Mr. Dickens's offices, the maid asking, "So, this man has money of yours?"

"He does, but I do not have access to my dowry until the first of June when I turn five and twenty. I do have other funds, however," she revealed. "The Dowager Duchess of Westfield has paid me quite a handsome sum for the work on her portrait."

It had surprised Margaret when the old woman had done so, since she had yet to see the work Margaret had produced. When the dowager duchess had named the figure at their most recent tea, it floored Margaret, and she told the older woman that it was simply too much.

"Nonsense, my dear," the dowager duchess had protested. "It is more than a fair price, one a man who is a portrait artist would command. I will slip, of course, and reveal how much I have paid you. By tonight's ball, I am certain that number will have doubled—if not tripled."

Margaret had been aghast at that idea, thinking no one would commission her at such a high price. The dowager duchess, however, assured her they would.

"You underestimate my influence," the old woman had said. "Even though I am but a widow, I still am a leader of the *ton* and can nudge them in any direction I choose."

Because of those funds, Margaret would be able to lease any place she wished for several months.

They arrived at Mr. Dickens's offices and Molly accompanied Margaret inside. The clerk went to notify Mr. Dickens they had arrived, and he came out wearing his hat.

"I think you will enjoy this property, Lady Margaret," he told her. "And your banker also informed me of the sudden windfall in your account, thanks to the Dowager Duchess of Westfield."

It should not have surprised her that her business was known by others. Men ruled the world she inhabited.

"Yes, Mr. Dickens, it was the commission paid by the dowager duchess for my work on her portrait. I completed it and hope to paint others of Polite Society."

"It must be some portrait, my lady. I look forward to seeing your talent on display at some point."

"I came in Lord Baxter's carriage," she informed him. "It is waiting outside. Shall we take it to see this property?"

The solicitor was agreeable to her suggestion and gave the address to the coachman. A footman helped them into the vehicle, and they rode in amiable silence. As she looked out the window, Margaret recognized the neighborhood they turned into as being the one where she had met Daniel for their tryst. Sure enough, the vehicle rolled past the very house and then turned west at the next street, pulling to the curb and coming to a halt.

"The neighborhood is a good one," the solicitor told her. "Not quite as fashionable as what you are accustomed to, my lady, but that would have cost a pretty penny. This way, you have the proximity without paying the high rent of Mayfair."

A part of Margaret did not want to like this house because she feared she might see Daniel and his mistress if she leased it. Then she decided they would not be out and about together in the neighborhood. His visits would be more of a late-night variety. By then, she would be snug in her bed.

Alone.

"Come along, Molly," she encouraged. "I would like your opinion on things."

The servant looked pleased to be included, and they approached the door. Mr. Dickens produced a key and unlocked it, ushering the women inside. He told them he had previewed the property the previous day, and knew it might suit Lady Margaret's needs.

"I will let you explore it a bit, my lady. You do not need me hovering."

He took a seat, and she noted the place was furnished, which was certainly a benefit. If she would have had to purchase furniture, her funds would dwindle rapidly.

She looked about the parlor before leaving Mr. Dickens there and then moved to a small dining room that seated four. The kitchens came next and were more than adequate. A small room stood off the kitchens, and she assumed by the twin beds in it that it was meant for two servants to share. If she hired a cook, the woman could sleep here, along with Molly.

There was no back staircase, and so they retraced their steps to the staircase opposite the front door. Upstairs, she found two rooms of decent size. One was larger than the other and served as a bedchamber, while the other stood empty.

"You could make your art here," Molly said enthusiastically. "Why, those windows are a good size and let in the light you would need."

Margaret had been thinking the very same thing. She deemed the place perfect for her needs. She doubted she would meet with clients here, thinking she would be summoned to their houses. If not, the parlor would serve as a perfect place to discuss the portraits she would paint with her subjects.

"I am leaning toward renting this," she told the maid. "Would you be happy to share a room with a cook?"

"That would suit me just fine, my lady," Molly said brightly. "Oh, this is so exciting!"

Margaret smiled. "I think so, too."

They returned downstairs and Mr. Dickens rose. "What do you think of the place, my lady?"

"I would like to lease it," she declared. "What are the terms?"

He told her she could let it for three months or six, the monthly rent dropping slightly for a longer lease. Three months seemed too short to her, and so she said, "I will sign a contract for six months. Is there an option to renew after that time?"

"There is. By then, you will know if this place suits your needs or not. If it does, you could continue to lease it or even make an offer to purchase it. If you find it is not to your taste, please let me know so I can explore other properties for you to see. When would you like your lease to begin?"

Without hesitation, Margaret said, "Immediately."

She was eager to have a place to work, anticipating she would receive a few commissions after the dowager duchess's portrait had been revealed this afternoon. She preferred privacy and knew Dolley and Baxter did, as well. The sooner she left their residence, the better for all. She had no desire to continue accompanying them to *ton* events because she did not want to see Daniel anywhere. She knew she would have to do so this afternoon at his grandmother's party. Beyond that? She needed the distance. It was the only way to begin to mend her broken heart.

"Then if you wish, my lady, we could stop at the bank and make arrangements for the funds to be transferred."

"Then let us do so."

The process went quickly and smoothly, thanks to Mr. Dickens handling the transaction. Soon, they were back at his offices.

"I will draw up the papers today and notify the owner of the property," he told her. "I can send these papers to you once they are signed so that you do not have to make a return trip here. I will include the key, as well. It should take a day or so, and then you will be able to move in."

"That would be most convenient, Mr. Dickens. I thank you for your help in this matter."

"It is always a pleasure to see you, Lady Margaret. Good day." He exited the carriage.

As they started for home, Margaret and Molly talked of the new place. Molly assured her that if it were only to be the two of them, she could handle the cooking for a while.

Margaret agreed, deciding she would eventually hire a cook. She did not want to work poor Molly to death. She would, though, need to speak with Dolley about taking the maid with her when she left.

They arrived at the Baxter townhouse, and she inquired of the butler where her sister was and went to Dolley's sitting room. She found Dolley lying on a chaise lounge, nibbling sweets and looking wan.

"How are you feeling?"

"Tired," Dolley admitted. "I am trying to rest now so that I will look my best at the Dowager Duchess of Westfield's party this afternoon."

"Speaking of that, she has already paid me my commission. I looked at a place this morning with Papa's solicitor. I had him searching for a property for me to rent, one that had a large place for me to paint."

"You are truly leaving us?" Dolley asked, seeming alarmed by the idea.

"You knew that was my plan all along. While I have appreciated being able to turn one room here into an art studio, I know how the smell of paints bothers you, especially now in your delicate condition. Mr. Dickens has found an ideal residence for me. It contains a perfect room to serve as my studio. I have leased it for the next six months and then will decide whether I wish to remain in it or find something else."

"I suppose if you are to be an artist, you need your independence," Dolley said. "You also will be . . . working."

"Yes, that lifestyle is not conducive to participate in the activities of the Season."

"You will no longer come to any *ton* events?"

It was obvious by the look of horror on Dolley's face that she thought her sister mad to consider such a change.

"I may go on occasion, but for the most part, my life as a member of Polite Society has ended. I will have my own money, Dolley. You and Baxter will no longer be responsible for me."

"Will you at least come to visit?" her sister asked. "The children have grown quite fond of you."

"Of course, I will come and see them. And you." She paused.

"I will need help, though. One of your maids—Molly—has been quite useful, helping me with my brushes and dressing me. She says she could cook and clean for me. Do you think it is possible to take her with me?"

"Of course. I won't miss one maid. I barely know any of their names as it is." Dolley studied Margaret. "Are you certain this is the life you wish to lead? You truly do not wish to ever wed?"

The only man she would ever consider marrying would be the Duke of Westfield. And that was impossible. Even though he had asked—no, actually told her—that they were to wed, she knew he did not value her art, just as her grandfather had been disrespectful of Grandmama's talent. She could not wed a man who sought to control her or take her art away from her.

"No, Dolley, I am meant to follow a solitary path. Art will be my constant companion."

She excused herself and returned to her bedchamber, needing time to reflect on all that had happened today. She sat in a chair, pleased that she kept her tears at bay, because she did not want to show up and have Daniel see her with swollen eyes. No, she had cried enough tears over the arrogant duke and was ready to move on.

Molly appeared without being summoned, ready to dress Margaret for the afternoon's party. She donned a gown of warm sunshine and allowed Molly time to dress her hair in a fashion to flatter both her and the gown. She even had the maid place the pearls Papa had given to her so many years ago around her neck.

When she rose from her dressing table, Molly beamed. "You look beautiful, my lady."

"If I do so, it is because of you."

"The butler called me in, my lady. They said that Lady Baxter had agreed for me to depart the household with you."

Molly took Margaret's hands and squeezed them. "Thank you ever so much, my lady."

"I am happy you wish to come with me, Molly. You might as well go ahead and begin packing my things because it looks as if we will be able to occupy the house starting tomorrow morning. The papers from Mr. Dickens arrived just before you came up to help me dress. I signed them, and they will be returned."

"Will you go to the ball this evening?" the maid asked.

"No. I will be packing up my art supplies," she explained. "I won't be missed."

Molly placed her hands on Margaret's shoulders. "No, my lady. Go to the ball. Everyone will be talking about you after they see the portrait you've painted. It will be good to be seen by others and accept their compliments."

The maid's advice did make sense.

"I will see your trunks are brought down from the attics," the servant said. "I will also pack up everything in your studio. It all will be ready to go by morning." Molly smiled. "You can count on me, my lady. I won't let you down."

"Thank you. Then I will do as you say and attend tonight's ball."

Margaret ventured downstairs. For once, Dolley had beaten her to the foyer, which let Margaret know how eager her sister was to attend this party. She wished it was because Dolley was proud of her but knew it revolved around being asked to a duke's home.

Baxter appeared. "Are we ready?"

Her belly filled with butterflies. She tamped down her anxiety.

"Yes, my lord," Margaret replied, knowing her future would most likely be decided within the hour.

CHAPTER TWENTY-SIX

Daniel anticipated Margaret's arrival more than the unveiling of his grandmother's portrait. She had summoned someone to frame the portrait in record time, as well as having two dozen invitations hand-delivered to some of the most prominent members of the *ton*. He knew every single person invited would forego their calls today in order to be at the Duke of Westfield's townhouse in Mayfair for the unveiling of his grandmother's portrait, done by Lady Margaret Townsend.

It was a bold move on Gran's part, listing Margaret as the artist. Daniel knew if people had been curious before they were now keen on attending, wanting to see not only the portrait itself, but the lady of Polite Society who had painted a dowager duchess. He was certain Margaret would claim more attention than Gran's portrait.

He still hadn't a clue how to convince her to marry him.

Daniel knew he had made several mistakes. He had assumed Margaret would want to wed him despite the fact that she had told him from their very first meeting that she was not interested in the *ton* or marriage. Her art was what captured her, body and soul. He had disparaged her art, making it seem small and unimportant—when it was everything to her.

He had hoped to be her everything and still was unhappy playing second fiddle to oil paints and canvas. But if it came down to it, he would do so. He would take scraps from Margaret and be proud to do so.

How could he ask for her hand? Yes, this time he must ask. He had not done so previously, merely told her where they could wed and announcing that a special license would be the solution. If anything, Margaret was independent. She did not take kindly to be told to do anything, particularly something she had no interest in.

Yet he knew the experience of making love with him had moved her. No woman could respond the way she had and be unaffected. He had to convince her they were meant to be together. If he had to grovel, cajole, plead, and persuade—he would do so. The trouble would be in getting her alone when he knew a swarm would be gathered around her this afternoon.

Perhaps he should remain in the shadows today. Let her shine in the sun. It was her time. Her hour. Her glory. Even though Daniel had yet to see what she had painted, he knew it would be brilliant. Gran would not have gone to such lengths to set Margaret up for failure. If anything, his grandmother wanted Margaret to succeed and bask in the recognition that her own grandmother had never received. He realized now that he had tried to squelch her talent, much as her grandfather had done to her grandmother. Margaret was not one to wait decades as her grandmother had to display her art. She would fight to do so—and win.

He entered the drawing room and saw the easel where the portrait rested, covered in a rich, burgundy cloth. Gran stood at the window and turned as he approached.

"Have you seen it?" he asked.

"I have," she confirmed. "Margaret is brilliant. If you are fortunate enough to make her your duchess, Daniel, you must allow her to paint."

He chuckled. "If I am lucky enough to land Margaret, there would be no allowing. She is not one to ask permission from me. She would act on her own. As my duchess should."

Gran smiled at him fondly. "You are already discovering the secrets to a good marriage." She paused. "I believe you are a love match."

"I do love her. I told you so. I only hope she loves me."

His grandmother cradled his cheek. "What's not to love?" she said.

Hampton entered the drawing room. "Lord and Lady Baxter and Lady Margaret Townsend," the butler announced.

A moment later, the trio entered the room. Daniel's eyes immediately went to Margaret, who wore a gown that made him think of sunshine in June. Her fiery red hair was curled and coiled high atop her head.

She was magnificent.

Daniel's eyes trailed Margaret as she moved across the room with the Baxters. Though he could acknowledge that Lady Baxter was a beautiful woman, in comparison she stood in darkness where Margaret shone brightly, her beauty rare and vivid.

They exchanged greetings, with Lady Baxter all smiles, graciously thanking his grandmother for inviting them today.

Daniel, his eyes on Margaret, said, "And what of your sister's role in this, my lady? After all, we are here to celebrate her work, are we not? My grandmother and I saw the portraits she did of you and your family. They were remarkable enough for me to also commission Lady Margaret to paint me, as well."

He saw the blush rise on Margaret's cheeks, but she still refused to look at him. Daniel longed to stroke her cheek. To allow his fingers to follow the curve of her hips. To kiss her everywhere, his lips moving over her satin skin.

Lord Baxter spoke up. "Yes, my sister-in-law has quite the talent, Your Grace. We look forward to seeing Her Grace's portrait revealed." The marquess's eyes went to the covered easel.

"All in good time, my lord," Gran said.

By then, Hampton had entered the room once more, announcing the new guests who had arrived. Soon, the drawing room held two dozen or so others. Daniel had yet to speak to Margaret, his gaze following her as she moved about the room.

Gran came to him and said, "When are you going to talk with the girl? You cannot win her hand by gazing at her from afar."

"Give it time," he said. "Have all our guests arrived?"

She nodded. "I suppose it is time to allow Lady Margaret to bask in attention because she is certain to receive plenty of it."

Gran signaled Hampton, who went to stand next to the covered portrait. Everyone seemed to notice the butler did so, and the room fell silent.

Gran spoke up. "Thank you, my friends, for coming today to celebrate with me. Not just the remarkable portrait that has been painted of an old woman, but the talented artist who accomplished such a task."

She held out a hand, and Margaret went to join her, taking it.

"Any words, Lady Margaret, before everyone sees your work?"

"While I am happy you are eager to show it off, Your Grace, I only hope you are pleased with my efforts."

"I am pleased with it—and you, my dear."

Gran nodded to Hampton and in a dramatic gesture, the butler whipped the cloth from the portrait. Daniel heard the gasps fill the room as he studied Margaret's work.

It was a remarkable likeness of his grandmother. It captured her regal air. Her goodness and dignity shone forth. Most portraits portrayed their subjects in a glowing light. Margaret's did—and yet at the same time, she captured the reality of who the Dowager Duchess of Westfield truly was.

He heard the words tossed about. *Stunning. Magnificent. Splendid. Astounding.* The portrait was all that.

And more.

Then those present surrounded Margaret, peppering her with questions about her work and even herself. Daniel stood close enough to hear the conversations without becoming involved in them. Margaret handled the attention with ease, her natural grace and goodness shining brightly. Their interest gave him an understanding of how her gift needed to be shared with the world.

Gran joined him. "She will make for a worthy duchess. That is, if you can convince her she can be both artist and duchess."

"I will do my best, Gran."

Daniel only hoped his best would be enough.

Finally, their guests began to depart as the clock struck four, telling Margaret how they looked forward to seeing her at that evening's ball. So far, he had not heard her commit to any commissions and decided he would speak to her of that now. He approached her a bit hesitantly, hoping she would not turn away from him.

"You have quite a few admirers now, Red," he said softly. "Gran is more than pleased. The portrait you painted of her will become a family treasure. Generations will view your work and feel as though they know her."

"Thank you, Your Grace," Margaret said quietly. "It was easy to paint the dowager duchess. When I have a personal knowledge of my subjects, my brush seems to know what to do without me even guiding it. It was an honor and privilege to paint such a grand dame. Her support will now launch my career."

"I did not hear you commit to anyone. I hope you recall that you are to paint me next."

She winced, and he wanted to cradle her cheek. He forced himself to keep his hands at his sides.

"You are certain you wish for me to paint you, Your Grace?"

"I would think it would come easily to you, Margaret. Because you know me better than anyone ever has. I spent many years being a carefree rogue. When my grandfather left us and I gained his title, I had to quickly settle down and take on many responsibilities. I have buried myself in work since his death, seeing few friends and having little-to-no fun."

He gazed at her steadily. "You broke through the walls I had erected around me, sweetheart. You have seen who I am. I—"

"I will be happy to paint your portrait, Your Grace," she said formally. "I have already begun my preliminary sketches of you."

"I know I hurt you, Red. That was never my intention. I—"

"I will be in touch with you, Your Grace," she interrupted, her tone one as if she spoke politely to a stranger and not the man she had made love with.

Even now, Daniel could see her in his arms, writhing beneath him, calling out his name in ecstasy. He realized words would never be enough for this woman. His actions would need to speak for him. This drawing room was not the place for it. He would bide his time and make his feelings known to her later.

"I look forward to seeing your sketches, my lady," he told her, adopting her formal tone. "When might we meet to discuss my portrait?"

"I will contact you," she said, her tone now distant, pushing him away.

Daniel's heart ached, knowing how badly he had injured her. He promised himself he would make it up to her, no matter how long it took.

"Shall we join the others?" he asked, and they moved across the room to where Gran spoke with the Baxters.

"You were quite the sensation," Lady Baxter told her sister. "Why, I believe everyone present today wishes for you to paint portraits of them and the members of their families."

"Did you commit to anyone?" asked the marquess.

"No, I did not," Margaret said. "I had already agreed to paint His Grace if he wished me to do so. After I complete that, I will see which subjects I choose to paint."

"I am very happy for you, Lady Margaret," Daniel's grandmother said, bestowing a rare smile upon Margaret. "You have made an old woman the topic of everyone's lips. My portrait—and your immense talent—will be the only thing spoken of at tonight's ball."

"I cannot thank you enough for the support you have given me, Your Grace," Margaret said sincerely. "Any future success I have will be because of you and your generosity."

"Do not sell yourself short, my lady," Gran told her. "Yes, I could bring attention to you and your art. It is your talent which will carry you through. I wish you the best of luck in these endeavors."

"I shall see you to your carriage," Daniel told them.

He offered his arm to Margaret, and she accepted it without emotion, her fingers barely touching him. He walked her and the Baxters to their vehicle. As Lord Baxter helped his marchioness into the carriage, Daniel took Margaret's hand and raised it to his lips, kissing her fingers tenderly. His gaze never left hers.

"I look forward to discussing my portrait with you, my lady. I also hope we might share a dance at this evening's ball."

"I do not think that wise, Your Grace. Please do not ask me to do so."

Frustration filled him. How was he supposed to grovel if he could not spend a single moment with her? He knew her hurt ran deep—and he was the one to have caused it. Daniel knew he must give her the distance she asked for.

For now.

He would bide his time and when she presented him with his finished portrait, he would then declare his love for her.

And pray she would not leave him in purgatory for the rest of his life.

CHAPTER TWENTY-SEVEN

D ESPITE NOT ARRIVING home until after three, Margaret was up early the next morning. Molly helped to pack up the last of Margaret's things, placing them in one of her trunks.

"I think that's everything, my lady," the perky maid said. "Once we arrive at your new residence, you can start on His Grace's portrait. I'm sure it will be even better than his grandmother's. You are so talented, my lady."

Margaret had worried about seeing the duke at the previous evening's ball. She had requested he not ask her to dance, fearing if he did that she might come undone in his arms. Instead, Daniel had not entered the ballroom all evening. Margaret had seen his grandmother arrive alone, thinking it odd. She had gone to greet the dowager duchess, who had mentioned that her grandson had headed straight to the card room upon their arrival and did not plan to dance a single tune all evening.

He had appeared during supper, though, arriving with two other peers who were several decades his senior. The three gentlemen had gone through the buffet together and taken a seat at a long table filled with more than a dozen others. Margaret had been sitting two tables away with five others, having danced with all three men seated there and been introduced to the other two women. It had been difficult to eat, knowing Daniel was so close and how she longed to touch him. Talk with him. Just as his scent had lingered on her skin after their hours of lovemaking, he now seemed embedded deep within her. She no longer felt whole. It was as if she were but half a person, one who would never be happy or whole again.

She told herself her art made her happy. That it was her reason for living. Nothing stood in her way now.

Except her love for a man who was destined for another.

"My lady?"

Turning, she saw Molly looking at her, concern on her face.

"Yes? Sorry, I was woolgathering. I do believe we have everything."

The maid nodded, satisfied. "I will go have a few footmen come up for your trunks."

"Be sure they also go to the studio, as well," Margaret reminded. "In fact, I will go there and supervise them. Send them upstairs first."

"Yes, my lady."

Molly left, and Margaret went to the portrait of her grandmother that hung on the wall.

"Oh, Grandmama, I am starting a new life today," she said to the familiar image. "One you wished for and never experienced."

A tear cascaded down her cheek, and Margaret hastily wiped it away.

"It is awful, Grandmama, I am so torn. I love a man who needs someone far better than I as his wife. He needs a woman who will give him children and put him first in everything." She paused, her throat thick with tears. "I could never be that woman. I love him. More than I ever imagined possible. But he needs someone conventional. A woman of excellent breeding who would devote all her time to him and their children.

"I want more, Grandmama. Not just for me—but for you. You were denied the right to pursue your own dreams. Stifled by a man who didn't appreciate you or your talent."

She touched the frame reverently. "I will become *the* portrait artist of the *ton*, Grandmama. I promise to realize your dreams—

and mine."

Margaret lifted the painting from the wall and took it upstairs with her, where she wrapped it carefully in a heavy cloth, the same kind she had used to protect the portrait of Daniel she had painted all those years ago.

She set these two paintings together as two footmen appeared.

"Be very careful with these," she instructed.

"We will, my lady," one assured her, taking both portraits and her easel and carrying them downstairs, the other lifting the trunk containing her paints and brushes and rags and hefting it onto his shoulder.

Once they left, she stood in the empty room. She had begun to discover herself again in it when she had arrived, not having painted for a good while. Painting Dolley and Baxter and then the children had awakened the need to paint within her, as well as bolstered her confidence that perhaps she could dedicate her life to her art and provide for herself so she was beholden to none.

Margaret went downstairs and stopped at Dolley's rooms, slipping inside. Her sister was still fast asleep. She kissed Dolley's brow and stepped back.

Dolley caught her wrist. "Are you leaving?" she asked sleepily.

"Yes. Go back to sleep."

"Will come see you. Soon. Bring . . . the children . . ." Dolley's hold on her relaxed and her hand fell to the bed again.

Despite how her sister had treated her, Margaret still held tender feelings for Dolley.

She left and made her way to the breakfast room, where her brother-in-law was being seated.

"I have come to say goodbye, my lord. And I wish to thank you. I appreciate you taking me in when my cousin wished me gone. It was very kind of you."

The marquess gave her a smile. "You were no trouble at all, Lady Margaret. You have a calming effect on my marchioness, and my children adore you."

"Spend more time with them, my lord," Margaret urged. "They will be grown and gone before you know it."

"Will we see you at the musicale this evening?" he asked. "Or will you be painting instead?"

"I am taking a respite from social affairs," she told him. "I will attend a few in the future in order to remind others I am around and hope they engage my services."

"You have a rare talent, my lady. Do not let anyone keep you from using it," he advised.

"Goodbye."

She went to the foyer. Molly waited for her.

"Everything is in the wagon, my lady. Except for the two paintings. I had the footman place the pair in the carriage. I can hold them steady for you."

Margaret smiled. "Already, you are looking after me so well, Molly."

They went outside to the carriage. She stared out the window at familiar sites as the vehicle drove away. Her new rented house awaited her. She had never lived on her own and actually looked forward to doing so.

Once they arrived, the wagon bearing her possessions was not far behind. Margaret told Molly to go to the market so they would have something to eat. She gave the maid some coins, and Molly ventured inside, claiming a basket from the kitchen and then setting out, as Margaret told her she would direct the footmen where to take the trunks.

It did not take long for her things to be brought inside. She left her trunks untouched in the bedchamber, knowing Molly would be put out if Margaret tried to unpack on her own. Instead, she went to the other chamber on the upper floor and went about setting up her paints. She returned downstairs and collected a few bowls to use in mixing and cleaning and brought them to her new studio. Then she went downstairs again, looking for a table she could set the bowls upon. One of the perfect size sat in a corner, and she carried it up the stairs.

She returned to the trunk and removed her brushes, placing them in the particular order she preferred. Finally, she took out the remaining items, her smock and her sketchbook.

Filled with pictures of Daniel.

Slowly, Margaret turned the pages, studying each drawing at length. Some she had drawn before their night together. Some came after. She blinked rapidly, trying to rid the kaleidoscope of memories from that night of touch and taste. Of pleasure. A night—for her—of love. It still bothered her that Daniel had assumed they would wed because they coupled together. She knew, though, that he was an honorable man. He had agreed to her request for a night together, not telling her that he would do the right thing and offer for her afterward.

Pushing aside those memories, she donned the paint-smattered smock in order to protect the morning gown she wore. She knew how to paint Daniel now. It was ready to burst from her.

And when she finished and delivered the portrait to him, she hoped she would never have to see him again.

DANIEL HAD STAYED away from the ballroom that first night because if he could not dance with Margaret, he would dance with no other. He had killed the long hours in the card room before going into supper with friends of his grandfather. Immediately, he had seen Margaret and through sheer willpower kept from running to her and kissing her senseless.

He had not called upon her at the Baxter townhouse, hoping she was putting in hours on his portrait. The sooner she finished, the sooner he could convince her they belonged together.

Always.

Daniel had now attended other *ton* events the past three

nights. She had been present at none of them. He didn't know if she avoided him—or the constant attention she now received. Gran had told him that Margaret had been the belle of the ball following the reveal of her first portrait. He had to listen at length to how Margaret danced every dance and how a line formed to speak with her after each dance ended and before the next began. His grandmother even mentioned that Margaret had agreed to accept three commissions, explaining she was currently working on a portrait of the Duke of Westfield, and that she would start on them after that had been completed.

He had not thought she would drop from sight so quickly and yearned to see a glimpse of her. Frustration grew within him, and he decided to go for a long walk. He ventured to Hyde Park and walked along the Serpentine, his only company being nannies with children. The fashionable hour to be seen was several hours away.

Returning home, he handed his walking cane and hat to his butler.

"A delivery came for you while you were out, Your Grace," Hampton told him. "They are the portraits you commissioned."

"They?" he asked, knowing he had only asked for one to be done and curious as to what else Margaret had completed. "Is Lady Margaret here?" he asked anxiously.

"No, Your Grace. A letter did arrive with them from her, however. I left it on the desk in your study. The portraits were placed in the drawing room."

"Thank you," he said, hastily making his way to his study.

As Hampton said, the letter rested upon Daniel's desk. Trepidation filled him as he picked it up. Suddenly, he did not want to know its contents, despite having been eager to read what she had written. It worried him that she was not here, in person, ready to see his reaction to her work. She had delivered Gran's portrait and visited with her at length.

Taking the letter with him, he dashed from his study, taking the stairs two at a time, racing down the corridor to the drawing room. He paused a moment, collecting himself, and then entered.

He spied the paintings immediately. Both rested against a large settee, covered in a heavy cloth. He moved slowly toward them as if in a dream.

Why two?

Would one be the portrait he wished the world to see and the other depicting him as Margaret saw him? Would he love one and loathe the other?

His hand shaking, Daniel removed the cloth from the one on the left, shock filling him.

He saw himself—as a young man.

It was the painting he had seen briefly that early morning he had visited her. He had looked upon it then in shock but left soon after. Now, he had time to truly study it at length.

Margaret had painted him as he had appeared ten years ago. He saw both eagerness and cockiness in his unlined face. She had captured a carefree university graduate, on the brink of entering the world, ready to find his place and make his mark. It was a remarkable likeness of Daniel at that age, the canvas revealing the man he had once been.

It still amazed him how well she had captured him because their meeting had been a brief one. Obviously, it had made an indelible impression upon her. His eyes fell to the bottom, left corner and he saw *M Townsend*—and a date under it—*1801*. He realized he would be the envy of Polite Society, having not one but two portraits painted of him by Lady Margaret Townsend.

Daniel now removed the protective covering from the second portrait, wondering what he might find.

It was as if he looked into a mirror.

He saw the slight wave in his hair. The exact shade of gray of his eyes. He even recognized the waistcoat and coat as being one he had worn in her presence. The cravat was intricately knotted, reflecting the diligence of his valet, as well as her skill in capturing the folds of the cloth. The portrait would command the eye of anyone who viewed it. They would see a man at the height of his looks and power. Every line spoke of his position as a duke in Polite Society. She had claimed his very essence, from his posture to the way he wore his clothes. There was a bit of arrogance in his face, which he preferred to think of as extreme confidence. It also showed a man of great humanity, one that others could trust and admire.

Daniel was not certain he was the man Margaret had painted.

But—could he become this man—for her?

His eyes returned to the first portrait and then roamed over the second one. He was fascinated by what she had seen. The subtleties she had observed and placed on the canvas. Margaret definitely had not only the talent but the soul of an artist. He could not keep this hidden. Rather, he knew it must be celebrated.

He was still standing in front of both portraits when Gran joined him. She came and stood alongside him in silence for some minutes, taking in the details of each portrait.

"I see by the date that she painted you when you first met," Gran observed.

"She did," he agreed. "I thought at that time she was special. She was merely a girl, however. It was the day before she turned fifteen." He paused and then added, "I looked for her, you know, during Lilly's come-out Season. I had figured them to be the same age."

"Were you so very disappointed when she did not appear that spring?"

"I was. But I hid it well. I thought I would never see her again and continued living the life of a young man in London. One who had everything he could possibly ever want."

"Then Westfield died, and you changed, Daniel."

"I had to, Gran. I never let you know, but the estate was a bit muddled. It took time to dig out from some of the debt which Grandfather left."

"Nothing that arse did would surprise me," she said dismissively. Then gazing deeply into Daniel's eyes, she said, "I hope you will be the duke—and the husband—that he never was."

"I hope I can be the duke seen in this portrait. It is me—but it is certainly idealized."

Gran touched his arm. "It is how Lady Margaret sees you, Daniel. Most likely, it is how others view you, as well. Do not let her down. Do not disappoint her. *Be* the man she has depicted here."

"I intend to be. I also want her to continue painting. It would be wrong to keep her from her art and to keep Polite Society from such a talent. Do you think it appropriate for us to hold another small gathering in order to introduce these portraits?"

Gran grinned wickedly at Daniel. "I thought you would never ask."

CHAPTER TWENTY-EIGHT

"I DO RECALL that," Margaret said as Lady Audley took a sip of tea.

She was sketching her old friend as they visited. She had accepted three commissions, the first being to paint Sylvia. She had chosen Sylvia because their fathers had been friends, and they were of the same age. Margaret had known Sylvia from the time she was very young, and they should have made their come-outs together.

Sylvia's life was very different from Margaret's now. She was married and had given birth to her third child six months ago. Margaret thought it would be more comfortable to begin painting someone she knew. This was the second time she had come to visit with Sylvia. The first time, they had spoken for an hour, catching up on their lives since they had last seen one another. Margaret had gone home and done a series of sketches and had returned today with them. Before she showed them to Sylvia, however, she wanted to add a few more into the mix.

Her friend had always been quiet. That had not changed. What had changed was the fact she had become a mother. When Sylvia talked about her children, her entire demeanor changed. She lit up when speaking of them and their accomplishments. That was what Margaret chose to capture in her sketches. She finished the one she worked on and then closed her sketchbook, setting her pencil aside.

"It is so interesting that you have chosen to paint," Sylvia said. "I remember you used to draw when I would come and see you." Sylvia smiled. "I recall your grandmother encouraging you to do so. She was ever so much fun."

"Yes, my talent comes from Grandmama. She wanted to paint as I did, but Grandfather was not in favor of her doing so."

"At least you have no husband telling you what to do," Sylvia said, chuckling.

Margaret did not want to talk about husbands and opened her sketchbook. "Would you like to look at a few of the sketches I have done for you in our past two meetings? I never use one, in particular. I usually combine two or three together to arrive at what I will paint."

She handed over the sketchbook and watched Sylvia's face as her old friend turned the pages.

Once Sylvia finished viewing the sketches, she said, "I can almost see our shared history in these, Margaret. Yet at the same time, you have captured the essence of me now."

Sylvia turned to one sketch and tapped it with her finger. "This one, in particular, is one I truly like."

"You were talking about your oldest losing his first tooth as I drew that one," Margaret told her. "You come to life when you speak of your children, Sylvia. It is very touching to see."

"All I ever wanted was to have a child," Sylvia revealed. "Being an only child, I longed for brothers and sisters. As I got older, I finally understood that Mama had trouble bringing a child to term. That she had lost several over the years. That is why I am grateful to have married Audley. He has become a true son to Mama and Papa. Because I had no siblings, I cherish the time I do spend with my own children. Audley indulges me in this. Oh, I know most mothers of the *ton* rarely see their children. I will never be one of them."

"Do you have a sketch you favor beyond this one?" Margaret questioned.

Sylvia shook her head. "No, I will leave that up to you. All of these are more than acceptable. Whatever you paint, Audley and I will like it. I do thank you for agreeing to paint me, especially since Polite Society is clamoring at your door for you to do the same with them."

"I have accepted two other clients, but I wanted to paint you first, Sylvia."

They talked another half hour. Sylvia extracted a promise from Margaret to attend the following evening's ball. Sylvia wanted to introduce her friend to her husband since Margaret had been caring for her ill mother and had been unable to attend their wedding. Though she was reluctant to go to any *ton* event, she agreed to do so, not planning on staying for long. It would be good to be seen at an affair every now and then. She hoped to avoid Daniel, though.

Margaret took her leave, returning to her small house, which was fast becoming home. Molly was doing a wonderful job of taking care of both Margaret and the house. Margaret still wished to hire a cook and she might have someone come in a few times a week to help Molly with the cleaning. That could be sorted out in the weeks to come.

She arrived home, and Molly greeted her at the door, whispering, "Her ladyship—Lady Baxter—is here."

She stepped inside and saw Dolley sitting in the small parlor.

"It is so good to see you," she told her sister. "Would you care for some tea?"

Margaret removed her bonnet and handed it, her reticule, and sketchbook to Molly.

"No, but we must speak."

She nodded at Molly, who left the room. She took a seat opposite Dolley and asked, "What is it?"

"We have received an invitation to view the Duke of Westfield's portrait. You, too, received a separate invitation. I wanted to deliver it to you in person. Have you not told the dowager duchess you are living on your own now?"

"No, I have not seen her. You know I have not attended any social affairs the past few days. I had not thought to write her and let her know I have moved."

Dolley handed the invitation to Margaret, and she set it aside, not bothering to open it.

"You will come?" Dolley insisted.

"I do not know," she said, actually knowing very well she had no plans to see Daniel anytime soon, much less now since she had delivered his portraits to him. It had been a stroke of luck when she came calling with them and strengthened her resolve to cut all ties with him.

"I do not like that look in your eyes, Margaret. You have always had a bit of a stubborn streak. Why do you not wish to go tomorrow afternoon? Did Westfield's portrait not turn out well? Are you worried you might lose commissions because of it?"

"Not at all," she replied confidently. "If anything, I did an excellent job of putting His Grace onto canvas. The *ton* will think so, as well. I may or may not attend this showing, Dolley, but that should not prevent you and Baxter from going."

Relief filled her sister's face and once more, Margaret saw it had been all about Dolley.

"I am glad you believe Baxter and I should go—even if you do not yourself."

Dolley rose. "I must be off. I have an appointment at my dressmaker's."

Margaret suspected it was to have larger gowns made up or to alter existing ones because of Dolley's condition.

Surprisingly, Dolley embraced her. "You must call soon and see the children. They have been asking for you."

"If I do not attend Westfield's gathering tomorrow afternoon, then I will come see them instead."

Margaret saw her sister to the door and closed it. Almost immediately, Molly appeared.

"Anything you need, my lady?"

"No, I have work to do now. I have completed my sketches

of Lady Audley and would like to begin on her portrait."

The maid asked, "Would you ever consider drawing me, my lady? I wouldn't need a full painting. I think it would be fun to have you draw me, though."

She was surprised the thought had not occurred to her.

"You have been incredibly helpful to me, Molly. I would be delighted to do so. Why don't I sketch you now?"

"Would you?" the maid asked eagerly. She looked about the room. "I could sit right here and be very still."

Margaret chuckled. "That will not be necessary, Molly. We are not strangers. Give me an hour, and I will show you what I have."

She went upstairs to her studio and removed the sketches of Sylvia from her sketchbook, setting them aside. Then she took up her pencil and chewed thoughtfully on its end before she began drawing her maid. Margaret did one sketch in pencil and then got charcoal and completed a second one with it.

When she finished, she took them downstairs, finding Molly dicing potatoes and adding them to a pot of bubbling stew.

"Come and sit at the table," she urged, and Molly followed her to the dining room.

Margaret set both sketches in front of a chair, and the servant took a seat. She watched Molly's face as she studied each sketch, a glow within her as she saw how pleased the girl was.

Suddenly, Molly burst into tears. Margaret went and put an arm about the maid, patting her shoulder.

"There, there. Nothing to cry about," she comforted. "I hope you are not disappointed with my efforts."

"More than pleased, my lady," Molly said through her tears. "I look . . . beautiful."

"That is because you are," Margaret told the girl. "This is what I—and others—see when we look at you."

"I want to pay you for these, my lady. We never talked about my salary, but you can take it out of my wages."

"I am sorry I neglected to mention your pay," she apologized.

ALEXA ASTON

"That was remiss of me. And no, I will not accept a farthing for these. I am happy to do this for you."

"Would you mind, my lady, if I gave one to my mother?"

"Where does she live? It would be a lovely gesture."

"In London. Near Covent Garden."

"I did not know you had family in town, Molly. We have been together such a short time, I should have discussed not only salary with you but time off for yourself. What did Lord Baxter give you?"

The servant named a figure, which Margaret thought entirely too low. Molly also mentioned having one Wednesday afternoon a month off, as well as every other Sunday afternoon.

"Your salary is doubled," Margaret proclaimed. "And you can have every other Wednesday off. Hopefully, you might be able to visit your mother then or on any Sunday afternoon. Those, too, will be yours. Take the sketch to her."

Molly, ever spontaneous, hugged her tightly. She pulled away and said, "I know I shouldn't embrace you, my lady, but you are such a generous soul. Thank you so much."

"I do plan to hire some more help." When she saw the look of dismay on the servant's face, she said, "No, I am not displeased in the slightest with what you have done. I feel you are doing too much. I would like us to have a cook because that takes up so much time."

"I wouldn't mind that a bit, my lady. You know already that I only know how to cook a few things. A cook would be most welcome. I can handle everything else at the house, though. The place is small, and you are not demanding in the least. Especially now, since you are not going to so many events and changing your gowns five or six times a day, it is easier to keep up with your wardrobe."

"Then it shall be a cook first. We will see if you need additional help with the rest."

Margaret went up to her studio and donned her smock, ready to get on with Sylvia's portrait.

CHAPTER TWENTY-NINE

D ANIEL DISMISSED HIS valet, trying to quell his nerves, knowing he would soon see Margaret. Though Gran had a headache and decided to forgo the previous evening's ball, he had gone simply to catch a glimpse of Margaret.

She never showed.

He saw her sister and was tempted to ask Lady Baxter about Margaret's whereabouts but remembered his conversation with the marquess and decided to steer clear of the marchioness. Instead, he had departed the ball and spent a quiet evening at his club, which was almost deserted.

He decided he would ask her to stroll in the gardens near the end of today's party. He certainly couldn't tell her he loved her in front of those invited and knew guests would be hovering about her both before and after his portraits were presented. Daniel would take her once again to the gazebo and fall upon his knees, begging her to give him a chance and declaring his love for her.

Even then, he worried she might not budge.

It would be important that she know he had no objection to her continuing to pursue her art. That had seemed to be the obstacle between them at their last encounter. He must assure her she could be both duchess and artist.

In the drawing room, he saw Hampton had both portraits still hidden as they stood upon easels next to the fireplace. He wondered how many would notice the date Margaret had placed beneath her signature on the first portrait and how she would answer any questions about it.

His grandmother joined him and within minutes, guests began to arrive. He mingled through the crowd, his eyes constantly wandering to the door, waiting for Margaret's arrival. He heard Hampton announce Lord and Lady Baxter's presence and turned, smiling, waiting for Margaret to appear. Instead, the marquess and marchioness entered the room, immediately going to his grandmother.

Daniel joined them, briefly taking Lady Baxter's hand and then releasing it. She gushed over the flower arrangements scattered about the room. The gown Gran wore. How select the guest list was for today's soiree.

When she finally ceased her chattering, he asked, "Where might Lady Margaret be? I thought she would come with you and Lord Baxter."

The marchioness flushed. "My sister . . . is visiting with our children."

He didn't like the hesitation in her voice, much less the guilty look she wore.

"Is that so?" he asked sharply.

"Yes," the marquess confirmed. "When we left, Lady Margaret was headed up to the nursery."

Gran frowned. "It seems odd she would miss the unveiling of Westfield's portraits."

"Portraits?" Lady Baxter asked, obviously confused.

"Did she not tell you?" Daniel asked. "She painted me twice. Once, long ago. Again, very recently."

"I did not know this," Lady Baxter said.

Gran looked around. "Come. We should show our guests what Lady Margaret has done."

He signaled Hampton and footmen began circulating with champagne as he and Gran made their way to where the portraits stood. Lifting two glasses from a tray, Daniel handed one to Gran.

The room fell silent, all eyes on him.

"Today, we are here to mark the occasion of unveiling old work—and new—done by Lady Margaret Townsend."

Murmurs began circulating through those gathered at his words.

"I had the pleasure of meeting Lady Margaret when she was but fifteen years old. Even then, she displayed a talent far above those twice her age. I had no knowledge until recently that Lady Margaret painted me after our brief meeting a decade ago."

Daniel turned and nodded to Hampton, who removed the cloth from the first portrait. He heard talk break out immediately as people took in the painting, some of them recalling what he looked like ten years ago.

He cleared his throat. "Lady Margaret graciously agreed to paint me once again. I think you will find it is a remarkable likeness of me."

The butler revealed the second portrait. A buzz began about the room. Daniel let it build before claiming attention again.

"As you can see, Lady Margaret Townsend has extraordinary talent. I hope each and every one of you might one day be fortunate enough to have your own portrait painted by her."

Daniel lifted his glass. "To Lady Margaret!"

"To Lady Margaret!" their guests echoed.

He downed the glass of champagne and looked to Gran. "I am going to her now."

Setting his empty flute on a tray, Daniel left his townhouse for Lord Baxter's residence. He didn't bother calling for his carriage. It would take too long and his street was already littered with carriages from those he left inside. No, he would walk to Baxter's residence and confront Margaret there.

Ten minutes later, he approached the door, his heart racing. The butler answered Daniel's knock, clearly surprised to find a duke on the doorstep.

"I am here to see Lady Margaret. Lady Baxter told me she is in the nursery." He brushed past the butler and moved toward the stairs.

"Excuse me, Your Grace," the butler called. "Lady Margaret has already left."

He halted and turned, returning to the servant. "Where did she go?"

"Why, her home, Your Grace."

"Her . . . home? I thought this was her home."

Looking flustered, the butler said, "It was. But Lady Margaret has leased a place of her own. It gives her the privacy she requires and ample room for her studio."

"Give me the address," he said, his voice low and deadly.

The butler now looked startled. "I . . . I do not have it, Your Grace. I am sorry."

Anger filled him. "Then find it!" he demanded.

A footman stepped forward. "I know where Lady Margaret lives, Your Grace. I helped move her there. I do not recall the exact address, but I would recognize the house if I saw it."

"Come with me," Daniel ordered, brushing past the butler and throwing open the front door.

Outside, he hailed a hansom cab and looked to the footman. "Get in. Tell the driver where to go."

The footman did as requested, telling the driver perched behind them where to turn.

After twenty minutes, Daniel recognized the street they turned upon as the one where he had Margaret meet him for their night together. Not needing the house, he had returned the key to his solicitor. The memories of that night tore at his gut.

"And a right here," the footman said. "It'll be third on the left."

He wondered how many times Margaret had passed the house where they had coupled and if she thought about what had happened behind those doors each time she did so.

The driver pulled his hansom cab to a halt. Daniel got out and said, "Take this man back to Mayfair." He handed the driver a sovereign and then turned to face where Margaret now lived.

The neighborhood was adequate, the house small but neat. A barrel filled with colorful flowers stood next to the door. As he knocked upon the door, he didn't have to wonder why she had left. Living with her sister must have been difficult at best. Lady Baxter was petulant and selfish and hadn't wanted to be responsible for Margaret. He supposed she had been able to leave because of what Gran had paid for her portrait. He couldn't see Margaret having any other funds to live on.

The door opened, and a servant stood gawking at him.

"I am here to see Lady Margaret," he said.

"Let me see if she is home, my lord," the girl said shakily, closing the door.

"It is Your Grace," he shouted through the barrier.

Daniel decided not to wait. The house was tiny. The maid knew if Margaret was home or not. She merely went to alert her mistress to his presence. Why, the girl hadn't even asked for his name or a calling card.

Opening the door, he closed it behind him, seeing the swish of the maid's skirts as she reached the top of the staircase.

He followed.

"My lady—*he's* here! The duke!" the maid said.

"Bloody hell."

That was his Red.

Daniel smiled and stepped up, now directly behind the maid. "I am delighted to see your studio, Lady Margaret."

The maid wheeled, gasping. "*You* were supposed to wait," she blurted out.

"I didn't feel like it," he replied. "Run along and fetch us some tea if you would."

"I will not!" the servant cried.

"She will not," Margaret voiced.

He shrugged. "Then she will have to witness this."

Daniel strode toward Margaret, who bravely stood her ground, arms akimbo, fury flashing in her eyes. Nothing would stop him. Not a meddling servant. Certainly not an angry

Margaret.

He reached her and yanked her toward him, his mouth coming down hard on hers. He heard the maid's shocked cry. Felt Margaret stiffen.

But he was one determined man.

Her hands clutched his shoulders and tried to push him away. It only made Daniel hold on even more tightly to her waist. His kiss was bruising. Punishing her for having abandoned him.

She turned her head, abruptly breaking the kiss and said, "Molly, you may leave."

"Will you be all right, my lady?"

"You should be asking His Grace that," was the reply.

It gave him a sliver of hope.

"All right," the servant said, reluctance in her voice.

"Close the door, Molly," Margaret prompted.

"Yes, my lady."

Daniel waited, hearing the click, his heart pounding against his ribs. Margaret turned her head toward him again. She didn't have to look up far because she was so tall.

"Release me now or I will be forced to do violence to your person."

He burst out laughing. "What are you going to do, Red? Dump paint over my head? Poke me in the eye with one of your sable brushes?"

Her knee slammed into his groin. White-hot pain flashed through him. Daniel stumbled back, his hands cradling his abused balls. Tears filled his eyes. He glanced up at Margaret, who glared at him.

"I would love to pour paint over your head, but it would be wasteful," she said, brushing her palms together. "You shouldn't have come, Your Grace."

"I had to see you," he wheezed.

"If you were pleased with your portrait, you could simply have sent a note," she said dismissively. "We have nothing to say to one another, Your Grace. I completed your portrait as you requested. I will expect payment in the near future."

She moved to a table and scribbled something on a piece of paper, coming toward him and tucking it inside his coat pocket.

"This is the name of my banker. He can help direct the funds into my account. I do not expect you to be as generous as your grandmother was. Good day."

Margaret left the studio. Daniel knew he could not pursue her since he could not stand erect at the moment. He took slow, deep breaths, and after a few minutes passed, he had recovered somewhat. Leaving the studio, he gingerly made his way down the staircase. The maid stood at the foot, her arms crossed.

He looked about and did not see Margaret anywhere.

"Has Lady Margaret left the premises?"

The maid frowned at him. "You chased her from her own home. Shame on you, Your Grace."

"I want to marry her," he said quietly, hoping to make this servant his ally.

Immediately, her features softened. "You do?"

He nodded. "I do. I have asked her once before." He passed. "Well, I did not quite ask. I told her."

The maid shook her head. "Oh, Lady Margaret would not like that at all."

"I understand that now. I want to ask her again. Properly. But I need to see her to be able to do so. Will you help me, Molly?"

The girl bit her lip, hesitating.

"I know you are loyal to Lady Margaret. I love her. I have yet to tell her, but I want to do so. I hope that will make a difference. That she will give me a chance. That she might try to love me, too."

Tears now filled the servant's eyes. "She's a good one, Lady Margaret."

"She most certainly is. I want to be her husband more than anything in the world. Help me, Molly. Please."

"Well, she is going to the ball tonight," the maid mused. "She is to meet her friend's husband. A Lord Audley. Perhaps you might dance with her there. And tell her you love her."

Daniel sighed. "I promise I will do so. You will always have a place in my household. Our household. Lady Margaret's household. The Duchess of Westfield."

Molly's eyes widened. "I could come with her?"

He laughed, hurting a bit. "I would insist upon it. After all, you are the woman who will help me win your mistress's hand."

"She'll be wearing an azure gown this evening, Your Grace. It'll be easy to spot her, with her red hair and blue gown."

Making an effort, Daniel bowed to the servant, something he never thought he would have done as a duke.

"Thank you, Molly. I hope to see you tomorrow under happier circumstances."

Daniel took his leave, his thoughts swirling as to how to get Margaret alone.

Then he realized he didn't have to do so. He didn't need to do so. In fact, he *wanted* to have witnesses.

Either he would become a laughingstock tonight—or he would win the woman he loved.

CHAPTER THIRTY

M ARGARET RETURNED TO her house an hour later, having walked for blocks, trying to allow her temper to cool.

Daniel wasn't supposed to be here. This was her space. Her place. This house was not a part of his world. It belonged to her. This house was fast becoming her sanctuary because it was somewhere she could relax. Be herself. Not put on any airs as the members of *ton* did.

He had invaded it, making her feel violated. She wondered if Dolley had given him the address since she knew her sister and brother-in-law were attending the party at the duke's residence today. She had not expressly told Dolley to keep where she was a secret. Then again, she did not want Dolley going about volunteering that kind of information.

Margaret needed to keep very separate lines as she hovered in one world yet lived in another. Daniel crossing into her house angered her. He was not a part of what she was creating. He was a leader of the very society that she felt uncomfortable in.

She wondered if she should write him a letter, telling him exactly what boundaries she had set and asking him not to ever visit her again, especially since he had received no invitation to do so this afternoon.

Would he be present at tonight's ball?

She would go as promised in order to meet Sylvia's husband

and then promptly leave. Of course, with the unveiling of the portraits she had painted of Daniel at different times in his life occurring today, it might be hard to sneak in and out. She hoped Polite Society approved of the paintings and would want to engage her services.

Finally, she decided an hour at most. No dancing, just conversations and perhaps agreeing to one or two more commissions. Just enough to entice others to wish for her to paint them.

Margaret headed back to her house. She had rushed away without anything, not even a hat. She hoped her cheeks had not burned since the afternoon was sunny.

She entered her house and was met by a worried Molly.

"Are you all right, my lady?" the servant asked, concern laced in her tone.

"I am calm now," she replied. "I was a bit upset to find His Grace inside my home without an invitation."

"Well, I told him to wait," the maid said. "Obviously, he doesn't take instructions very well." She sniffed.

Margaret couldn't help but laugh. "No, His Grace is used to being the one giving the orders, not obeying them." She placed her hand on Molly's shoulder. "You did nothing wrong. He was the one who was ill-mannered."

"You look a bit tuckered out, my lady. We need to get something for you to eat. Then I will draw a bath for you, and you may bathe before tonight's ball."

She remembered she had told the maid of her plans this evening. After her long walk in the heat, a bath would be just the thing to soothe her further.

"Let us go into the kitchen. I will help you finish up anything there."

While Margaret dished up the stew and ladled it into bowls for them, Molly removed fresh bread from the oven and gathered a crock of butter. They ate together at the small table. This had become their habit. Margaret saw no need for her and Molly to eat separately. Besides, she enjoyed the servant's company immensely.

"I thought about what you should wear to your ball this evening," Molly said. "The gown is pressed and ready for you."

She usually didn't care what she wore, but she knew she would draw more than her fair share of attention tonight and asked, "Which gown did you select?"

"One you have yet to wear, my lady. It is as blue as a summer sky and will go well with your hair and eyes."

Margaret knew the one Molly referred to. It had been among her favorites the modiste had made up. She thought tonight might actually be her last ball of the Season. With three commissions and possibly a few more this evening, she might only need to attend a few smaller, more intimate events in the next few weeks. One thing she did need to learn, however, was which families might remain in town once the Season ended. She knew several couples would leave by mid-June when temperatures began to rise and the smells of the city overwhelmed its citizens. The remaining members of the *ton* would stay until mid-August or so, when the Season ended. Margaret, having no country home to adjourn to, would remain in her rented house. It would be wonderful if she could continue painting for at least a few months to help tide her over until next spring. She looked forward to exploring London when it was a quieter, less crowded place. She thought of long walks through the park along the Serpentine and visiting several museums would be an ideal way to pass her time.

They finished with their meal, and Molly told Margaret to leave the dishes. The servant had already put on water to heat while they ate, and it was about ready.

"No need to lug the tub and water upstairs," she told Molly. "I can bathe right here in the kitchen since it is only the two of us."

Margaret went to find a large bath sheet while Molly dragged the wooden tub into the kitchen from the small alcove where it sat. She went to her bedchamber and claimed a small vial of scent. Returning to the kitchen, she poured it into the bath and allowed Molly to help her disrobe.

"No time to wash all that hair of yours, my lady," the maid said.

As she bathed, they discussed various hairstyles which might be appropriate for the gown she was to wear.

Then Molly said, "My lady, I think you should wear your hair in the chignon you favor. You have the bone structure for it. Not many women of the *ton* do."

"I will take your advice," she said and stood, allowing Molly to pour clean water to remove all signs of soap.

Molly opened the bath sheet, and Margaret wrapped it around her, carefully stepping from the tub. The two women went upstairs, and Margaret sat at her dressing table while Molly laid out the gown and various undergarments to wear with it. Once she had donned the layers, the maid held up a pair of silk stockings of pale blue.

"You have yet to wear these, my lady. They will go well with your gown."

Margaret slipped a foot into one stocking and eased it up her calf. A flash of memory haunted her as she recalled Daniel removing her stocking, bringing it slowly down her leg and lifting it from her foot. She chastised herself for even thinking of him.

Molly handed her the other stocking, and Margaret put it on and stood. The maid lifted the azure gown over Margaret's head and, it skimmed her body as it fell to her ankles.

"What slippers do you suggest?" she asked.

"Hmm." Molly went to the wardrobe, where Margaret's shoes sat on a shelf, and contemplated the choice. Then she removed a pair of blue and gray satin slippers.

"These, my lady."

Margaret sat and allowed Molly to ease on the slippers, tying the ribbons in a clever bow.

"I like this bow," she said. "Perhaps I will even have to lift my skirts a bit in order for others to admire it."

Both women laughed, and then Molly had Margaret sit at the dressing table. She unpinned the hair, letting the heavy tresses fall to Margaret's waist. The maid brushed Margaret's hair until it shone.

"It is too bad you cannot leave it down, my lady. You would be the envy of every woman at the ball."

She shook her head. "No, I seriously doubt that. Red hair isn't the least bit fashionable. Neither is being two inches under six feet. The belles of tonight's ball will be tiny blonds who weigh little more than a feather."

Molly crossed her arms, a dark cloud descending upon her face. "Well, I believe you will be the envy of every woman by the end of this evening's ball."

Margaret studied the servant a moment, thinking Molly left something unsaid. Then she thought she was reading too much into the situation. Molly was always asking for details about the balls and other events Margaret attended.

She took the items she wished to carry tonight from her everyday reticule and placed them into one of blue satin, which Molly brought out. They went downstairs, and then Margaret stopped in her tracks. She had forgotten there would be no carriage waiting to take her to this evening's ball. She was spoiled, having lived with Lord Baxter and having his carriage always waiting at a moment's notice to convey them to events.

Molly must have come to the same determination because she let out a small cry of dismay. "I shall summon a hansom cab for you. I am sorry I did not think to do so sooner."

"I would not have wanted to keep a driver waiting for long anyway," Margaret told her.

"Wait here, my lady. I will be back shortly."

It was closer to ten minutes until the maid returned, telling Margaret she had a driver to get her to the ball. Margaret thanked Molly and went outside, telling the hansom cab driver where she wished to go.

He smiled at her. "Don't get anyone from these parts going to a fancy ball. Happy to take you there, though, Miss."

She did not correct him. In this neighborhood, perhaps she would not be Lady Margaret. Instead, she could be Miss Townsend, the artist.

She liked the sound of that.

The horse clopped along and Margaret sat back, trying to relax. She would stick to her plan. Meet Lord Audley. Speak to a few members of the *ton* regarding their portraits. And most of all, not dance. She did not want to give Daniel an excuse to come and sign her programme because she would most likely leave before the opening number was played.

They reached Mayfair, and the streets became clogged with vehicles, the many carriages, heading to the evening's social affair. They finally reached a standstill, and Margaret glanced over her shoulder.

"You can let me out here. I fear this is as close as we will be able to get."

"Shall I wait for you, my lady?"

"I do appreciate the offer, sir, but I do not know how long I will be. I would not want to keep you from other fares. Thank you for your kind offer, though."

The coachman quickly climbed from his perch and helped her descend from the vehicle.

Smiling at her, he doffed his hat and said, "Enjoy your ball, Cinderella."

Margaret laughed and gave him a few coins, waving as he drove away. She lifted her skirts and walked the two blocks to her destination, falling in with others who did the same. By the time she entered the townhouse and joined the receiving line, two other gentlemen—an earl and a baron—had already approached and asked her about painting their portraits.

As she stood in the receiving line, several others stopped to compliment her on the pair of portraits she had done for the Duke of Westfield. She wondered how Daniel had reacted seeing the two portraits side by side. She hoped he liked the contrast between the pair. It had been hard on her part with the original portrait she had completed of him after their first meeting, but she needed to cut all ties with him—else her heart would never begin to heal.

She reached her host and hostess, who both complimented her on the paintings she had done of the Duke of Westfield. She thanked them and moved toward the ballroom.

Once inside, she began looking for Sylvia and her husband. Then she saw Dolley waving her over and joined her sister.

"I did not know you would be present at tonight's ball," Dolley said. "The duke was most annoyed that you did not come this afternoon."

"Did you tell him where I live?"

"No," Dolley said. "He asked where you were, and I truthfully answered that when Baxter and I left, you were with the children."

Margaret supposed he must have gone straight there and just missed her, getting out of one of the servants what her new address was.

"Why did you come this evening?" her sister asked.

"Do you remember my friend, Sylvia? Her papa and ours were good friends. They used to visit us upon occasion."

Dolley thought a moment. "Oh, you mean the rather plain girl. Yes, you were very close."

She had never thought of Sylvia as plain, though someone of Dolley's beauty would have.

"I am painting her portrait next, and she wished for me to meet her husband, Lord Audley. I promised I would come and do so this evening."

"You will be besieged by others," Dolley predicted. "The response to your portraits of Westfield was tremendous this afternoon."

"Thank you for passing that along," she said.

As Dolley predicted, a wave of others surrounded them,

many of them pestering Margaret to commit to painting their portraits. She deflected all requests as graciously as she could, realizing by doing so, it only made those of the *ton* more eager to engage her services.

Finally, she bid her sister goodbye because she spotted Sylvia. As Margaret approached, she saw Sylvia on the arm of rather tall man who looked to be close to thirty. He was smiling down at his wife as she told a story. The look on his face let Margaret know that Sylvia had found love. She was happy for her friend.

"Oh, there you are, Margaret," Sylvia said. She turned to her husband and smiled and then looked back to Margaret. "I wish to introduce you, Lady Margaret, to my husband. This is Lord Audley."

He smiled broadly at Margaret and took her hand, kissing it.

"It is a pleasure to meet you, my lady. My wife has told me of your childhood friendship. I am sorry for your loss of both parents."

"Thank you, my lord."

"My wife is delighted you have finally come to town and hopes you will be able to renew your friendship." He turned and bestowed a sweet smile upon Sylvia, who looked up at him in adoration.

Turning back to Margaret, Lord Audley said, "Would you allow me to engage you in the opening number?"

Though Margaret had not intended to dance any number, she graciously accepted. After that dance ended, she would slip from the ballroom without notice.

They spoke for another few minutes, and then the musicians began warming up.

Margaret turned to Sylvia. "Are you certain you do not wish to dance the first number with your husband?"

"Oh, Margaret, it is not fashionable to dance with one's husband. I have not danced with Audley since our marriage."

Margaret thought it merely another quirk of the *ton*.

"I say if you wish to dance with your husband, do so. Who

cares what Polite Society thinks?"

"You always were a bit of a rebel," Sylvia noted. "No, I never was one much for dancing anyway. I recall the first time I danced with Audley, I stepped on his toes—twice!"

They both chuckled, and then Sylvia said, "You always were a graceful dancer. I remember us practicing together before our come-outs. I am so sorry, Margaret, that you did not make yours when I did. It would have been a much happier Season for both of us if you had."

She knew her life would have been quite different if she had made her come-out years ago. Still, she was beginning to do what she had always dreamed of doing. Paint others. She knew regrets could eat away a person's soul and pushed them aside.

Lord Audley asked, "Might I escort you to the dance floor, Lady Margaret? It looks as if it is time for the dancing to begin."

"Thank you, my lord." She placed her hand upon his sleeve, and they began moving to the center of the floor.

"I hope you will get to see more of my wife," Lord Audley said. "She is the best woman I know. When she speaks of our children, her face lights up. To me, she is the most beautiful woman in the world."

"I am happy to see my friend has such a good man as her husband and that he values her."

She realized they did not form any squares with other couples and as Lord Audley took her hand in his and slipped an arm about her, she knew this would be a waltz. Her throat thickened with unshed tears, thinking she would never waltz with Daniel again.

Smiling brightly at Lord Audley, they stepped as one when the music began. They danced only a few measures before he released his grasp on her. Confused, she called out to him as he melted away into the crowd.

Suddenly, someone else had taken his place and she was twirling.

In Daniel's arms.

CHAPTER THIRTY-ONE

D ANIEL FELT HE had come home the moment he had taken Margaret into his arms. Thank goodness he had known Audley and made his request of him before Margaret came to speak with Audley and his wife. He had told Audley he wished to marry Margaret and that dancing with her was the most important thing in the world to him this evening. Audley had readily agreed to the request, telling Daniel he would ask to dance the first number with Lady Margaret and then Daniel might cut in. After that, Daniel had gone to the section of musicians and found the man in charge, asking that they play a waltz for the first number. Though one was not planned, no one ever turned down a duke's request, and Daniel had been certain they would do as he asked.

As he waltzed with Margaret, he saw yearning in her eyes and knew she had missed him as much as he had missed her.

"Do you have a habit of cutting in on people as they dance?" she asked.

"I have never done so, Red. Only for you." His gaze searched hers, and he saw the blush rising in her cheeks.

"I think it quite rude of you, Pestfield."

"It was the only way I could get you alone."

She snorted. "And why would you wish to do so? We had our time alone. Now, you can spend all the time alone you wish with your mistress."

Daniel caught the jealousy in her tone and bit back a smile.

"I have no mistress, Red. I haven't since I became the Duke of Westfield. I do not plan to take another because I would not break my marriage vows to you."

She stiffened in his arms, and he twirled them about once again.

"We are not going to wed, Daniel."

"Why?" he asked earnestly. "We are perfect for one another."

"No, we are not. I am not suited to be a duchess. You need a woman of great beauty, one who can effortlessly lead the *ton* because of her position in society."

"Don't you realize that you are the most beautiful woman in this room? The most beautiful one I have ever seen—or will see?"

She shook her head vigorously. "You are plying me with pretty words. I know I am too tall, and my hair is too red."

He smiled tenderly. "Those are two of the reasons I love you."

She stumbled, her feet coming to a halt as dancers swept around them. Daniel proclaimed, "I love you, Margaret Townsend. I absolutely adore you. I want to spend my life with you. Grow old together."

"I cannot wed you, Daniel," she said stubbornly. "I will not be my grandmother."

"And I will not be your grandfather. I know he kept her from her art. That was wrong. I see that now. Painting nourishes your soul. You have a rare talent, Red, and I would not ask you to set it aside when we wed. It should be shared."

"No duchess should offer services to others," Margaret insisted. "No duchess would paint and accept fees for her work."

Daniel beamed at her. "Mine will. She will blaze her own path—and I will support her on every step of her journey—whether I walk behind you or by your side."

"But what would Polite Society say?"

"We don't care. We will be a duke and duchess."

"What of our children?" she insisted. "I would not have them ostracized by the *ton* because of their scandalous mother."

His hands cradled her face. "Their mother will be much beloved by Polite Society and her children. And adored by her husband." His thumbs caressed her cheeks and Daniel realized the dancers around them had stopped, watching the little drama unfold. He knew he had to make a bold statement to Margaret, in front of the entire *ton*, before she might truly believe him.

He took her hands and dropped to one knee, hearing the gasps around them. By now, even the musicians had halted their play and all eyes focused upon the couple in the center of the ballroom.

"Lady Margaret Townsend, I worship the ground you trod upon. You have brought love and laughter into my life, and I cannot live another moment without you by my side. I love you more than life itself, and I will honor you and support you in any endeavor all the days of our lives. You have a rare talent and can capture the very essence of others on a canvas. I want you to continue to paint because it will make you happy. And the rest of the time, my darling, I will make you happy, as well."

Daniel squeezed her hands, seeing how she trembled at his public declaration in the middle of a ballroom.

"Daniel, you do not know what you are saying," she protested.

He rose. "I know exactly what I am saying, my dearest love. I want you as my duchess. You will be my wife. Friend. Lover. Adviser. Most of all, you will be the best artist and best mother I will know. Seize the moment, Red. Make us both happy beyond our wildest dreams. Tell me that you will marry me."

He swallowed hard, waiting for her reply, praying she would agree.

"Yes."

"You said yes?" he asked anxiously. "You said yes?" he repeated, excitement rippling through him.

He turned to the ballroom of guests and shouted, "She said

yes!"

Daniel wrapped Margaret in his arms and gave her a kiss that would be talked about for many years to come. A public kiss that let all of Polite Society know that this duke would always stand by his duchess. That Daniel Judson, Duke of Westfield, had found the love of his life and would never let her go.

When he finally ended the kiss, Daniel wasn't about to let Margaret go. He swept her into his arms and carried her from the center of the room as the sea of dancers parted, their mouths agape as the now betrothed couple left the ballroom, the duke beaming and the soon-to-be-duchess's laughter ringing into the night.

He raced down the stairs and into the foyer, a startled footman quickly opening the door, allowing Daniel to rush out into the night.

The street was lined with carriages, coachmen sitting atop them and looking down with interest as he carried her through the empty street.

"Do you have a destination in mind, Your Grace?" Margaret asked, her arms entwined about his neck, her fingers stroking his nape.

"I most certainly do," he told her as he strode along the lane, turning the corner and arriving at his own carriage, where he'd had his driver park at a distance, hoping he would be making his escape with his one, true love. Pausing, he asked, "Would you like to go to your house—or mine?"

She considered the question. "Mine. It would be less scandalous, I suppose. I only have Molly, where you have a bevy of servants who would see us."

"Then your house it is."

He called up to his coachman, giving him Margaret's address, and then allowed a footman to open the carriage's door, the steps already in place. Climbing them, he ducked his head and fell onto the bench inside as the door closed behind them, Margaret on his lap.

They both began to laugh and then hunger filled them, his mouth suddenly hot on hers, both greedily taking from the other as they kissed the entire way there. By the time they reached her rented house, they were both out of breath.

Daniel broke the kiss and rested his brow against hers, breathing in her scent, happy in the knowledge this woman would forevermore be his.

"We will build a good life together," he told her. "Because the foundation of that life will be our love for each other." He paused. "You do love me, don't you, Red? You agreed to marry me but . . ." His voice trailed off, uncertainty suddenly filling him.

Margaret pushed her fingers into his hair, holding his head steady. "You are the only man I could ever love, Daniel. Even when I didn't much like you, I loved you," she admitted.

"But you like me now?" he teased, relief filling him.

"I like you ever so much," she declared. "Probably more than I should. I like you. I love you. I worship you."

"No, it is my job to worship you," he told her.

She frowned. "And I say we shall worship each other."

Her lips hovered a moment over his and then touched them, passion exploding between them. The kiss grew needy. His body heated, as did her skin.

Breaking the kiss, he said, "We should go inside—else I will have my wicked way with you here and now."

Margaret cocked her head. "Hmm. A rolling carriage and two very eager lovers. I think we should give it a try, Your Grace."

Daniel grinned shamelessly and kissed her hard. "Very well, Red." He rapped on the roof of the carriage and shouted, "Drive! Drive until I say stop."

The coachman drove the streets of London—for the rest of that night and well past dawn.

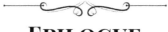

EPILOGUE

Six years later . . .

D ANIEL DESCENDED FROM his carriage and entered his London townhouse. Hampton greeted him.

Handing over his hat and cane to the butler he asked, "Where is my duchess?"

"Her Grace is in her studio with the children, Your Grace," Hampton replied.

"Thank you," he said, taking the stairs two at a time until he reached the top floor.

He had hoped he had timed everything perfectly, getting to see his children before their naps began, and then spending precious time alone with Margaret.

He went along the corridor and then paused at the open door, taking in the scene.

His wife sat in front of an easel, their five-year-old daughter, Norrie, standing in front of her. Norrie had a paintbrush in her hand and was asking how to do a certain brushstroke.

Margaret took her daughter's hand. Together they dipped the brush into the paint, and she helped Norrie guide it along the blank canvas.

"Like this, Norrie," she said. "Do you understand now?"

His bright little angel, the very image of her mother, nodded with enthusiasm. "I do, Mama. Watch me!"

Norrie stroked the brush along the canvas, pausing to dip the tip into her paints again, and then added more to the canvas.

"That's it, my precious," Margaret praised. "I think you will become a better artist than I am."

Daniel's eyes dropped to the floor, where his son, Edward, was using his fingers to paint. The three-year-old had more paint on him and the tarp spread out under him than he did the actual parchment before him.

Daniel stepped into the room and sat on the ground beside Edward. It might mean another pair of breeches ruined, but he didn't care. He treasured these times with his children and could always wear the pants out on his country estate as he helped tenants.

"Papa!" cried Edward. "I'm painting." His son held up a palm to show his father his paint-covered hands.

"I see that," he said with a smile. "What are you painting today, my boy?"

"Dogs," Edward declared.

Dogs were Edward's new passion, and they already had two of them. Knowing Margaret's tender heart, more would be added to their household.

His lovely wife and daughter turned to him, and Norrie said, "Papa, I am painting the sun in the park."

"I cannot wait to see it when you complete it." He looked at her canvas. "I like the shades of orange and red that you are mixing into your yellow sun."

Norrie nodded solemnly. "The sun isn't just one color, Papa. When it goes up or down, it has lots of colors. Mama is helping me mix my colors so I can paint it going down."

His eyes met those of his wife's, and he gazed upon her tenderly. "Mama is doing a wonderful job teaching you," he told his daughter.

Margaret continued helping Norrie, and Daniel sat and watched as Edward painted what he identified as three more dogs before their nursery governess appeared and told them it was time for their naps.

A maid had accompanied the governess, bringing soap and water for the children to wash up. Margaret supervised Norrie cleaning the brushes, the little girl already knowing this was an essential part of painting. Once both had clean hands, they left with their nursery governess, Norrie pausing to give Daniel a kiss on his cheek.

Once they left, he rose and went to his wife, kissing her.

"I think a nap is called for, don't you, my dearest?" he asked.

Her eyes lit with amusement. "Somehow, your naps never have anything to do with sleeping, Your Grace."

He pulled her into his arms. "Adults take different kinds of naps, Red. Surely, you have discovered that by now."

Her fingers caressed his cheek. "Oh, I rather enjoy adult napping," she told him, mischief in her eyes. "Shall we go downstairs?"

They went to their rooms, rooms designated for the Duke of Westfield. He had bucked tradition and had made certain his duchess slept in his bed every night of their marriage. The only exceptions had been when she gave birth to Norrie and Edward in her own, little-used bed. She did use the duchess's rooms for bathing and dressing, but her nights were spent with him. He wouldn't have it any other way.

They found his valet there, replacing shirts in a wardrobe.

"We are not to be disturbed," he instructed the servant.

"Yes, Your Grace," the valet said, quickly vacating the room.

"He knows exactly what we are up to," Margaret said, as Daniel had her sit on the bed as he began removing her shoes and stockings.

"I am sure the entire household will know in the next half hour or so. You have never been quiet when you nap," he noted, his lips twitching in amusement.

She laughed. The sound was music to his ears. "Do you know that I fall in love with you more each and every day?"

ALEXA ASTON

He cupped her cheeks. "I do, my love. Because I also fall in love with you a little more with each passing day."

Daniel's lips found hers for a tender, lingering kiss. As always, though, his blood began to heat in her presence, and he quickly removed her clothes and then his own. He kissed and touched every inch of her beautiful flesh, joining with her in the age-old dance that he would never grow tired of.

An hour later, spent, they lay together, his arms around her, her cheek nestled against where his heart beat. For her. Always for his Red.

"How is your latest portrait coming?" he asked.

She toyed with the hair on his chest as she said, "The countess has been easy to capture. She is an open book, very effervescent and easy to know. The earl is more enigmatic—but I will figure him out."

"Of course you will, my darling. You figure everything out." He pressed a kiss to her hair, thinking how truly happy he was in this moment. Daniel did not think he could be happier.

Then Margaret changed his mind.

"I have some news to tell you," she said, her fingers still dancing along the muscles of his chest.

"Oh? Have you received a new commission?"

"In a way, I suppose you could say that." She was silent a moment and then said, "It is a commission from you, Your Grace. It should take me about another seven months or so to complete."

Joy filled his heart. "You are with child again?"

"I am. I hope you are pleased."

"I was pleased with Norrie and didn't think I could love anyone as much as I did her. Until Edward came along—and then I saw how love is limitless. My son and daughter bring me incredible happiness, and I know another child will do the same."

Daniel kissed his wife tenderly. "Red, I am glad you came into my life."

His duchess smiled up at him. "And I am glad that you accepted me for who I am and allow me to be a duchess, artist, wife, and mother."

"You are—and always will be—my everything," Daniel told her, kissing her again.

Their future would continue to be bright.

About the Author

Award-winning and internationally bestselling author Alexa Aston's historical romances use history as a backdrop to place her characters in extraordinary circumstances, where their intense desire for one another grows into the treasured gift of love.

She is the author of Regency and Medieval romance, including: Dukes of Distinction; Soldiers & Soulmates; The St. Clairs; The King's Cousins; and The Knights of Honor.

A native Texan, Alexa lives with her husband in a Dallas suburb, where she eats her fair share of dark chocolate and plots out stories while she walks every morning. She enjoys a good Netflix binge; travel; seafood; and can't get enough of *Survivor* or *The Crown*.

Printed in the USA
SIA information can be obtained
w.ICGtesting.com
081417211223
988LV00091B/4575